WELFARE

Tyrant Books

Via Piagge Marine 23

Sezze (LT) 04018

Italy

www.NYTyrant.com

ISBN 978-0-9992186-6-2

Cover: Brent Bates
Book Design: Adam Robinson

First Edition

WELFARE
A NOVEL

STEVE ANWYLL

tyrant books

1.

I probably remind my old man of the woman he lost. Maybe that's why I always feel like I don't belong. And why he gives me so much space. I don't know if it's that that made me distant. Independent. But what I am sure of is that it makes leaving pretty easy.

In fact, I've been thinking about it for years. But where do I go? And how do I pay for food? So I've had to wait. Until after my 16th birthday. When the fighting with my dad's new wife gets to be too much. I just pack my bags.

And when I come through the kitchen. She's standing there. She asks me where I think I'm going. I tell her the fuck out of here. That I can't take it anymore. That she's had it out for me since the day she moved in. Scared that I might remind my father of what he used to have.

She makes threats. Like I'll never make it. That I'll be back in an hour. That I'm too stupid to last a day on my own. The whole time I'm by the door. Lacing up my boots. Certain she's the stupid one.

I walk down the slope of their driveway. A backpack full of t-shirts and socks and underwear and books on my back. I have $50 and two packs of cigarettes in the pocket of my army surplus jacket. But no lighter. You can't have everything, I tell myself.

When I get to the main road the sun is setting. I stick out my thumb. It's the quickest way I know to get out of the shitty little lakeside village we live in.

After about ten minutes of walking backwards. A beat up sedan skids to a halt on the gravel shoulder and I don't hesitate. It's got all the signs of a bad time. Chipped blue paint. Rust showing through. And a greasy longhaired fisherman sitting behind the wheel.

I hop in and sit down. There's a hole in the floor between my feet half covered by a greasy pizza box. He shrugs his shoulders. Mutters oh yeah and tells me to watch out. As we speed down the highway I watch the asphalt blur like running water.

'I used to hitchhike all the time when I was your age, man,' he tells me through a cloud of second hand smoke. 'Some of the best years of my life. Where you off to on a school night?'

And I don't know why I do it. Later, I tell myself it must've been the hole in the floor. The road going by between my feet. A calming effect washes over me. And instead of keeping my mouth shut, or lying, like I always do with my family, scared of them getting to know me, I answer him.

I lay it all down to the man in the cloud of smoke. He lets me talk. And I tell him how this town and my family and school and my friends and the future feels like two hands around my throat. And how everyday a little more of my life is slipping away. And how I don't think I'll make it much longer if things don't change.

When I'm done he pauses. Butts out the third smoke he's smoked since I got in the car and lights another. He takes a long drag. Fills the interior with a fresh cloud.

'You're doing the right thing, man. It's time you're out on your own,' he says. And he's telling me exactly what I want to hear. And even though I probably shouldn't, I listen. Mistaking his advice for truth.

When he drops me off at a gas station on the edge of town he gives me five cigarettes. I ask for a pack of matches. He holds out his hand and I give him mine. We shake by interlocking thumbs and wrapping our fingers around the back of each other's hands.

'Best of luck, brother,' he tells me as I shut the door behind me. And before I can take a step back he squeals off onto the highway, past the sewage treatment plant. Into the night and out of my life.

He was here when I needed him.

Even though I'm appreciative of the ride and the advice, I wish he'd dropped me off a little closer to where I'm going. It takes me almost two hours to walk across the city. To where my friend Greg lives.

He's almost 20 and moved out of his parent's house a year ago. He works as the night janitor of the YMCA. The pay and the work are shit. But he has enough to pay his rent and get drunk every night.

In my eyes, he's a real success.

I knock on the door even though it's early. There's no lights on. When there's no answer I get ready to wait for a while. I sit on his broken concrete porch for hours. I smoke cigarettes.

I think about how if I were home I'd be lying in bed. Watching TV. Wondering when someone was going to bang on my bedroom door. Start yelling.

And how I'm freezing sitting here. And don't know if Greg will let me stay when he shows up. Or when I'm going to eat next. But this still feels better than lying in that warm bed, ten feet from a full fridge.

When Greg rolls up on his bicycle, I'm freezing and exhausted. He's drunk. I'm not sure if that'll work in my favour. His reputation doesn't include alcohol-induced kindness. And his face is screwed up into a frown.

'Stan, what are you doin' here?' are the first words he slurs out.

I go over my story again shivering on his steps. He nods along. But I know I have to keep it short. He's fading out.

I ask him. If I can crash here for a while. I'm certain he'll say no. So I start thinking of other places I can go. Like under the train bridge a couple of blocks away.

And he surprises me. Says I can sleep on the couch. But I'll owe him half the rent. I don't know what else to do. Because spending a night under the train bridge doesn't feel good already. So I agree. Unaware of how awful things are going to get.

That night I get a glimpse. Greg stays up until dawn. Drinking cheap malt liquor. The kind that makes the strongest drunk alive turn into a piece of shit. Argumentative. And ready to fight. But Greg's not strong.

I spend the night lying on the couch. Hoping he'll go to sleep. Or at least start sharing the piss he's drinking. Listening to him rant and rail. And the more I agree with him. The louder he gets.

The next month is a complete fucking nightmare. Between his bullshit and not eating that much. I don't make it to school much. I'm too tired. The long nights taking their toll.

So I sleep the mornings away. Catching up. In the afternoons I try to find ways to make money. But it's tough. No one wants to give me a real job. I don't have a resume. Or experience. Or a very good attitude.

They all ask me why I'm looking for work. And I'm too fucking honest. I tell them I'm hungry. That I need to pay for the roof over my head. Which always results in a queer look. My age and story not matching up. So I get advice instead of a job.

'You should go back to your parents, son. Get an education.'

And it's hard for me. To keep my mouth shut. To not tell them to go fuck themselves. Spit on the floor by their feet. And I'm not sure what stops me. But I usually just walk away before they're done talking.

So on the weekends I get up early. Go around the neighbourhood. Knock on doors. Offer my services as a workhorse. I'm given odd jobs cutting lawns. And weeding gardens.

Sure. It's demeaning. And I hang my head when I do it. But more often then not I end my day midafternoon with a sandwich in my stomach. And $50 in my back pocket.

But it isn't enough to keep afloat. I quickly learn eating and drinking is a pricey luxury. I give up on things like milk. Vegetables. Fruit. And any meat not dumped out of a can.

And living here isn't easy. I have to start drinking more. Because it's the only way to stand Greg. His late night benders. All we do is sit in front of the TV. Yelling at one another. And I feel as though I'm as close as I've ever been to strangling someone most nights.

So when the end of the month rolls. I'm short. More than half. All I can do is give him $75. I tell him it's all got. He looks at the money in his hand. Disgust on his face.

'Well, then you better go apply for welfare I guess.'

But I'm not ready to do that. I have too much pride. I come from the kind of family that looks down on people on welfare. Openly makes fun of them. I'm ashamed of what I'll have to tell people. Because they'll ask. And I won't be able to keep it a secret.

Luckily about a week later an aunt of mine gets married to her long time boyfriend. I go. My parents are there. We sit at the same table. Match each other free drink for free drink. By the time they leave I've been given $500 and an invitation to come home any time I want.

That night when I get back I throw the remaining $125 I owe Greg in his face while he plays a video game. It takes me another two weeks to burn through the other 375$. Lavish meals and name brand whiskey.

I move back in with my folks the next day. A week before I owe Greg another month. One last burn for having to deal with his nightly terrors.

But my folks and I were never meant to get along. We all should've known better. But the cheer of the wedding. The booze. The rose-tinted glasses. We foolishly fell for our lie.

We fuck up. Unable to believe that if we really want it to work, we're going to have to stay drunk. But of course when they catch me taking some of their white rum things turn nasty. And after a few more days of sober relations we're right back where we started from.

Then one day my stepmother tells me to shape up or ship out. And I just look at her. And she asks me for the thousandth time why I think I'm so much better than her.

My answer is to turn around and walk to my room. Her yelling behind me. Certain of what I'm going to do with my life.

In my room I lie in bed. Hands behind my head looking at the ceiling. Thinking it's not entirely up to me to fucking shape up. Sure, I'm not that old. But I've learned a thing or two. And one of those is that no one is free from being a piece of shit.

So the next day around noon. While they're out at work. I pack my bags. Leave a note.

'Thanks for the good times. But I'm shipping out.

Stan.'

And I walk down their driveway again. The sun shining this time. I have the same shirts and underwear and books and backpack but less than $50 in my pocket this time. I don't know why I think I can do it. But I'm determined to never come home again.

I walk across the village. Over kettle creek. Towards the beach. Where another friend of mine lives. He's a ward of the catholic aid society. An orphan. He gets a nice fat check every month. Rents half a beach house.

To me, he's the coolest guy in the world. He's a year older than me. Has read all the good books. Knows all the best movies by heart. Lives by his own rules. I look up to him. Because he's exactly what I want to be.

We came to an agreement about two weeks before. That if I ever need a place to stay, I could come live with him. And when I show up with my backpack he knows I'm not going to be leaving for a while.

I sit down on the couch. Light a cigarette. I can't be more than two or three kilometers from my parents. But it feels like thousands. I feel free. There's none of that weight of them in the same house as me. I feel good.

And it's just like when I was waiting on Greg's porch. But I have a better handle on where things are going.

. . . .

The next morning I get up early and apply for student welfare. I'd rather just drop out. Give up. Hitchhike off into the sunset. Lie in grassy fields all day. Stop caring about anything in the world.

But all my life has been leading up to something. This fucking shitty moment of graduating school. And moving on. But not to anything much better. Because all I ever see for myself is the same shit my old man has.

A steady good paying mindless job in a factory. It's easy to believe in. Because it's all I've seen. And it seems so easy. Because places like that don't ask for much. Just a high school diploma.

I have to finish high school. It's all the training I need to stand in some hot, dark steel box all day. Doing the least amount of work. Kept safe by a union. And becoming as lifeless as my old man over the years.

The reason I apply for welfare is so I can go to school to get a job I don't want in the future. Securing a rotten existence until the end. But to me though. The whole thing makes a lot of sense.

I have to meet with an agent to qualify for welfare. The office is in the middle of nowhere. On the side of a two-lane highway right between the village where I live and the city I go to school in.

On the day of the appointment the sky pours down rain. I have no way to get there but to hitchhike. No one wants to pick me up. And by the time I make it into the office I look like shit. Watered down. Smelling damp. Pathetic.

I look at my reflection in a window and think I couldn't be in a better situation to look like shit.

I walk up to the counter. Tell a woman sitting behind three inches of plexiglass that I'm here. She chews gum. Slides several sheets of paper through the slot at the bottom of the glass. Tells me to fill them out. Wait.

It takes about thirty seconds to fill them out. And the next hour and a half I spend my time staring off into space. My clothes and shoes making a puddle under the chair I'm sitting in. Wondering if I'm a not a little young to be so wretched.

Off to the side of the waiting room a door opens. My name is called out and I'm asked to follow. Since my only other option is to walk back out in the rain and starve to death I do as I'm asked.

Just on the other side of the door is a desk. I sit down in front of it. Before she has a chance to sit down I look the woman over. And just as much as I look like my role she does too.

Her face is screwed up. A long beige skirt covers her thick thighs. Tucked into it is a white blouse buttoned to the top. Her hair wound in a tight bun.

'Why do you need to be on assistance?' she crows at me.

'My parents gave me the boot.'

'What for?'

'We didn't see eye to eye on things.'

'Don't you have anyone else to take you in?'

'I got no one, lady.'

I fill out more forms that seem exactly the same as the last ones. Answer her questions about school. What my plans are. This is it for now, she says. They'll call in a couple of days. Set up an appointment.

'An appointment for what?' I ask.

She tells me that they need to see where I'm living. To make sure it's not some awful drug den. That they only pay for suitable lodgings. I assure her with my best lie that they'll certainly be impressed.

She stands up and leads me back out. We say our goodbyes. The first thing I do when I get outside is light a smoke. It helps me think as I walk back out to the highway in the misting rain.

By the time I stick out my thumb I'm pretty sure where I live isn't going to be considered suitable.

The small home is filled from wall to wall with it. Trash. We have one main path that runs from the front door to the back. Breaking off to give access to points of interest.

Like the sink. The fridge. The toilet.

And even then, some of those are rarely used. Like the kitchen sink is a total waste. Most of the dishes are covered in mold. The drain is regularly filled with maggots. I've never seen the counter tops.

We have a second floor. With bedrooms. But instead we sleep in the living room on filthy old couches. Because all three rooms up stairs are stuffed full of shit.

Like old Christmas trees. Bed frames. Stolen library books. Bags of burnt stuffed animals. Balls of wire. Thousands of clothes hangers.

So as I walk backwards along the shoulder of the highway in the rain

I convince myself there is no way it's going to pass the test. And that starving to death is a realer consequence than I'd like.

· · · · · · · ·

I get home from school the next day and there's a message on the answering machine. It's the welfare office. The agent will be coming by in two days.

I take a look around.

I haven't even started to clean.

I'm fucked.

I sit down on the couch. I put my head in my hands. What the hell am I going to do.

The next day I wake up with the alarm. When my roommate gets out of the shower I tell him he should skip school. Stay home with me. Help me clean. It's his goddamned mess.

'I'd love to help you, Stan. But I got a big test today. And sure. The mess is mine. But I don't need it to be clean. That's your problem.'

He lights a cigarette, wishes me the best of luck. Leaves laughing. The screen door slams behind him.

'You fucking piece of shit,' I say out loud. 'You're god damned lucky you walked out when you did. Or I'd bury you under this mess and not think twice about it.'

I sit down on the couch as my threat fades. I smoke a cigarette to calm down. Think about where to start.

The upstairs is a complete waste. I know that. I can spend days up there. Nothing can be done. There's no time. So I shut the door at the bottom of the staircase, forget about it.

If she asks I'll just tell her that it's a closet. That there's another tenant living upstairs. Pray she doesn't get up to investigate.

I butt out my smoke. Start jamming magazines and pop bottles and dead houseplants under the couches. Which helps. And I can begin to see the floor. There's carpet. Who knew.

I know there used to be an ashtray on the coffee table. But I can't see it. Just a mountain of ash and cigarette butts. A few bowls with sour milk and dried cereal in them. Mold threatening to form. I get a garbage bag and sweep it all in.

All the empty booze and cigarette packs I put in the cupboards. Start doing the dishes. Gag and dry heave. Give up. Throw them in the garbage bag. Drag it to the curb.

There's no vacuum so I do my best with a broom. I almost put my back out several times because of my vigor. The dirt in the paths is too much. It's ground in there. And I can't see myself scrubbing it.

'Shit, I can lay that on the landlord. Slander him. Call him a fucking slumlord.' I tell myself. I feel giddy with pride. I take a break. Sit down and smoke a cigarette.

I sit there with my feet up smoking. Feeling good about myself. This is the most strenuous thing I've done in ages. I'm sweating. I smell. I can't remember the last time I took a shower. I think about cleaning the tub.

I notice a shirt of my roommates is on the edge of the couch. I grab it. Stand up. Wipe the dust off of everything. Run it between the blinds of the window while smoking and ashing on the floor. An old habit.

The shirt was a faded orange when I picked it up. One of his favorites. But now it's dirty black. I use up every available inch of it. Put it right back where I found it.

I laugh.

I look forward to future confrontations.

The clock says it's half past three. I've been at it for six hours. I'm fed up. Hungry. It's as good as it's going to get.

The place is a dump. She'll have to deal with it.

I pick up my jacket. Lock the door behind me. Go for a walk around the village.

I walk towards the beach. I go through the parking lot of a bar all the fisherman drink at. Their cars are always unlocked. They always have smokes. Money lying around. I need to eat. There's no other way.

So I take what I think I need. Go to the beach.

I sit in the sand. Count my haul. Fifteen bucks. Thirty cigarettes. It should hold me over for a while

I smoke. Look out on Lake Erie. And I imagine Cleveland across all that water. Some other city. In my head it's glamorous. Full of life. Not this fucking shithole that's killing me.

But when I try and picture myself walking the streets there I can't. To me it seems like there's no way of getting farther than 45 kms in any direction. And I'm doomed to stay here. Or close to doomed.

I start thinking about how things have turned out so far. I've spent a day cleaning up after someone else so I can impress a caseworker from welfare. I had to steal cigarettes and change from open cars to eat.

I'm sinking faster than if I just walked into the lake and tried to make it to Cleveland.

I get up and go home. Spend an hour scrubbing the bathroom and then I take a hot shower. And even though I put dirty clothes back on I feel better. Like life isn't going to crush me.

I lay on the couch I call my bed. Letting my hair dry. Staring at the stained ceiling, smoking until my roommate gets home.

'Shit! This looks great,' he says when he gets in.

'Really?'

'Yeah.'

'But do you think some welfare lady is going to like it?'

'Not a fucking chance.'

· · · · · · ·

The appointment is for ten in the morning. I get up early. Nervous, I guess. I walk my roommate to the bus stop. Wait with him. Smoke some of the stolen smokes.

When the bus comes we throw our smokes down. Squish them under the soles of our shoes. He wishes me luck. I turn around and light another one before I walk back home.

I wait in the living room. Panicking. Watching TV. Smoking. Pacing. Even though the paths are cleared I stick to them from memory.

Pathetically I try and do some more dusting. But all it does is spread it around. It's too far gone. I smoke more cigarettes. Watch the clock. It ticks off the minutes. I start to worry.

This is never going to work.

At ten to ten I empty the teacup I'm calling an ashtray I've filled since 6:30 this morning. I sit on the couch like a proper little boy. Channeling the behavior I need to fool her. Hands on my lap. Affecting good posture.

At five past, I hear her knock.

I get up. Hope for the best. When I open the door I put on my biggest fake smile. Tell her the lies we all like to hear. Like I'm glad to see her. Invite her in.

She takes a look around.

I can only imagine what this woman thinks of me. By the look on her face she'd like to crush me under the heel of her boot.

I offer her a seat on the couch. She declines. She chooses an old kitchen chair that's in the corner. She sits on the very edge. Trying to stay clean. Trying not to look so nervous.

I sit back. Arm over the back of the couch. Trying to seem nice. Trustworthy.

'Are you living here alone?' she asks me.

'Ah, no. This is my roommate's place. I just moved in. This is his mess.'

'Oh. Is he on welfare?'

'No, he's an orphan. Catholics give him money. Parents were dead-beats, you see.'

'I do.'

She tells me all the conditions. The same damn shit I heard when I hitchhiked in. Since I'm on student assistance I don't have to look for work. I just have to make it class. Not get kicked out.

I nod my head the whole time. I'm not going to disagree. And I wonder if anyone ever does. Because welfare isn't about making demands. Getting picky. This is the end of the line.

She gets up from her seat and I do the same. We shake hands. I walk the three steps to the door. Before she leaves, she turns around. She stops. She wants to say something.

But the words are not easy coming.

'Please tell me that you'll give this place a proper cleaning. I don't want to come back here and see it like this. Ok?'

'You bet ma'am. I'll get to it the second that you leave. Like I said. I just moved in. My roommate has some issues. But I'll definitely put things in order. You have my word.'

'Thank heavens,' she sighs. I close the door behind her. Lock it. Make sure she can't get back in. I walk over to the couch. Fall down on it.

I'm shaking. Terrified. A cold sweat comes over me.

With trembling hands I reach for a smoke. I grab my lighter. I inhale deeply. Feel the nicotine take me home. I begin to feel better.

I lay back. Head on one armrest. My boots on the other. It's over. I did it. I won. I think about cleaning the place a little better as ashes fall on the floor.

2.

The whole process of signing on and getting a check takes about two months. I call and ask why, what's the holdup. And all the answers I get never satisfy me. Leave me confused. I wonder if it's because I have too much on my mind and not enough in my stomach.

So one day I skip school. Walk over to my parents place when I'm sure they're both at work. I still have a key and I hope it works. My stepmother always kept a large stock of canned goods. Non-perishables.

Something her sisters and brothers joke about.

But to me it's no joke. My mouths watering two blocks away. While I take the short cut behind the post office. Past the bench on the side of the building. Where my buddy Saul and I spent countless hours.

Because we always agreed that anywhere was better than being at home.

The closer I get to their house I start to consider creeping into the backyard through the woods. So I won't be seen by the neighbours. But that'd take a ton of work. Like climbing a steep hill. And then coming back down through a heavily wooded lot.

I like the idea of it. But I'm lazy and I've never been graceful. So I walk up the drive like nothing is out of step. Pull out my keys like I've done a thousand times before.

Act casual. This is the easy part. You better pray there's no one home. Because I know you don't have a lie.

And that's exactly what I do. For a second before I see if the key turns I send out a prayer to any deity that'll listen. Asking for an empty house. A smooth run.

When the door shuts behind me I stand still. I'm in between floors on their split-level home. There's six stairs to climb on either side of me. Every three and you're on a new level.

From where I am I can see into the kitchen/dining room and down into the living room and the bottom of the stairs into the basement. I listen for any sign of either my father or stepmother.

My father would be easy. He'll understand. He's always considered me a free man. But if she's in the house, I won't be surprised if she calls the cops.

So I wait for longer than I need to. Still and silent. Taking in the smell of my stepmother's incessant baking that I'd forgotten. The air sweet like fresh flowers. Instead of the damp fungal odor of the beach house. I'm ready to run at the first sign of them.

But I get no sign. So I creep down the six stairs into the basement like a thief. I must be suffering some kind of delirium. Because when I see all those cans of beans and tuna fish and soup and stew and boxes of macaroni and cheese I can swear the whole room is glowing.

I know that my backpack isn't going to cut it. So I run up nine stairs into the kitchen. Go straight for the second drawer down on the far left of the counter. Grab a handful of plastic bags and go back down stairs mad with the thought of the white trash feast I'll be gorging on tonight.

I fill up three plastic bags full. A couple dozen of my old man's home-made beer find my way into their backpack. I'm sure he'll just think my stepmother's brother came over.

Any remaining space is filled with frozen hamburger patties, sausages and hotdogs. The last thing I grab is a bottle of whiskey from behind their bar. By the time I lock up behind me and start walking back to the beach house I look like I just came from the grocery store.

A huge smile on my face.

I feel like I've done something.

. . . .

But I have to come up with the rent. And I can't just waltz into my folks place, pocket $200 and sail on for another month. I don't want to have to go back to doing yard work either. I feel like it's beneath me now.

I'm on welfare. I have standards.

And I remember the day I cleaned up the apartment for the social worker. How in the late afternoon I rifled through a few cars with unlocked doors. And came home with a pretty good take.

So I figure there's a future in this. At least for a little while. So I take to car hopping through rusting sedans. Beat up minivans. The occasional Camaro or Monte Carlo. My work is done at night. With my head down blindly sweeping under driver's seats. Digging through sticky centre consuls and tightly packed glove compartments.

I can hit up the bars a couple nights a week. And creep into the garages of homes whose lights are off the rest of the time.

It's not a bad living.

Because at the end of the week I come home with $125 and enough smokes to last for days. I find bags of weed. A large hunting knife with a beautiful bone handle. Engraved lighters.

I smoke the weed and keep the knife. The lighters I sell to the highest bidder on the schoolyard.

I hand over $75 a week to my roommate. It keeps him off my back and in the possession of good whiskey and delivered food. I can't throw around money like a fucking millionaire. That's for sure. But all in all, I can't say I'm not having a good time.

But I know I can't keep the car hopping up. Because at some point these drunken fishmongers are going to get wise to what's going on. And before I know it I'll be surrounded in a sandy parking lot down by the beach. Begging them to take it easy, that I'm just a kid.

So the day I come home to a message on the answering machine saying that my first check is ready it's like every Christmas and birthday I've ever had. I can give up my life of crime.

I can go back to being a respectable citizen.

. . . .

To get my check I have to go in person. Pick it up with my actual hand. And when I call to ask why I'm told, 'It's procedure,' by the woman on the phone. The voice she uses makes me feel small. Like how my stepmother and teachers speak to me.

So by the time I get off the phone with her I know why I'm supposed to go. They want me to come in with my head hung. They want me to come in on my belly. Wearing my appreciation like a new suit.

The whole day at school is a complete fucking waste. I only go in because it's slightly closer to the welfare office. And they might start asking questions like 'Why the hell am I not in class?' when I show up at 10 AM with a great big smile across my face.

All day I can barely sit still. I don't listen to any of my teachers. Because I can't. I'm lost in dreams of the kinds of foods my roommate orders in every night. Pizza. Chicken wings. Gyros.

The fucker. Those nights I hate him. As I sit on the couch spooning the same damn macaroni and cheese I've been eating for weeks down my throat. The rich smell of food driven to the doorstep subduing the stink of stale cigarette butts and dampness in the air.

When school ends I catch a ride with my buddy Saul. We've been inseparable since we were kids. In fact, I think he's the only reason I've managed to keep it together for so long. He was my only friend when everyone else in the world seemed against me.

Saul got himself a part time job washing cars on the weekends. Saved up and bought his own car.

Now here we are. He's driving me to pick up my first welfare check.

And I can feel our lives veering off on entirely different paths. He has money for booze and drugs and girls. He eats his parent's food. Makes payments on his car. Is saving for college.

He's getting ready to be an adult. Just like our parents.

And sitting in the passenger seat I have to admit I don't really know what the fuck I'm doing. And I'm scared. And I don't know if my plan is a sound one.

But I am becoming an adult. Just a shittier one than our parents.

'Thanks for the ride, man,' I tell Saul as we drive from school. Passing the cornfields of southern Ontario. My future just around the bend.

'No problem, you fucking welfare bum.'

And this is what I'm going to start hearing more and more. But I don't feel any shame that it's supposed to illicit. I tell myself it's my only answer. I need to eat. I need to pay rent. I can't go home. I have to finish school.

We're racing down the highway. Saul pulls out a joint. The papers are thickly covered in black hash oil. He takes both hands off the wheel. Lights it. Thick blue smoke fills the car. He passes it to me.

'I don't know if I should go in there stoned, man. They might have some questions for me. I'll have to prove myself. I don't know if I can handle it.'

'It's your loss, man. You're going to stink like it anyways.'

'You make a point, give it here.'

By the time we park I'm feeling pretty good. But still. I have to give myself shit for smoking any. I might have to talk when I get in there. They'll know I'm baked. I take a look at Saul sitting there. He winks. And who am I to distrust a stoned 16 year old?

I walk up the stairs and pull the heavy glass door open. The building is old. Originally offices for the mental hospital across the street. It has marble floors and high ceilings. Gold accents on the edges of thick wooden doors. All evidence it was built in a time of Canadian prosperity.

The joint is making me feel pretty light. And I can't remember where I'm going. I wander around the main floor. Try and make out the placards on doors. Open the wrong ones and barge in. Upsetting the receptionists only to back out slowly when I'm asked if they can help me.

After about ten minutes of fucking around I decide to go to the second floor. And as soon as I get to the top of the stairs I see it. The welfare office. It's sign gold lettering against black.

I go in and walk up to the plexiglass separating me from the receptionist. You know, I think to myself, there weren't any protective shields in any of the other offices I walked into today.

I stand in front of the little holes cut in the plastic to let our voices get through. The woman sitting there ignores me. Looks at her nails. I clear my throat. Announce myself.

She looks up at me. Rolls her eyes and tells me I have to wait. They're busy.

I look around. I'm the only person in here. I have my pick of the fifteen empty chairs. I sit down. Stare at the floor between my feet. It gleams. I can see myself in it. I don't look so great. Run down. Thin. Red eyes.

The money'll help, I tell myself.

After about five minutes the woman tells me I can come over. I walk slowly.

'What can I do for you?'

'Ah, I'm here to pick up a check.'

'Oh,' she groans, 'What's your name?'

'Acker, Stan. '

'I'm going to have to see your drivers license, Mr. Acker.'

I tell her I don't have one. She looks at me like it's a federal offence. I tell her I'm just a kid. And all I have is a social insurance card and my birth certificate. She rolls her eyes and tells me she supposes this will do as she pulls them through the slit at the bottom of the glass.

'Ok. We do have a check ready for you,' she slides my ID back through the slit, 'but I'm going to need you to sign this first. '

'Sure thing,' I take the paper. Sign it without looking at a word on it. I couldn't fucking care less. I'd give her my first-born. All I can think of is a pack of smokes. Hot food. Something prepared by a short order cook.

'Here you go.' She slides a brown government envelope through the slit. I snatch the check from under the plexiglass. Her manicured fingers still grasping it.

'Thanks a lot. Have a nice day.'

She gives me one last dirty look as I turn around and walk out the door.

'Th'fuck took you so long?' Saul says as I get back in, 'Was it busy in there?'

'No, they just wanted to make me wait.'

'Nice. Well…how much did you get?'

'Fuck. Been too excited to open it.'

I work my index finger under the flap. Tear it open. I pull out the check. I look at the numbers. I look at them again.

'Holy shit.' I whisper.

'How much man?'

'$1800.'

'Fuck. I'm gonna go on welfare.'

For the rest of the ride home, Saul tells me about his job. His boss. How he's a fat fucking pig who doesn't lift a finger. But I couldn't be further away. Staring out the window. Thinking that life might work out.

Saul drops me off out front of the bank. I go in. Walk up to the woman behind the counter. She gives me a big smile. Says hello. But when I hand her my check, she looks at it. See's where it came from. That's the end of the smiles.

'Would you like me to put this in your account, Mr. Acker?'

'No, I'll take it all in cash thank you very much.'

'Of course, ' she says while rolling her eyes at me. And I know she thinks that I'm shit. Garbage. A fucking leech. But I don't care. Her and her fancy job and her nice clothes can go fuck themselves.

All she has to do is count the cash and fork it over.

Which she does. And I walk out of that fucking bank with my head held high. Feeling like a new man. Like I can do anything. Go anywhere. Eat the best food. Talk to beautiful women.

But this is a little Canadian fishing village. And both of those are in short supply.

So instead I stand on the corner outside the bank. A wad of bills thick enough to make a bulge in my pocket and I know I'm going to walk in the opposite direction of responsibility.

Towards home.

Where it's easier to order something.

'You'll go to the grocery store tomorrow...or maybe on the weekend. When you have more time,' I say out loud. To the empty streets. And the setting sun.

But I know I won't.

I just like to lie to myself.

I walk along William Street. Past the town hall. The library. I cross the river over the old green metal lift bridge. I stop in the middle. Where the two pieces come together. A foot on either side. Look down and lose myself in the current of the river.

The world feels like a beautiful place.

And I don't know how long I'm standing there. But the wind picks up and I know I need to get drunk. I can see the liquor store from where I'm standing. Which doesn't help.

When I get there I have to wait around the side. I'm way too young and the village is too small. They'll all know I'm the wayward Acker boy. The one that ran away.

I light one of the discount cigarettes I still have. Take a long pull. I wait around for fifteen minutes. I see a stumbling fishmonger coming up the deserted street. I stop him. He tells me he'll do it for $5.

A brokerage fee.

But I can spare the expense.

When I get home my roommate's there. He's sitting on the couch playing video games like always. He sees the bottle of whiskey in my hand. The cigarette hanging from my smile.

'How'd it go?'

'Fuck man, not too bad.' I count off and throw a third of my money on the coffee table. It lands half in an ashtray. Knocks over several plastic bottles. They spill on the floor. Neither of us pays much attention.

'Get yourself a glass. Call the pizza joint. Tonight we eat,' I announce.

He puts the controller down. Follows the path to the kitchen. Rustles around in the sink. The tap runs. He brings back an empty pop bottle with the top half cut off. I pour out four ounces or so. He picks up the phone. Starts dialing.

'What do you want to eat?' he asks me.

'The most expensive fucking thing they have on the menu.'

3.

Instead of going to school one day my roommate and I go to the beach. It's past the season for it. Sure, there are far less girls in bikinis wandering around. But the tourist hordes stay home. And there's nothing more than the wind and the sand and the seagulls.

It becomes the kind of place I can take a deep breath and have it mean something.

We throw rocks in the lake. Smoke cigarettes on the shore. My roommate goes on and on about all the places he wants to go. The universities he wants to apply for.

He's got a lot of dreams, I tell myself. And I wonder where they all come from. Because I've never thought about going to university. And other cities were just places from television. For other people.

It doesn't occur to me I can just move anywhere I want. And it isn't that hard.

He likes to talk so it's easy to tune it out. I offer up base responses like grunts and the occasional oh yeah but it's from a level of mind that's not thinking. And the rest of me fades out.

To thoughts of the shitty future I have. At best in a factory. With a wife and kids and a kitchen table full of bills. And I know I'm young. But I have confidence in the fact I don't have what it takes to repeat my father's life.

But I also don't feel like I have what it takes to stop it from happening either.

And by the time we get up to go I'm covered in sand from having sat in it. And I'm feeling like I don't have much of a reason to carry on.

I'm looking at my feet as we walk. So my roommate sees it first. He nudges me with his elbow and says 'Dude, look at that.' And about a block away. In the gravel strip between the street and a lawn is a great big l-shaped couch. My roommate is ecstatic.

'Man, we should take this,' he yells at me.

And as I take a step back from his excitement I wonder where he wants to put it. I've got to do something I tell myself. We've got no fucking room as is.

'Um, where the fuck do you think we're going to put that, pal?' I ask in my calmest voice.

'We're gonna put it on the lawn.' His eyes light up. And at this moment, I know I'm seeing a childhood white trash fantasy coming true.

And the more I think about it the more I like it. I imagine cool clear nights. A roaring fire. Booze. Chicks. My life will be like a rock and roll video.

And I find my reason to look forward to things again.

By now it's late afternoon and the school bus should be on it's way back to town with most of our friends on board. My roommate says he'll go over to where it stops. Grab people to help drag it home as they get off.

So I stay with the couch. I sit down. And even though it's peppered with piss stains it's pretty comfortable.

When my roommate comes back in ten minutes he's got four other kids from around town with him. They all look up to him the way I did. Before our lives became so similar.

We get the piece of shit home in no time. Drag it into the side yard. My roommate's interior decorating skills come out from hiding.

We set it up with one back to the house and the other to the hedges hiding us from the street. This way on one side we're looking at the neighbours to the left of the house. And on the other side we're blocked by shed.

And after we drag a 40-gallon drum into the middle for a fire pit the perfection of our efforts is evident. I go inside and grab the whiskey I have. The six of us sit down. Smoke cigarettes and share the bottle.

· · · · · · ·

By Friday there's at least 15 people coming. Far more than the couch can hold. But I'm happy. My roommate has promised girls. And since I left my folks house, the girl I was seeing wants nothing to do with me. So I'll make sure I get squished in beside someone pretty.

The sky has been threatening to rain all weekend, all day the sky has been grey. One of the downfalls of the great lakes. Which cause bouts of anxiety in me. But we get lucky. It holds off. And the couch doesn't get a chance to turn into a sponge.

People start coming over right after school. Everyone has booze and beer stolen from their parents. We start drinking right away. Because none of us know any better. And we're young. And we don't care.

But we have no wood for a fire. And without that the night's a waste. So after a couple a drinks and before the sun goes down I round up some help. We make our way to a neglected part of the harbor a couple of minutes walk away.

It's a sure bet that we'll find something to use. The whole village dumps their shit there. And we do find something. A pile of 2x4 pieces. Several busted up sheets of chipboard. Branches galore.

The jackpot.

Darkness is coming quick. We make a couple of trips before it gets dangerous. We bring home enough of the shit to burn the entire village down. We're determined.

And we're not really thinking straight.

Because next thing I know I'm jimmying open the landlords shed. Stealing the gas can he keeps there for the lawnmower. And I'm dousing a pile of wood in the bottom of the 40-gallon drum.

My friend max throws a match in and I can hear the oxygen get sucked out of the air. And a 15-foot flame shoots up out of the old oil drum into the twilight.

We whoop and shout. Dance around like savages. Freedom in the air.

· · · · · · ·

All of our neighbours have 40 years on us and we seem to keep different hours. We only see them from time to time. There are nods and waves. Gestures of acceptance. But up until now we've had no reason to get friendly.

So after 20 minutes of fire lighting up the sky, the man who lives across the street comes over. There's a drink in his hand. His eyes are watery like every old drunk.

They shine in the light of the fire.

'Hi, I live across the street. My name's Tom Collins,' he says with a slur.

'Like the drink?' I say.

'You betcha,' and he raises his glass, swirling the ice.

'Is that what you're drinking?'

'Christ no. I can't stand the fuckin things. I'd rather drink a tall glass of warm shit. '

'Yum.'

He tells us he came over as a courtesy. To let us know that the fat bastard who lives next door is the county fire marshal. We've seen him a bunch. We laugh at him in his bathrobe. Taking his Chihuahua out for a piss. It's head so heavy that when it lifts its leg it does a handstand. Dribbling urine down it's belly.

Tom tells us he can be a prick if he's feeling just right. Which Tom implies can be achieved in about five drinks.

We give him our thanks. Offer him a seat on the couch. He says why not. Which I take for approval of our lifestyle. And before long he's talking to my friends Jenny and Susan. They're both young and pretty and laugh at his jokes. I figure he'll never go home.

But sure enough when his drink's finished he gets up. Comes over and shakes my hand. Thanks me for the good time. And to watch out for the fire marshal.

'Of course.' I tell him, 'This will not get out of hand.'

But my words are lies. And I know it before they leave my lips. Of course it's going to get out of hand. We pour more gas on just to watch it explode up out the top of the can. And each time we do, we all scream a little louder.

So an hour later. When I see the fire marshal come around the hedge with a highball glass in his hand I'm drunk but not surprised. He walks over slowly. Careful not to stumble. Or to spill. Or lose respect.

Just as the fire marshal steps into the yard my friend Max throws a can of brown beans in the fire. I hear it land with a thud in the bottom. It rings through the oil drum. Max howls with laughter. There's no getting it out.

And fuck, I could've eaten that.

'Who lives here,' the fire marshal demands when he comes over. Before we can answer he pulls out a smoke and lights it.

'Um, him and I do…what's happening?' I ask.

'Well. I live next door. The names Russ. I'm the fire marshal. It's my duty to come over. Check these kinds of things out. Make sure everything is on the up and up.'

He's drunk in the way only older men get drunk. Complete incapacitation. No acknowledgement of his shame. His drink spilling over his huge gut. His eyes unable to focus.

And all I can think about is that can of beans. Sure, I have to be polite. But I need him to get the fuck out of here.

'Well, as you can see, things are rolling pretty smoothly. No need to keep you.' I say.

'Oh yeah. Some fire you got 'ere. Really going.'

'Thanks.'

Christ, I think. That can has to be a 1000 fucking degrees by now. I picture it bright red. Pulsating in the embers down there. And he's just gonna stand there sipping his goddamned drink running his mouth until we're all covered in them.

'Well you see,' he slurs, 'the dog does handstands cause his head's too fucking heavy,' he laughs obnoxiously.

And that's when it happens. A loud pop. The tin of the can took as much as it could. I try and tell myself that the oil drum makes it sound worse then it is. But a hot jet of baked beans shoots up out of the top. Into the sky.

Fuck, here we go, I think. We're cooked now. As soon as those red-hot beans hit his skin he's going to shut us down. Call the cops. The rest of the night answering questions. Getting tickets.

And I look for Max. So I can start strangling him as soon as possible. I see him smiling at me as he makes his way into the shadows behind the shed.

'Shit. You must'a 'ad some wet pieces in there, eh?' Russ slurs.

'Oh yeah, man. Wet wood. I'll keep a better eye on things sir.'

'Thanks boys. I better get goin. Thol ladyll begin a wonder where ahve gotten to. Think I'm out with a young girl. Enh?' He winks. Stumbles back off around the hedge.

'Christ man, we gotta watch it,' my roommate says.

'What? About him. He'll be asleep in ten minutes. Throw some more logs on the fire. And give me a slug off that whiskey.'

4.

A couple of weeks later the landlord dies. It happens on the lawn. Right where the couch was before it rained and we had to drag it down to the neglected part of the harbor.

I find out from Tom. He catches me one morning when I'm going to get the bus. Tells me the landlord fell down clutching his chest. That the police and the ambulance and the fire department showed up right after.

It all took place before noon on a Saturday morning.

So I tell Tom that I don't know what the fuck he's talking about. That we must've slept through the whole ordeal. And the look of shock on his face makes me laugh.

'Jesus, Stan, there were sirens and lights and everything,' he says.

'You know what it's like going to school,' I tell him, 'It can really wear you down,' before running the two blocks to the bus stop.

Sitting on the bus I stare out the window. The flat cornfields rolling by. And I wonder if my roommate knows. So when I see him around lunchtime I ask him. He says yeah like it's no big deal. That the son of the landlord had called him. That he was taking over.

'I just forgot to tell you man,' was his answer.

And I don't question him. But I start to think about what else he's forgetting to tell me.

Like did he know that the son was going to start renting out the other half of the duplex? Because up until this time it had been empty. And even though we only lived on one side of the house, it felt like we had it all.

Which was a comfort I was taking for granted.

I come home from school a couple of times and see the landlord's son. Running his mouth on the front porch. Boasting about all the benefits of living so close to the beach

About a month later he comes over to tell us he found someone. He's all smiles about the money he'll be bringing in. He says he rented it to some goodwill charity. They plan on using it as a group home.

'You know, for them retards,' he says.

He tells us that whatever god damned charity it is that's footing the bill thinks the quiet beach life will be good for them. They can take the crisp lake air, and relax.

But his fucking words and smile give me the fear. That these bastards don't know what they're getting into. And everything will end terribly. Like he said, they're here for the peace and quiet.

I tell myself they've been told we're students. And that they imagine two nice boys in argyle sweaters spending their time studying under lamplight. Not two teenage drunks free to wallow in their own filth.

So a week later when they move in I can't help feel a little sorry for them.

I watch from the window. The charity hired movers for the big pieces. Couches and beds and dressers. But throughout the day five families drop off scared adult children with backpacks.

The place next door is the same size as ours. So I wonder how they're all going to fit. Sure their upstairs bedrooms aren't filled with trash. But still. With the full time keeper, it's going to be close quarters.

And no matter how much I learn to hate them I have to give them credit. Because in no time they destroy our quiet life like professionals. They cry and yell. Stomp. Howl late into the night.

'These god dammed walls can't be any thicker than cardboard,' I tell my roommate at 3 AM.

His only agreement an angry grunt. And I wonder how much longer I can put up with it.

. . . .

Since the beginning of the year the teachers and the school board have been at each other's throats. Teachers demand higher wages. The school board says its pockets are empty. And fevered rumors circulate among the students.

Then one Tuesday afternoon it happens. The principal announces it over the school PA system. That there won't be any classes until they get what they want.

All the other kids in the class jump up from their seats. Yell and scream. Act like apes. I sit there smiling quietly. Hoping that this goes on forever. And that the teachers never get what they're after.

Because it gives my roommate and I an advantage.

The one thing the neighbours have had on us is their lack of an organized life. When a good day is not shitting yourself, it's easy to stay up all night moaning. And listening to the television at full blast.

But now we have even less fucking structure. They've got their goddamned keepers breathing down the backs of their necks. Without school or parents and only loosely watched by bureaucratic institutions our lives lose all purpose.

I start car hopping at nights again. I'd been meaning to for a while. After that first big check from welfare the proceeding ones were pared down. And it was getting tougher to smoke, drink and eat for 30 days a month.

Now with nothing to do all day I smoke more. Drink more. And since I cant steal from the school cafeteria or eat at their breakfast club for poor kids, I eat less.

My youth keeps me going. But I know it can't last forever.

The car hopping isn't bad either. I like the excitement of walking the empty streets at night. Hiding in the shadows. Rustling through the glove boxes full of maps and garbage. Sticking my hand down into the seats of old beaters and pulling out handfuls of sand and lost hair.

Always wondering when I'll feel the grip of some drunk on my collar.

I get home around midnight. Any later and I risk being seen by those leaving the bar to go home and sleep it off. And when I do my room-mate is always sitting there. A video game controller in his hand. A bottle of whiskey on the table. And the smell of hash oil in the air.

We stay up til dawn every day. Drink whiskey. Smoke dope. Yell. Scream. Turn the television up as loud as it will go. We're young, free and drunk. So of course we're selfish.

One afternoon we get a knock on the door. My roommate answers it. It's a woman who looks after them. She's in her mid-thirties. Still pretty. But she looks run down. Weak. Tired.

'Um, hello. I hope I didn't wake you…I live next door, and I was wondering if I could ask a favour?' she asks my roommate.

'Yeah, what do you want?' he asks.

'Well, I was wondering if you can keep it down at night. It's getting tough to sleep. And one of the tenants, Darren, is becoming unpredictable.'

I don't know any of their names but I know who she's talking about. He's a nasty little dwarf with a cracked face. Long filthy beard. Rolls his own cigarettes. Wears cowboy boots. Treats everyone like shit.

He's a full-sized asshole.

And my roommate tells her sure fucking thing. Giving her hope. But the poor woman doesn't know him. And doesn't hear the sarcasm in his voice. Not like I do.

But I'm no better. Because I'm lying back on the couch smoking. Thinking to myself, fuck this lady and her simple, neighborly request. A part of me wants to see what this Darren is like when he gets unpredictable.

And my youthful stupidity never allows me to contemplate what the fuck we're getting ourselves into.

· · · · · · · ·

Then one morning I hear Darren through the wall. I recognize the stomp of his little boots going to the door. Which the little fucker slams behind him.

I hear him stamp his way across the wooden porch. Then a brief period of silence. Followed by our windows and door and whole front of the fucking house being pelted with what sounds like gravel to me.

'Jesus. What the fuck is that?' my roommate says from the kitchen.

'No idea.' I tell him. Even though I have my suspicions. So I get up. Walk to the window. Lift one slat in the blinds. Peek out. And here's the little asshole standing on the side of the road. Picking up handfuls of mud and rocks. Flinging it at the house.

'Someone needs to teach him a lesson,' I say after I explain what's happening.

'Are you going to do it?' he challenges me.

And fuck. There's nothing I'd like better than to go out there and beat that little dwarf like he's been asking for. But I'm smarter than that. I can see the headline: *Local Drag on Society Murders Happy Dwarf in Fit of Rage.*

It has no chance of ending well for me.

I tell my roommate this as he sits down and half listens. Instead of caring about anything that's going on he picks up a video game controller. Turns on the TV.

So I lie back. And stop giving a shit myself. It's not my name on the lease. Fuck him.

I smoke a cigarette. Listen to rocks hit the front of the house for a while. Until his little arm gets tired and he stops. Which is nice. Because the night's catching up. And I was never going to get to sleep with all that racket.

· · · · · · · ·

After a couple more weeks of us fucking around, Darren completely loses it.

He starts banging on the wall. Cursing us. Making threats. Yelling in the face of the poor woman left in charge. When I hear her say *Put it down* I'm certain she's holding back tears.

And I can't help but see the image of her over there. Short of breath. Scared. Trying to remember her training concerning neighbours without empathy. And how far sleep deprivation can drive some people.

I laugh a little to myself. Amused by the level of stress in the air.

The front door of their place cracks against the wall when Darren kicks it open. His little feet pound across the porch. He rips open our storm door. Starts kicking the wooden one with all his might.

I'm glad I slipped the chain across earlier. Because I don't know if the bolt is in place. And I want to avoid a face-to-face confrontation. Unsure how I'll manage against this angry troll who's beating my door and screaming like a wounded animal.

As the whole front of our apartment rattles under the force of Darren's kicks my roommate blurts out 'Jesus fucking Jesus. What the fucking Christ is going on?' Language I'm sure his benefactors would not be so proud of.

'Any ideas if he gets in?' I ask my roommate.

'This is it, man. Your chance. An excuse to teach him a lesson. Think of it now. Local welfare recipient quells angry dwarf. Saves village.'

I convince myself and my roommate that this is not the time for heroes and brave deeds. But to make sure this little fucking monster stays on the other side of the door.

A point that I couldn't make at a better time. Because just as I do Darren grips the door handle. He gets it open as far he can before the chain stops him. But it's enough to slide his hairy, grey hand through.

And I don't think I've ever been more afraid in my life.

His long yellow fingernails scratch at the door. He gets a hold of the curtains. Tugs and rips them. Manages to knock over a pile of science fiction novels that had been teetering next to the door for ages.

I start laughing. My roommate gives me a dirty look and I tell him this is the nice thing about living in a fucking a mess. Because I can't even tell the god damned difference.

The caregiver starts pleading on the other side of the door. Which gives me hope. She's sorted things out I tell myself. Remembered all the right tactics. She'll have this tiny asshole calmed down and in bed in no time.

But I couldn't be any more wrong.

I can't hear exactly what she's saying to him. But it's not helping. Darren screams with twice the fury. He pulls his grotesque hand back through the crack. But only for a second.

And when he sticks it back through he's holding a long, sharp looking knife. It's half the length of his stunted arm. And despite his limited ability to wave the blade he exhibits skill while he does.

'I think it's time to call the cops,' my roommate says.

Fuck off, I tell him. The closest police station is a 20-minute drive. By the time they get here we're sliced up like a holiday roast. And I can only imagine the ridicule the cops will give us when we tell them we're afraid of a dwarf.

Instead I start yelling through the door. I want the caretaker to know we mean business. I tell her we don't have to stand for this. That we're calling the cops. And that I'm certain this isn't Darren's first violent meltdown.

She yells back, 'Please don't. He's just riled up. He just hasn't been sleeping well.'

All I can do is laugh.

My roommate gets up and goes to the kitchen. He comes back with a frying pan. It still has dried tomato sauce and bits of ground beef in it. I try and remember the last time either of us cooked.

He walks over to the door. Raises the pan above his head and smashes the dwarf's hand as hard as he can. Darren drops the knife. Pulls back his hand. And when he does my roommate kicks the door shut and turns the bolt.

Darren flies into a rage on the other side and starts growling. Throws himself at it a couple more times.

Jesus, even if we didn't call, the cops must be coming by now. How can they not be. The neighbours have to have heard this. Where the hell is that fat drunk fire marshal when you need him.

Darren gives up. Or just tires. We hear the nurse walk over to him. Consol him like a child. Then walk him back to through their front door. With our victory in the air I can't resist. So I yell at them one more time.

'Keep that thing under control. Remember. We have the knife now.'

After things calm down my roommate and I order a pizza. I pull out a bag of weed I found while car hopping a couple nights before. The rest of the night a blur.

A couple weeks later the group home moves out. The experiment a failure. We hear from the neighbours that they've gone to another village. One down the lake. A whole house to themselves.

A better chance of success.

For both of us.

And then the strike ends.

5.

I got used to things. Gave in to the idea that this was it. I'd live out my days with nothing to do but steal from cars and drink every night. These thoughts came easy with no direction.

I was going to have to get up in time to catch the bus. Sit in a class all day. Listen to some boring asshole go on and on. Which didn't seem important anymore. Not when I had to worry about other things.

And all I really I wanted was to sleep til noon. Steal from cars at night. But welfare wasn't going to keep paying my rent while I did that. Not when I could be going to school. Or finding real employment.

And going to school is the easier of the two.

So when my roommate suggests we move, find something within walking distance, I think he's a genius.

Because I can already see myself missing too much class. Which is something I can't swing. Not with welfare up my ass. And if I don't graduate I'll never get a job in one of the factories. Like every other man for miles around.

But of course getting an apartment isn't easy. We're too god damned young. When they ask and we say we're 16 and 17 we get bad looks. Like we can't be trusted. And when I think about our current place they're right to be wary.

When we get asked about our finances things start looking even worse. No one wants a teenage run away welfare recipient and an orphan renting out their attic or basement.

Sure, the landlords do us the favour of a walk through. A reason for the drive over. They take our application forms. Never call us back.

At night I lie on the filthy couch I call my bed smoking cigarettes. Wondering who these landlords are looking for. People who'll only be there in their sleeping hours. People who'll keep everything in working order. Someone they can count on to pay the rent.

But to me, those sound like the kind of people who buy homes. Have a good job in the factories. Or with the government. People with money. And cars. They don't need to rent.

The only people who rent are deadbeats. And teenage runaway alcoholics. Like us.

. . . .

We find a great place. It's in a neighbourhood we like. Some of the girls we run around with live close. The streets are lined with trees. A convenience store on the corner that's sympathetic to underage smokers.

A 20 minute walk from school.

The apartment has hardwood floors. Lots of windows. A sunken living room. Good sized bedrooms. A nice kitchen.

It's got it all.

We walk around looking at it with the landlord. A quiet looking older man. Liver spots along his hairline.

And in my head I'm already telling my roommate he can have the small room. The one with a disproportioned Spiderman painted on the wall. I'm thinking of the parties we can have. The girls I can bring back. And all the good times ahead of us.

'So what do you boys think?' the old man says.

'It's great. Just what we've been looking for.' I say

'Yeah we love it. It's close to school. We have friends nearby. We'll take it.' my roommate pipes in.

Then this kind looking old piece of shit breaks the bubble. Tells us that because we look a little young he's going to need some more convincing. Like a hand written letter from our folks, a principal, or sports coach, or priest.

We look at each other.

We're fucked.

We don't have anyone. That's why we're looking for a fucking apartment. Both of us are on the outs with our folks. The school hates us.

We could ask our current landlord. But he's been showing the place. And isn't happy with the state of things. Then again, he might just give us the reference to get us out of his hair for good.

'Oh, of course. We'll contact our preachers. The principal loves us. But it's going to take a couple of days. Could you hold the place for us?' my roommate tells him.

'Sure thing, boys.'

'We'd appreciate that.' I say.

We shake his hand. Leave. Walk down the creaking wooden stairs and stand on the sidewalk. The sun is shining. It's midmorning. It's going to be nice day. My roommate pulls out a pack of smokes. I ask him for one and he gives it to me. He lights his. Then mine.

I inhale deeply. We never see that landlord again.

'So, that's too bad hunh?' I say exhaling.

'Yeah. No one is going to stick up for us. Fuck. That place is the nicest one yet.'

'A priest. Who the hell does he think we are. Who the fuck is religious anymore. What year is this.' I ask.

'Yeah, that was surprising,' my roommate says.

'Christ. This isn't easy.'

We keep looking. At basements and attics and three storie walk-ups. But it's the same thing over and over. They don't like how young we are. They don't like how I'm on welfare. They don't like how my roommate's an orphan.

So all we can do is keep losing.

And all this rejection is breaking me down. I'm not strong enough for it. The line of questions. Not to mention all the school shit I'm dealing with. It's getting to be too much. So one night staring at the ceiling above the dirty couch, I give up.

Without looking at my roommate I tell him it's over for me. That he's going to have to do the rest of the searching. That I'm just a fucking bad luck omen skid mark on the whole operation.

He does his best to convince me otherwise. That this is how things work themselves out. You never find a place until you're almost out on your ass. It's one of life's great stresses. And that I'm letting it get to me.

'Listen. I'm out.

'Ok. If that's how you want things.' he says.

'It's too much for me right now. I'm overwhelmed.'

I lie there and tell myself I'm a kid for fuck sakes. I shouldn't be out pounding the pavement looking for apartments. I should be worrying about my fucking drivers license. Getting good grades. Graduating. The rest of my goddamned life.

But I don't have the time. I'm too caught up in this trying to figure out where I'll live in two weeks bullshit. Will it be an apartment or the street. And what the Christ am I'm going to eat for dinner tonight.

Then there's school. Ever since we got back they've been trying to make up for the lost two months. So we can finish the school year on time. I have to write a fucking poem for English that was due four days ago.

I'm coming undone.

· · · · · · ·

Two days after I abandon the search my roommate finds a place. It's a 15 minute walk from school. All I have to do is sign the lease when we move in. He tells me the superintendant already loves him. That we both have a bedroom. And the rents only $250 a piece.

So it's easy to see I was the problem all along.

'Fucking eh. When do we move?' I ask.

'He says since the place is empty we can move in next Friday. A week early.'

I take a look around at the beach house. At the black garbage bags bursting in the corner. The pop bottles scattered across the living room floor. The smell of mold in the air. And I tell my roommate he has a lot of work to do.

All I have is the same backpack I moved in with. The same shitty stained t-shirts and underwear and socks. Even with a couple of books I'm carrying around and a knife I found in the backseat of an old Camaro it's as light as a feather.

My roommate on the other hand is a completely different animal.

His load is heavier.

First off he decides to abandon everything that's been rotting upstairs. We have no room for it. And there's not enough time to even start. So a couple days before moving out we close the door at the bottom of the stairway. And neither of us says a thing.

Pretend it never happened. Like a nightmare.

But even still. He has a ton of shit. Way too much for some one his age. He digs through it all. Unearths items I didn't know were here. Another couch. A dining room set. He pulls out what he wants. Leaves the rest.

He packs all of his books. Hundreds of them. Some English literature classics and an overwhelming collection of science fiction. I've been tearing through them at night. While he plays video games. And I'm glad he's bringing them along.

When he gets to the kitchen he begs me to help him clean. Tells me it's just as much my mess. And I laugh. Tell him to go fuck himself. That this mess was here long before I showed up at the door.

So as he washes dishes and swears, I lie on the couch. Smoking. Not lifting a finger. He really should've helped when the welfare lady was coming.

· · · · · · ·

We're excited to be leaving this place. My roommate grew up in the city where we go to school. So it's a bit of a homecoming. But I'm glad to be putting some distance between the village and me. My parents. And my memories.

So we can't even wait until Saturday morning.

We plan everything for Friday night. My roommate stays home to do some more packing. But I go to school in the morning. Not because I care about it. But I want to make sure everyone is still coming to help.

I see my friends Billy and Saul. They can both bring their parents pick up truck and van. They'll be by around seven. My ex-girlfriend Sam tells me she'll be there too. Her dad is lending her the van for the night.

And I wish I hadn't been such a piece of shit to her. And I wish I could convince her I'm still good.

But I'm too busy for that today. And instead of telling her how much I love her or going to class I say fuck it. Walk out to the highway and stick out my thumb. I get a ride in no time. A nice old man who wants to tell me stories while symphonies play on the radio.

I get the old man to drop me off at the edge of the village. I don't want to g back to the apartment. I don't want to see my roommate. Or help him. I want to walk around. I want to be alone. I want to think.

About all the years I've been here. Wishing for this moment. When I could shake off this village like a shoulder full of dandruff. To me it represented my father remarrying. A reminder of my mother dying.

So I see the beaches and safe streets tinted with a smear of shit. And there's nothing I can do to wipe it off.

Except run even farther away.

Like always I end up at the beach. Looking out at the water is the only time I feel at ease. I sit on a bench in front of a hamburger stand closed for the season. I stretch out my legs. The wind off the lake in my hair. I smoke cigarettes for hours.

When I stand up the sun is going down. The wind is beginning to bite into my knuckles. I feel tired. I want to lie down for a while before anyone shows up.

But when I get there my roommate and Carl are there. Drinking beer and smoking weed. I have no will power. So when I get passed a joint and a beer I forget all about resting. Riding high on the excitement in the air.

· · · · · · · ·

We drive up the long driveway in convoy fashion. Billy and my roommate up front. Carl and Saul in the next car. And Sam and I last. It's just about 9 o'clock.

It's the first look I've got of the place. I imagine our apartment will be in one of the five 3-story walk-ups on the lot. Two on either side of the driveway. And one at the end of the other side of the parking lot.

'So this is it eh. Is it nice?' Sam asks me driving up.

'We're gonna find out at the same time. I've never been in.' I smile at her. And then I tell her how I couldn't take it. All the bullshit. And that as soon as I stopped looking my roommate found this place.

She laughs. And tells me it sounds about right for me. That of course I have no problem moving into somewhere I haven't even seen.

Everyone parks in the lot at the end of the driveway. We get out. Look to my roommate for answers. Like what the fuck are we doing, where do we go. He tells me to follow him inside the closest building. To the super's office. And everyone else can wait out here.

'I ain't got all night,' Sam says laughing as we walk away.

'You and her getting along tonight?' my roommate asks as we get inside.

'Yeah, of course. Why wouldn't we?'

'Well I guess you're not that drunk then.'

As I follow behind him down the hall I wonder what it'd be like to kick him right in the lower back. And how happy it'd make me. Fuck him and his opinions.

At the end of the hall my roommate stops and knocks on a door. We can hear a television on the other side. Some shuffling. And the lock turning. A kind looking older man opens up. Recognizes my room-mate. Shakes his hand and invites us in.

We go into his kitchen where my roommate introduces us. He tells me his name is Joe. That he's retired and that him and his wife look after the building. They get the apartment in trade.

As I'm signing the lease he tells us that we look like nice boys. And that it does a man good to get out on his own young. My roommate and I smile along with him. But I'm not sure if I agree yet.

Maybe when I'm his age. And I'm looking from the other side of a free apartment. Before we leave he gives us keys and tells us to use the side door. And a staircase that's right beside our place.

Walking back through the hall to the front door I ask my roommate, 'so, which apartment is ours?'

'Oh, it's right above Joe. Looks exactly the same,' my roommate replies like it's no big deal.

'Hunh? Above him? Exactly the same?' and I try to imagine us sitting around drinking. Smoking weed. With all the same shit on the walls as Joe and his wife. Commemorative plates. Needlework of black labs bringing ducks back to their masters.

And I can't help but wonder if this might not be a bad idea. I ask my roommate if he remembers the blow out with the halfway house. The dwarf. He answers me confidently that he's certain the same thing will not repeat itself.

So I figure fuck it. And stop asking questions.

Outside my roommate starts organizing everyone. He always wants to be in charge. Thinks all his ideas are the best. I don't know about anyone else. But I find it easier to just let him run his mouth. And do things my way in the end.

Billy is friends with two guys across the hall from where we're moving in. He goes up and gets them to lend a hand. We unload one vehicle at a time. With the eight of us we get all of our shit up and into the apartment in about an hour.

And to me it feels good running up and down the stairs. Carrying couches and boxes of my roommate's garbage. Because I'm doing something. And it makes me feel like my life is on its way. Success is within my reach.

The last thing we have to move in is a pull out couch. It's my roommate's. It's heavy. We've gotten fat and weak from lying around the beach house. The only people left are Billy and the guys from across the hall. But they've had enough. All they do is stand around. Smoke cigarettes.

I remember my roommate before we left. Tying the pull out mattress to the frame of the couch with a piece of twine. Even then I thought the knot was shitty. But if I'd said something, he wouldn't have bothered to listen.

We have the side door of the building propped open with a used copy of *Stranger in a Strange Land*. The door is the kind that is just a metal frame with thick, wire mesh glass running through it. It's strong. Designed to withstand a late night kicking.

A few of the neighbours have stuck their heads out into the narrow hallway tonight see what the racket is. Who the new tenants of apartment 201 are. And I have to admit. They look like an unruly bunch.

So the security door is probably warranted.

Of course, when we have the couch halfway through the door my roommate's knot comes undone. The bed unfolds. The metal frame tapping against the middle of the glass.

Which shatters into hundreds of little cubes. We both hang our heads. Groan. Fold the bed back in. Hurry up the stairs. I lose sight of my chance at success.

'What do we do, man? We have to tell the super.' I say.

'No. Fuck that. If he asks don't say a thing. We'll play stupid.'

'C'mon man. He knows we're moving in. He's gonna know it's us. I don't think he's a fucking idiot.'

'Yeah, but he can't prove that it's us. We just say we know nothing. This is how things work in the real world, pal.'

We argue back and forth for a while. I'm naïve. I think that if we state our case, tell him it's an accident. He'll be sympathetic. He'll understand.

But I'm new at things.

. . . .

Like an idiot I go down and knock on Joe's door in the morning. He answers in his housecoat. The smell of coffee in the air. He smiles and invites me in.

I hang my head as I stand in his kitchenette. Family photos look on from the living room. His wife's voice is coming from the back bedroom. She's humming a song that I remember my grandmother singing to me.

So it makes my confession come harder. I feel like I'm admitting a horrible crime to my grandfather.

'No trouble this soon I hope,' he says.

'Oh no, no trouble.' and I tell him what happened last night. About the window. And how it was an accident. And he smiles at me. Says he must've been right. We are good boys. Because most of the other people in the building would've just played dumb.

He has no proof.

And I start to feel a warmth rise up through my body. This'll show my prick roommate. I did the right thing. Joe's happy about the whole thing. Even proud of me.

The world is a good place.

'So, I'll call the glass guy to come and fix it. I'll send you the bill when I get it.'

'Um, what's that?'

And he tells me the same thing over again. That a bill will be on my doorstep. And I'll have to pay it. Which is bad. But now I'm going to have to go up there and admit to my roommate what happened.

Fuck.

This old asshole. I want to strangle him. Watch his eyes go blank. How can he do this? I hope there's cancer eating away at him.

I'm really surprised here. I thought things we're going to go well. That it'd all be chalked up to moving expenses. But no. Instead I'm fucked. And I can't believe it.

I turn around and leave without saying a thing. I feel like an idiot. My roommate was right. I should've listened. Instead of going back to the apartment, I go and sit on top of a washer in the laundry room for a while. I can't bring myself to face him.

When someone comes in to do their laundry I get up. Walk back upstairs to my new home. When I come in my roommate is on the couch smoking a joint.

'How'd it go? Did he let us off?' he asks me just before he starts coughing.

'No. The old fucking cock sucker told me he'd send us a bill.'

'What'd I tell you. You can't trust these people. It's his job.'

'Is everyone a piece of shit?' I ask while looking up at the ceiling.

A couple weeks later Joe comes by with a smile and a bill for three hundred and fifty dollars. Neither of us have the money to pay it.

6.

I didn't think the move would affect me. Outside of getting to school quicker. But I was wrong. Like about everything. And my claim with welfare didn't just transfer over.

So I have to reapply. And again it isn't good enough to make a phone call. They need me to come down and tell some sour face that I'm a bum in person.

And what can I do. Other than show up with my head hung down. Beg for their help and charity.

But this is what you have to do if want to live for free, I tell myself. It's better than back home. All that yelling. All that bullshit, so I don't worry much. It'll be easier this time knowing the flavor of shit I'm going to be served.

And what keeps me going is thinking about the big first check I'll get. Because after the move I don't have a lot going for me.

Except this is the kind of apartment a government employee can't raise a stink over. It's a series of crisp, bland white boxes strung together. Christ. Even the grey/blue carpet looks like the cheap shit in offices everywhere.

There's no fucking stained paths leading you deeper into the mess. And instead of stinking dishes and newspapers littering the floor sunlight streams in all day though a large patio door.

It's completely bland. A sign I'm on my way up out of the gutter.

So the next day I skip school and walk downtown to city hall. The office is in the basement. I tell the woman behind the plexiglass my story. She rolls her eyes and nods along. She couldn't give a fuck about me or my circumstances.

The familiarity of it gives me confidence.

She flips through an appointment book. Taking her time to slowly scroll through all the columns of about seven pages. When she finds an empty slot she asks my name and address. I'm told someone will be by a week from Thursday.

And in the ten days between then and now my roommate does his level best. Works hard. To turn the place right back into the dump we moved out of.

He gives up completely. Starts ordering food nightly. Leaves the empty chicken and pizza containers on the coffee table until they get too high to see the TV. And he kicks them on the floor.

I never see him cook but somehow the dishes pile up in the sink. And really I find it amazing how quickly the sink stopper becomes a maggot hatchery. Even as I'm dry heaving I have to admit I'm a little proud of him.

At night I lie in bed in my room in the dark. Smoking cigarette after cigarette. Wondering if the asshole sleeping on the other side of this thin wall is trying to fuck me over. Or is he just so god damned oblivious that he doesn't see he's taking a shit all over my bright future.

· · · · · · ·

I have to go to school the day before they come. I can't afford to miss any more days. Things aren't going so well there. I rarely know what class I'm in or what work I should've done.

So I have to spend the night before cleaning. My roommate sits on the couch smoking pot while I run around. Picking up his trash. Washing his shit-smeared dishes.

And I feel so doomed. Defeated before I even get a chance to fuck it up. As I empty the ashtray on the coffee table my roommate decides to take a second to tell me what he thinks.

That I'm wasting my fucking time. And I shouldn't be so uptight. He says the government owes me the money while laughing at me cleaning. All I have to do is say I won't finish school without it.

All I manage to say in defense of myself is go fuck yourself. But what the fuck does he know. He gets money handed out by Christians. A compassionate organization. Someone with an interested ear.

He doesn't know what it feels like to go down to that office. He doesn't know what to feels like to admit to another human that you're not really worth anything. He doesn't know what it feels like to be looked at like that.

And I know what I have to do. Better that he does. So I go on cleaning the place from top to bottom. More than I'm sure that I have to. Because when this fucker comes through the door in the morning they want to see someone who looks like they're on their way up.

Not some bag of shit laying around in an extension their own rotten existence.

When my roommate goes to bed I decide I'm hungry. In the cupboard I have enough cans of tomato sauce and pasta to last a couple weeks. While I boil some noodles and heat up the sauce I wonder what I'll eat when this runs out.

I sit on the couch and eat. Take a large roach from the ashtray. Smoke it down to nothing. Fall asleep watching local television.

· · · · · · · ·

In the morning I wake up when I hear my roommate banging around in the kitchen. I lay on the couch with my eyes shut pretending I'm asleep until I hear the door close behind him and his foot steps down the hall.

I roll over and smoke a cigarette. After I finish I get up and go into the bathroom. I pick up my razor. Look at the chips in the blade. All the old hair stuck in it. I know it's just going to rip the hair from my face.

But what do you do. I ask the mirror while shrugging.

I take a shower. Then put on the cleanest clothes I own. Comb my hair. Smoke a cigarette staring in the mirror. Try and believe myself when I say I look good. Respectable. Friendly.

When I hear the knock on the door I butt my smoke out in the sink. Wet my hands with cold water and rub them into my face. This is going to go well, I lie to myself.

I open the door with a smile on my face. It's a small woman. She looks scared. And I find it strange they keep sending ladies into the unsupervised apartments of the lowest common denominator.

I invite her in. She takes a look around. Something's off I worry. Maybe it's so clean she can't believe her eyes. But I doubt it. I wonder about the places other welfare types live in. And should I be setting my standards higher.

Or lower.

I offer her a seat on the couch. She says she'll stand. We lean against the living room wall.

She tells me all the shit I know. I have to go to school. It's my duty. If I miss more than ten days a month they'll reassess my needs. All the same shit as before. But this time they want me to meet a caseworker.

I ask why. I'm told they want to see how my progress is coming along. Make sure that I'm doing my best at school. That I'm not just lying around. They want to make sure I become a functioning member of society as quick as possible.

Which was something the county never even brought up.

She tells me that she has to be going to her next appointment. That the apartment seems suitable. Although it could be better she says. As she leaves she tells me I should be getting a call within two weeks. It takes up to that long to process my claim and authorize a check.

I tell her she's an angel. Shut the door behind her. Go over to couch and sit down. I light a smoke. I can do this, I think as I exhale.

I just have to make sure I get up early every morning. Make it to school before they stop giving out breakfasts to poor kids.

At lunch I can swipe half eaten meals off cafeteria tabletops. Cold french fries. Chewed on hamburgers. Plates of toyed with spaghetti. Things kids with families and full stomachs don't need.

· · · · · · ·

The night before I go to pick up the check I don't feel the pain any more. Or worry. I lie on the floor of my bedroom in my sleeping bag hallucinating food dancing across my vision. Bricks of cheese. Tuna fish. Ramen noodles.

I fall asleep with a great big grin on my face.

In the morning I get up early. Drool soaking my pillow. Those damned food dreams. I wipe the side of my face dry and unzip my sleeping bag. Get dressed and leave. Without anything to eat the best thing to do is walk.

When I get downtown I'm early. I have to wait outside. Bouncing back and forth on my feet in front of the door. I'm full of delirious excitement. I pass the time imagining hot breakfasts from filthy diners.

The lock in the door turns and I wait. I don't want to seem too anxious. But it's tough with my stomach growling and when I throw the door open the asshole behind the bullet proof glass is just getting back to her chair.

I tell her I'm here to pick up my check. She tells me I'm pretty early and that I must be anxious. I smile and nod while thinking she'd be pretty anxious too if her cupboards had been bare for the last few days.

When she asks for my name I give it to her and wait for her to scan the computer screen in front of her. She takes her time. Stops to look through some papers on her desk. My stomach growls.

'Did you hear that?' she asks me.

All I can do is shake my head no.

'Yep, you were right,' she says, 'there is a check her for you. Just wait a minute.' She gets up and goes though a door behind her. When she comes back she has a brown envelope in her hand.

I'm so excited I think I'm going to faint. She slips it through the slot at the bottom. I grab it and stuff it in my pocket. Sign for the check. Turn around. I hear her muffled voice through the glass. I don't hear her. Or care. I'm out the door and on my way to the bank.

It's a long walk. But with a check in my pocket I don't notice. I get lost in the sounds of the city. Smile at people walking by. The thought of hot food turning me into a nice person.

At the bank I have to wait in line to use the machine. So I pull out the envelope. Rip it open. My mind is expecting three months back pay. So the $500 that the check is actually for comes across as a little disappointing.

Five hundred bucks. My rent is $300. How the fuck am I going to eat? How am I supposed pay the landlord for the broken window?

There's no way I'm going to to pull it off. There must be some kind of mistake. Where's my back months pay? I walk home with my head hung low. The thought of a hot breakfast disappearing with each step.

Instead I buy a loaf of the cheapest bread I can. A jar of peanut butter. At home I sit on the couch with it laid out in front of me. And if I look at in the right light, I'm pretty sure it looks just like my future.

· · · · · · ·

In the morning I call up the welfare office. I ask to speak with my agent. They transfer me. I wait. I listen the calming music being played and remember I have to be nice. I can't give them a reason to take away my pittance.

When my agent picks up the phone it's the first time I've spoken with her. Her voice is soft. And for a second I forget that I was ever angry. Or starving. Or expecting anything other than what I got.

I tell her my problem. And in her soft voice she tells me I don't have one. That sure, the county gave out money for time waiting the processing of a claim but the city didn't. And there was nothing I could do.

She asks if I have any more concerns. And I don't. But she wants to make sure I won't miss my first meeting with her. And that if I do I won't see another cent.

When I hang up I sink back into the couch. I can't move. I'm fucked. This is going to be tough. I make a peanut butter sandwich. Drink a glass of water. I think about how the fuck I'm going to do it.

I know other people on welfare. They all do something. Sell drugs. Tattoo. Work odd labour jobs. The kind that pay in cash at the end of the day. If I want to survive I'm going to have to find something.

I walk over to the patio door. I can see into the windows of apartments in the other three story walkups on the property. Overweight families blending into their couches. Shoveling food from bowls into their mouths.

And I feel like I've been given another look into my future.

I go down to the Joe's apartment and knock on the door. He opens it and invites me in. His wife is doing the dishes. The smell of bacon and eggs is still thick in the air. I think about my peanut butter sandwich.

I want to lick their walls.

'Here's the rent, sir.'

'What about the money for the window?' Joe asks.

'Yeah, I'm going to have to pay you a little each month. Is that ok?'

'Sure thing, Stan.'

'Thanks a lot. I really appreciate it.'

After Joe writes me a receipt I leave. Walk down the hall and out the front door of the building. I don't want to go to school. I'm feeling too low. But I can't afford to miss another day.

It takes me about half an hour to get there. I stop for a while and sit by the pond in the park. Smoke a cigarette and watch the ducks. My ass is damp when get up but I barely notice.

I don't have what it takes to care.

When I get to school it's the break between 1ˢᵗ and 2ⁿᵈ period. Everyone is outside smoking. I see my roommate at the edge of the woods with Carl and Billy and Saul. I walk up and bum a smoke from Saul.

'Hey. What's going on.' Billy asks me.

I tell them about yesterday. And my morning. And about how I'm fucked. And how I'm not sure how I'm going to make it. But they don't want to listen. They have easier things to think about.

The bell rings. It's time to suck it up. To go sit in the back of a classroom and fade out until lunch. I take the last drag of my smoke and follow everyone in.

From behind I hear some one yell, 'hey Stan, is that goose shit on the back of your pants?'

7.

After the guys across the hall helped us move in we've been hanging out ever since. They come over all the time. And their horror movie collection is unrivaled in the city.

They're the kind of guys that say their Satanists. But only in regards to a lifetime of long greasy hair. Death metal. Pentagram tattoos. And getting fucked up. Of course I look up to them.

And they were good guys to have on my side. One of them. Mitch. Was a fucking brute. He had a feral look in his eye. A temper. And a habit of going around town and beating the shit of the biggest guys he could find.

This was a habit he'd picked up during a childhood on the east coast. He told us horrible stories. Things that shattered my visions of the Canadian east coast. Of sleepy fishing villages and good-natured people smiling like morons.

All his stories involve horrible beatings. Blood. Broken limbs. He tells the tales like they're nothing. Just something you to have to do when you get up in the morning. A twinkle in his eye during the moments I have a hard time stomaching.

Like when he tells us about this game they used to play. It's called broom a coon, he said. A giant smile on his face. The sunlight coming in through the screen door illuminating his broken teeth.

And I think about going into the woods. A broom over my shoulder. Searching for some poor sleeping raccoon. And when I find it start beating the creature viciously. And run away before it has a chance to retaliate.

To me it seems more like a dare than a game. But I'm still a naïve little boy sometimes.

'How'd you play?' my roommate asks.

That's when Mitch's face really lights up. And it has nothing to do with sun this time. He's just so fucking proud of what he's about to say. That this is a special childhood memory. And we're about to get a look passed his cruel eyes.

'Well we'd get a broom handle right? Then we'd go over to the black part of town and the first nigger we saw we'd drive up behind him and whack up side the back of his head as hard as we could. Never even had to get out of the car.'

'Christ, are you serious?' I blurt out.

'Don't use his name in front of me.'

'What? Christ?' and he looks me in the eyes. His nostrils flare. There's hate all over his face. I think he's going to hit me.

I explain myself. Tell him I'm taking the lords name in vain. It's a sin. Which should make him feel better. But I'm sure my words come out sarcastically. And I can't stop myself from rolling my eyes.

It's a curse.

'If you say it again, I'll fucking crush your windpipe.' He makes a fist. Punches our coffee table. All of the ashtrays and empty bottles and dirty plates shoot up into the air. Come down with a clatter and spill on the carpet. Mitch storms out.

And I'm glad he gave me a chance. Or a warning. But I have watch myself. So when the door closes I tell myself it's because of how shitty he is that makes us better allies than enemies.

Mitch is on student welfare like me. But I guess he's smarter. Because he tells people he's an artist. Spends his time painting. Most of the pieces are poorly rendered demons. Flames. Pointed emblems that I'm told hold satanic meaning and significance.

Really unlikable garbage. But when he comes over with a new one in his hand it's hard to tell him it's shit. For fear of a busted face. And we end up with a few on the walls.

Torture in the form of a gift.

So he never finds out that he fucking stinks. And he makes the natural transition from local tough guy to tattoo artist. He finds someone to sell him a machine. Starts dishing tattoos out from his home studio/ kitchen table.

And there's never a shortage of clients.

I tell myself that he must be bullying them into it. But I can never tell. Or ask. Or know. And it doesn't really matter anyways. Because it'd be no consolation when I see him eating good food. Drinking beer. And know there's more of both in his fridge.

Instead of like at home. Where the only thing in our fridge is a terrible smell.

But what makes hanging around Mitch worth it is his roommate. Kelly Reeceback. Everyone calls him Greaseback though. It's not the kind of nickname that has the girls running to him. But the consequences of being a boy named Kelly are far worse.

Greaseback is rail thin. Never wears a shirt. Has a pentagram tattooed on either side of his chest. He smokes and drinks like it's necessary for him to stay alive. Been out of high school for years.

I never ask him if he completed all the grades. Or just walked out one day. And I don't want to find out. Because I'd prefer to imagine him telling off a teacher. And storming off while lighting a cigarette.

I do know that since whatever the fuck happened he's been on and off welfare for years. Sometimes he has the luck of a well-paying construction job. Or as a painter. Or the helper of some man with a van.

And whether the times are high or low he's always smiling. Looking for a good time. Never threatening anyone. He just wants a drink. Smoke. A few laughs.

He has nothing to prove.

He makes no waves.

And he reminds me of the Japanese poems my English teacher loves so much. But I'm not sure she could find the same beauty here. In this apartment. With the walls covered in pictures of demons. And oiled women with big tits. And a cloud of cigarette smoke in the air.

These days Greaseback's riding pretty high on the hog. He collects a check on the 1ˢᵗ of every month. Just like I do. But he's also helping out some guy he knows with a shitty old van.

The two of them do just about anything for money. Haul trash and scrap metal. Cut lawns and tar driveways. Trim bushes. Paint houses and clean out leaves from troughs. The only thing that influences their choices is the time of year and the weather.

And Greaseback comes home on those nights with a great big smile on his face. A smoke hanging out of his mouth. A bounce in his step. Cash in his pocket and a dozen beers under his arm.

So I look at him. And his life. It seems like he's got it all figured out. When I take a step back and look at his life from where I'm sitting. Other than not having a girl under his other arm it sure don't look bad.

I'm young. And it's easy to look up to him. So I just tell myself night after night. As I lie in bed. Hungry. That my life will look a whole lot better if I can make it to the end of the school year. Graduate. And get a job.

So I don't have to covet what the neighbours have.

. . . .

One night I'm sitting around watching TV. All we get is the local channel. My parents always had cable. So it took some getting used to not having any choice. But now I don't even blink when I sit through a half hour drama about bike cops.

During one of the commercial breaks I see one I've seen a thousand times. Church of Jesus Christ and Latter Day Saints. Images of depressed, lonely men and women. Which reminds me of where I am right now. So I turn on a light.

But not until after I pick up the phone. Dial the number along the bottom of the screen. Prepare myself to talk to a stranger. And when a kind sounding woman answers I tell her I'm interested in one of them free bibles.

'Oh that's great,' she beams. And her smile travels through time and space. I can see it my mind. Her perfect teeth glowing in front of me in the darkness. It's contagious.

So I go full bore. Tell her how I'm sitting her watching TV. Alone. And how the commercial spoke to me. How it brought tears to my eyes. How it made me want to change my sad, depressing life

'Sir that's exactly why we play those commercials. Knowing that people are out there alone, with no idea of the love of Jesus Christ just pains us.'

She asks me my name and I give her Mitch's. I follow it up with his address and telephone number. Smiling just as wide as I imagine the woman's on the other end of the line. She tells me it's going out right away.

And that it's the church's policy to send out some missionaries about a month after the bible shows up. Just to make sure that all the love of Christ is penetrating my soul. And to clear up any problems I might be having.

'That'd be great,' I tell her, 'then maybe I won't be so lonely.'

After I hang up I laugh to myself. Imagining Mitch getting that fucking bible in the mail. I wish I could see behind his face when he opens the mailbox. That'll teach the son of a bitch. The fucking bully.

And Jesus. When they show up to talk about it. He's going to blow his fucking top. I won't be surprised if he hits one of them. And I almost feel bad about it. But they probably deserve it. Spreading the word of Christ all over.

So I don't give it a second thought.

Then a couple of weeks later I'm over there in the afternoon. From where I am I can see Mitch in the kitchenette. Tattooing some kid I've never seen before. The machine buzzing. Greaseback is in the same worn armchair he's always in. Him and I are smoking. Watching a shitty horror movie about puppets.

And as I reach over to ash my smoke I see it under a gun magazine. The copy of the bible I had sent over. And I decide to play dumb. Ask about it. Get some more satisfaction from the situation.

I pull it out. Look over at Greasback. Smile. 'What's with the fucking bible?' I ask almost laughing.

'Mitch got it in the fucking mail,' Greaseback says while laughing. He chokes on his cigarette smoke. Starts coughing.

'Going soft on us Mitch?' I ask.

The machine in the kitchenette stops. Mitch goes on a tear. Saying that if he ever finds out who gave them his address he's going to fucking kill him. I nod. And tell him I sure wouldn't want to be that poor sap.

Greaseback's the only one who can laugh at Mitch and get away with it. He exercises his liberty with force. And ends up coughing so much I wonder if he's not going to die in front of me.

When he stops, Mitch goes back to tattooing. I take a drag off my own smoke. Happy with myself. Confident that they'll never find out who called the number. But of course they do.

Because I'm not smart enough to keep my mouth shut. And I tell a couple people who think will find it funny. But I put too much of my trust in them. And think they'll do better than me. And keep the secret.

But when the Christians come to the door. One of the people I told is sitting on the couch. Mitch is out so it's just him and Greaseback. And he see's the whole thing. The knock. And Greasback getting up. Opening the door shirtless. Pentagram tattoos on display.

The missionaries stutter as they ask for Mitch Agneau. How they'd like to talk to him about the power of Christ. Greaseback laughs but goes along with it. Tells them that he's worried about Mitch too. How he thinks Mitch needs someone to talk to.

In a week when I get an apology from my friend he says it just slipped out. He forget he wasn't supposed to say anything. That he was laughing too hard to think straight. And at that point what could I say.

So when Mitch gets home a few hours later Greasback tells him someone came looking for him. And that they'll be back. He also passes on all the other messages he has for him. Like who was behind it.

That's when I find out Mitch knows. Because he comes across the hall and starts pounding on my door. How he knows that I'm to blame. And that I'd better come to the door. He can hear the TV and knows I'm in here.

There's nothing I can do. I'm sure he's holding back. And that he can kick through the door like a cardboard box if he wants. So I get up off the couch. A cold sweat comes out of nowhere. Soaks through my clothes. And by the time I get to the door I'm shivering.

Before I open it I yell at Mitch. Tell him that I'll open up. But he has to stop kicking the goddamned door. He stops. I undo the lock. I tell myself I'm going to get the shit kicked out of me. And I better be ready.

I pull it open as fast as I can. It's inevitable. So I might as well get it over with. Mitch is standing in the hall. His apartment door is open behind him. He's standing there. Shaking. His fists are clenched. He has that wild look in his eye.

So I don't say a thing. Because I don't want to set him off. And slowly his words come to him. He tells me he knows I did it. And that if those degenerates come by his place again I'm going to be in trouble.

When he's done talking he turns around. Goes in his door. Slams it behind him. I shut mine. Go back to the couch. And tell myself to stop taking for granted how lucky I can be from time to time.

A couple minutes later there's a more gentle knocking on the door. I get back up. A little worried. That maybe this is his ploy. Confuse me. Calmly beat me into the ground. But that luck again. It's Greaseback.

He tells me how close I'd come to a beating. That he's never seen him this mad before. At least not without someone ending up in the hospital. And that right now Mitch is over there in his room. In the dark. Breaking shit. Swearing.

Which is impossible not to laugh at. So the two of us do.

· · · · · · ·

The whole thing blows over pretty fast though. I see Mitch in the corner store the next day. And before I get a chance to run away he smiles at me. Says everything's all right. And that he can see how funny the whole thing is.

I can relax again. The beast has been tamed.

But a couple days later my roommate and I are over at their place. Mitch is at the kitchen table. Drawing. My roommate is sitting with him. Greaseback's in the same chair as always. I sit on the couch

It's hard to see anything. Because all four of us have cigarettes going. And none of us are saying a thing. So I wonder, what the fuck am I even doing over here. I could be in my room alone doing the same thing. But at least the air's a little cleaner.

The phone starts ringing. Greaseback picks it up. Answers. Passes the phone to Mitch without saying a thing. Mitch answers. Says hello. And as whoever it is talking to him he looks over at me. There's that glint again.

That's when I know who he's talking to. And I want to avoid what I know is going to happen. I jump up. Greaseback starts laughing. I curse him silently and run for the door. Mitch gets up.

And the last thing I see before I make it out the door is Mitch clocking my roommate in the jaw. And the last thing I hear is my roommate crumpling onto the floor. I make it out and into my apartment. I try to shut the door but Mitch is there. His fat body blocking it. I'm running out of options. And not thinking straight. So I slam the door on him. He groans.

'You're fucking dead now,' he snarls.

I run for the bathroom. I tell myself that if I can get in there that the cheap shitty door will stop Mitch. All I have to do is lock it. Then wait things out. Cower in the tub until he calms down and goes home.

I hope.

I tear down the hallway. And for some reason tonight it feels like its a thousand miles long. Which I attribute to the fear of death. And the sound of Mitch kicking my door open. The sound of it banging off the wall. For a second all I can think about is my landlord. And if the handle left a hole it's going to cost me a fortune.

I get into the bathroom. But Mitch is down the hall in three steps. I can't shut the door in time. How the fuck did he get here so fast. And now I'm trapped. Which was probably going to happen no matter what.

But I was happy with the lie I was telling myself. There's nothing left to do. So I start trying to talk my way out of it. I'm too scared or too young to act like a man and take the beating.

'C'mon Mitch. It was a practical joke. It's funny,' I say.

'You're not going to find it funny when I break all your teeth.'

'You gotta be kidding me.'

He answers my question with a heavy fist to my temple. I get dizzy and feel sick. I take a step back. Trip into the tub. I crack the other side of my face off the tiled wall. And tell myself this isn't shaping up to be my day.

I haven't even hit the tub before he's punching me. I try to pull my hands up over my face. Protect my good looks. But he gets a few good pops in before I can. After that I lie back. Let him tire himself out.

And for a chubby smoker the fucker has some stamina.

To me it feels like the longest thing that's ever happened. But it's probably less than a minute before he stops. He stands up over me. Looks down. Tells me that he didn't want to do it. That it's principal. He had to. And I have to understand.

He turns around. Walks down the hall. I hear him close the door behind him.

What a gentleman.

I turn over on my back. My ribs scream out. I stare up at the ceiling. The yellow stain in the corner. The mark of water leaking through. I should probably tell the super. Maybe in the morning.

8

Joe, the superintendant, is a nice old man. He doesn't really want any trouble. But the landlord on the other hand is a real contemptible cocksucker. He dresses like an out of work cowboy. The boots, the jeans, the floral patterned shirts.

He comes to the building once a month. To pick up his fat wad of rent checks from Joe. And it's always the same. I can hear him driving up. Classic rock pumping loud enough to send anyone into delirium. Madness. And if I'm home I get up. Watch him from behind the curtains.

And every time he gets out of his car he does it with a strut. His shoulders thrown back and his head held high. A pop in his step. He's real proud of his looks. He thinks he's something else. He thinks he's better than all of us.

Which is fine. Because he is. But he doesn't have to rub it in.

I run into the other tenants. Sometimes they stop me in the hall. Strike up asinine conversation only to ask me what I think of him. Which is really a precursor for telling me what they think of him. And not once have I heard a flattering word.

They tell me horrible stories. About why everyone in the building is on welfare. Or some other kind of assistance. We don't have much when it comes to bargaining power. And he knows we have to hand over rent receipts at the end of the month.

Or the money stops rolling in.

And they pass on the urban legend of him phoning in tips to welfare. Telling them you're committing fraud. All for the offence of being a day late with the rent. Which always gives me the fear.

I leave the conversations reminded of why my roommate had such an easy time getting the place. No questions asked and all that. We fit the requirements. We were dependent.

Normally he never deals with us. Leaves things to Joe. Except it's been awhile since we busted the side door window. And neither of us has bothered to pay him a cent. After I pay rent I'm not left with much. And I just don't feel like handing it over to the landlord.

I don't think he deserves it.

Joe's told us that he's pissed. And that he's going to come looking for us. My roommate says he can't do anything. And I like the sounds of that. So I believe him. But still. I don't want to be here when he shows up.

But of course I am. Because I barely leave the apartment. And he catches us early on a Saturday. We're both sleeping. So we didn't see the purple Cadillac come up the drive. And he must've had the classic rock turned down low I tell myself when I hear him banging on the door.

I lie there in bed. Hoping my roommate will take care of it. I don't know what to say to an angry man yelling at me first thing in the morning. It was a late night last night. And I'm feeling like shit.

So when I hear my roommate's bedroom door open I take a deep breath. I roll out of my sleeping bag. Pull on some pants and walk into the hall. My roommate is standing there. A green bathrobe covering him.

We don't say a word.

'I know you're in there,' the landlord yells, banging on the door again. 'I can hear ya, open up or I'm coming in.'

My roommate looks at me. Shakes his head. And to me it seems like he's more annoyed than anything else. He walks over to the door. Waits a minute. Then opens up.

'Hey there, how's it going?'

'Don't give me that shit. You owe me three hundred and fifty bucks. I fucking want it now. I shouldn't have to pay for your fucking around.'

He figures we're kids. That he has the upper hand. That he can scare us. Get us to cough up the dough. He never figures on my roommate being a smart, cocky little asshole.

And from there the conversation takes a turn he never saw coming. My roommate asks him for the bill. Which is something we'd never been shown. He tells the landlord that we just can't give him this much money on good faith alone.

The landlord flies into a rage. Calls my roommate a cocksucker. And that he better give him the fucking money or else. I'm still standing down the other end of the hall. Positive that this asshole was going straight home to call in some tips.

'Or else?' my roommate repeats. And tells him he thinks he should leave. That he's sure that more than a few of the neighbours have heard his threat. The landlord's face goes bright red. It's the purest anger I've seen in a long time.

And my roommate just stands there. Calm. Like this is the easiest thing in the world. I stand there envying his confidence. Wishing that I believed in myself the way he did in himself. Even though he was a total asshole sometimes.

'You little piece of shit,' the landlord snarls. But he looks like he knows he's whipped. Without the purchase order he's got nothing. The fool. He'll have to come back with something. 'Don't think you've won you little fucking faggots. I'll get ya.'

'Oh, I'm sure you will, now have yourself a nice day.' My roommate shuts the door. Walks back over to the couch. Sits down. Waits.

The landlord doesn't move. I can hear him snorting on the other side of the door. And I'm a good three meters away. Jesus, I think to myself. He's really worked up. And I can't help it. A small laugh escapes. Maybe he hears it. I don't know, but he kicks the door one last time. Stomps off down the hall.

In a minute I hear him revving his engine outside. The sound of classic rock fills the air. Tires squeal. I look out the patio doors. The landlord peels out. Goes up over a couple of parking curbs. Some fat children playing in the grass start squealing.

'You really pissed him off there, eh?' I turn and say to my roommate.

He tells me the landlord can go fuck himself. That he knows his rights. That he has to show us a bill. He can talk a wide yard. And I feel myself being swayed by his argument. I bring up the point of what happens when he shows up with the bill.

'Sure. Who cares. We'll just keep putting him off. Move out during the middle of the night. Fuck him if we can,' is my roommate's only answer. Which cinches it for me. Because forgetting about things is easier than doing them.

My roommate pulls out a joint. Lights it and passes it to me. I take a couple drags off it. Pass it back before I sink into the couch already more concerned with what I'm going to eat then where I'm going to get the money to pay that screaming asshole.

And then there's another knock on the door. Lighter this time. No force behind it. My roommate puts out the joint. Stands up and wraps his bathrobe around him. Answers the door with bloodshot eyes.

It's the super. Joe. He's standing there meekly. With his head hung. He's not the kind of man who likes scenes. I get the feeling that if he had his way, the whole world would be quiet. Only broken by the murmur of polite chitchat.

'Hey Joe, how's it going?' my roommate asks.

He says that he's doing fine. But he came up to give us a warning. That we've really pissed off the landlord. That we should watch out and lay low. Because he's liable to do something rash.

'Well Joe, I'm within my limits. He can't come up demanding money and threatening me. He needs to be taught a lesson. He needs to learn some manners,' my roommate tells him in a tone I find a little abusive from my spot on the couch.

Joe tells him that he knows the landlord's not the nicest guy in the world. But he has his reasons. He's been screwed over by a lot of tenants. My roommate doesn't give a flying fuck. But thanks him for the warning anyways.

'I like you guys, I just don't want to see anything bad happen to ya,' Joe says.

'Thanks Joe, have a good day,' my roommate says as he shuts the door. Walks back over to the couch smugly. He looks happy with himself. Like he's won.

And I almost want the landlord to come back with the bill right now. Shove it in his fucking face. Because even if I had to pay out my share for the 350$ it'd be worth it. To see him get that awful satisfied smile wiped away.

He knows his rights. And he has his faith in them. But I'm not the same. I'm too young to have the experience to justify my feelings. But a part of me knows that the world is full of ways to fuck over your fellow man. And I'm certain the landlord will find one.

A couple minutes later there's another knock. This time I get up. Open the door. It's Mitch and Greaseback. I let them in. Greaseback has a smirk on his face. His walk is like laughter. Mitch looks happy for once. They sit down on the couch. Start smoking before saying a word.

They ask us about what went on. They tell us they could hear the landlord yelling from their place. That they haven't heard him get so mad before. We sit around for a while laughing at this man's anger.

. . . .

In the end we never give the landlord the $350. He even comes back with the work order. Signed by the man who did it. My roommate tells him it looks doctored. Which of course sends the landlord into another rage.

We make a compromise. Tell him we'll pay a little each month with the rent. But when the 1st rolls around neither of us ever have any extra money. Eventually we move out. Disappear.

And there's nothing he can do.

9.

I keep telling myself the same thing over and over. I just have to make it to the end of the school year. It's a breeze to keep my grades above 50. Just enough to graduate. I have no hopes of making it into any universities.

That's just not the next step for people like me.

And even if I had the grades. Good luck getting a loan. There was no money squirreled away. And I'm hardly in a position to go groveling to my folks for that kind pay off. A couple of times I'd called my old man. Asked for $50. He'd given it to me. But I felt like shit taking it. And my hunger was always replaced with depression.

So I figure the best I can do is the same as my father. Go up to the one of the big factories. With my head held down. Tell them that there's nothing I want more in this is world than to give up. Toil under their roof day and night. Start a family.

Dig in.

These are the kinds of things these places like to hear. The words of guidance counselors. Teachers. My old man. Friend's dads. They've been telling me it all through high school. I guess they saw my destiny.

So I believe in it. And I believe that there's nothing else out there in the world for me.

And on nights when the can of tuna doesn't fill me. And I lie there staring up at the shadows on the ceiling of the plain white box I call my bedroom. I tell myself tall tales of the life I'm going to have. The one I remember from living at home.

Because working pays a lot more than loafing. And my old man brings home what I live off of now eight times in a month. He has it easy. No education. He just walked up one day and it was like winning a lottery that paid out until death.

And the factories like to hire their own. Generations of families giving up their lives. My old man's been there for years. And I've been told I'm a shoe-in.

So it's easy for me to dream of. And it's the only way for a guy like me to make any money anyways. To buy cars. And boats. And fucking gigantic bbq's. And pools. And mountains of food.

You know. All the amenities of having a bit of the good life.

Because my friends' fathers who didn't get lucky like my old man. I've seen their homes. And they have the same worries as I do right now. Like how I am going to eat. How I am going to pay rent. But piled on top is the weight of sweaty children and a fat wife screaming.

And if you're going to have a fat wife, then you better have the money to feed her.

So I keep going to school as much as I can muster. I miss all the days that I'm allowed by the guidelines of welfare. I try and spread them out throughout the month. Making it so I'm never there more than four days a week. Which is an easy way to bare it.

On my walks to school I smoke cigarettes rolled from yesterdays butts found in the ashtray. They're harsh and tear my throat up. But they still have a calming effect. They aid in the lie. That I'm working towards a life that I want.

But I'm not working hard towards anything. I'm throwing my life away but not doing anything at all. I left home and stalled. If I couldn't handle living with a family now why do I think it'll ever get any better.

I take short puffs as I walk and tell myself that the job is what I need. Then I can get all the shit I'm supposed to have. The big fucking car. A house somewhere on the ever-growing edge of town.

In between coughing fits I convince myself that if I get all that. Then I'll be able to win back Sam. The girl who decided I wasn't worth hanging around with after I left home and became a full time piece of shit.

I'm too delusional to admit that she left because I was never anything other than a piece of shit.

By the time I get to school. In my garbage mind. Sam and I are already back together. Married. Children. A piece of green grass I can call my own. And how it all hinges on the job in the factory.

After that things will change boy, I tell myself just loud enough to drown out the voice that holds the opposing opinion.

That things in this town will never change. And a boat or a car or a wife or a house or a son or a job or a refrigerator full of food won't change things. Like how I've been sad and angry and confused for as long as I can remember.

· · · · · · ·

My grades have been slowly tapering off. I can't remember the last time I brought a schoolbook home. Most of my tests I guess the answers and come up lucky. At the end of the day I just don't give a fuck.

Because it seems like my future is already locked in. And I don't have the strength in the face of things to change it. So why bother.

One day I'm in art class. Not doing anything. Just sort of staring at the table in front of me. A voice comes on the intercom and asks the teacher if I'm in class and could she tell me to go to guidance counselor's office.

I get up and walk out. Saving her the trouble of having to relay the message.

When I get to his office he's waiting in the doorway for me. He's leaning in the frame with his arms crossed. A smile on his face. I don't know what it is. But I've always felt comfortable around this man. I feel like he understands.

'C'mon in, sit down,' he says when I get close enough to do both. I walk into the office and sit down. I stretch out my legs. He follows me in. Closes the door behind him. Sits down behind his desk.

He stares at me. Doesn't say a thing. I look everywhere except in his eyes. On the walls lining his office is every grade nine class picture going back to the 70's. I look for the one I'm in. For my stupid blonde bowl cut. For my innocent face.

And I remember how scared I was then. And how far I've come in the last three years. How I finally got what I wanted. Some breathing room. And even though it's not all that great, I still wouldn't want to be back there. At home.

Because I might go home hungry now. But I never worry as I'm walking up to put my key in the door. Scared. Of what fault my stepmother had found in me that day. And how long she was going to scream at me. And how late I'd be up crying. Wishing I'd died. Instead of my mother.

'How ya been? Everything alright?' he finally asks me.

'Of course, sir. I'm doing great,' I lie, 'just checking in on me?'

He gives me an odd look. Like he can see through the lie. And I'm not sure if it's my answer. Or his tactic from the beginning. But he drops the bullshit. And tells me he noticed that I've really been slipping.

'You used to get good grades. You're a smart kid,' he tells me, 'Have you gotten into drugs?'

I laugh. I can't help it. It's not the booze or the dope. I tell him that's not it. That there isn't a need to worry. That I'm getting on all right. But he doesn't want to give up.

'Then what's the goddamned problem. You can get into university. You're sharp.'

And he's making me feel like shit. I'm not used to being complimented. Or told I can do things. That was never the dialogue at home. And I get embarrassed. Because there's no fucking way I'm going to any university. Guys on welfare don't go on to that.

But he needs some kind of answer. And he's not going to let me go until I give him one. So the easiest way out of here is to tell him the truth. That my parents kicked me out. That I've been living on my own for the last few months. That it's not easy. And I admit my studies suffer. I don't eat a lot. It's tough to concentrate.

'Oh my god. I didn't know. How are you getting by? Do you have a job?' and it seems to me that his concern is real. And I let it all it out. How I'm on welfare. And that things are tough.

He asks questions about how I get on. I tell him. Some days all I eat is here at school. In the mornings. At the church run breakfast club.

'Good god,' he reaches into his back pocket. He pulls out his wallet. He hands me twenty dollars. 'Take this. Get yourself something good to eat. Get a nice meal. Some nutrients.'

'Oh, sir, I can't,' I lay it on real thick. But the sight of that bill makes me start to sweat.

I imagine the things I can buy. A pack of smokes. Some cans of beef-aroni. Maybe a pint of whiskey.

But lucky for me he makes me take it. Forces it into my hand. Tells me not to tell anyone about this. That he could get into trouble. I let him know I won't as I put the money into my pocket. Already hours away from here. Enjoying the spoils of his pity.

He tells me he's going to talk to my teachers. Get me some extensions on my work. But I tell him I don't want it. I might've taken his money. But I'd never be able to suffer the looks of my teachers.

'Just do your best, Stan,' he tells me after we shake hands. I get up and walk to the door. Pull it closed as I leave.

I don't want to go back to class. I'm not in the mood to sit there. Listening to Mr. Morrison blather on about his paintings. So I go outside. Sit on a parking curb. Put my hand in my pocket.

And the weight of that bill in there is some off my back for at least another day. A windfall I didn't expect this morning. It represents a couple meals. And something to make me forget for a little while.

I pull out a smoke. Light it. Now that I have some cash I can afford to smoke. I think about fucking off for the rest of the day as I take my first drag. Which is an easy thought to make a reality.

The sky looks perfect right now. Big and blue and lazy. I drop my ass off the back of the parking curb. Lie back in the grass. Stare up and smoke. I figure there isn't time left until class is over. So I'll go. I'm full of dreams and nicotine. I can handle it.

I get up. Walk back to class about as slow as I can. Open the door. Sit down. There's only fifteen minutes until it's over. I'm set. This is all I have to do to make it through and then I'm free.

There's no way I'm going to next class.

'Where you been,' the girl beside me asks when I sit down.

'Oh, you know. Intensive guidance session. It was something else.'

'Yeah right. You reek of cigarettes.'

'Which is nice for a change, no?'

10.

I can't lie. Being a teenager on welfare has it's advantages. Like never having to answer to anyone. Once a month I have to go down to the apartment directly under me. Hand over some money. And that's basically it.

School for the most part is just as easy. As long as I sit in the back and don't say much. I'm left alone. Just another kid falling through the cracks. Every once in a while the principal or a teacher might be breathing down my neck. But it's nothing to sweat.

And as long as I keep going to school and handing over my rent receipts I'm in the clear with welfare. There was some talk about having to meet with a caseworker. But that hasn't managed to be scheduled yet.

One of the things I can't stand though is all the people who come over to sit around all the time. Other fucked up kids who don't like being at home. And like the freedom to smoke pot on a couch in front of a television.

Instead of in a park. Or under a bridge. Where you can get caught. Here they all feel safe. There's never the threat of anyone's parents coming over. So it's a good place to hide.

Which was one of the reasons I left home. The house was too small to breathe in. I ran away to hide. Not harbor other pathetic kids. But it's now a rare night there isn't some friend of my roommate sitting there with us.

And what kind of friend are they? Just some kid who wants to smoke dope or drink. Someone who wants to act grown-up for a few hours. I don't think they like my roommate. And definitely not me.

Because I have a hard time hiding my feelings. And if they ask me how I'm doing I usually just stare at them. Dead-eyed. Then go spend the night lying in my bedroom. Watching the ceiling fan turn around and around and around. Wishing they'd hurry up and fuck off.

But my roommate likes the audience. He needs someone to listen to him talk. To tell him how smart he is. Or how he's got his whole damn life figured out. Or watch him eat the kind of food he orders in.

So macaroni and cheese becomes a private affair for me.

I sit on my sleeping bag. Eating it from the pot. Thinking about before we moved. When I used to carhop and live like a king. And instead of sitting in my room cursing my roommate and his pizzas and bbq chicken I was right there beside him. Living it up. Grease running down my chin.

Get back out there, I tell myself. You little pussy. You used to have it all. Now it's just these four walls and that pot of garbage you're eating. All you got to do is rummage through a few cars. Get back on track.

And I get up off the floor. Look out the window. It's dark. The sound of televisions chattering floats like mist from other apartments. I don't see anyone out. So I have a little confidence. I go over to my closet. Look through it for a black hoodie to go with black jeans and shirt I'm already wearing.

But when I grab hold of the door handle I give up. This is a bigger city, I tell myself. There's people everywhere. One's more likely to call the cops than beat me up. Like back home. The old man never dished out much advice. But getting a beating was always better than dealing with the cops he said.

So I sit back down on the floor. Pick up my pot of food and eat it while frowning. Because since I got up it's cooled down considerably. And I don't have long until it becomes like wet concrete. Inedible.

When I finish I drop the spoon in the pot. And an arms length away I put the pot on the floor. I lie down. Listen to the sounds of televisions coming in the window. Hating myself for my lack of courage. The suburbs of this city are full of unlocked cars. And none of their spoils will be mine.

Fuck this, I tell myself.

I get up. Leave the pot on the floor. Because as bad as my roommate is at keeping things clean. I'm not much better. I open my bedroom door. Look down the hall. I can't see who's here. But I can hear my roommate playing a video game.

I can't do the living room yet. I know this. So I take a left and go into the bathroom. Shut the door behind me. Turn on the cold water tap. Let it run. Look in the mirror. Tell myself I'm shit. Then rub cold water into my face with my palms.

This will do.

After I turn off the taps and walk down the hall I sit on the couch. It's just my roommate and our friend Carl. Who barely ever goes home to his parents. And the food they cook. Even though he just lives a couple blocks away.

Which I chalk up to a throwback from the place by the beach. He was there almost every weekend. And during the strike he rarely went home. When his folks dropped him off or picked him up they always seemed like good people. But I guess they had their problems.

When I sit down he smiles. Nods his head at me. Asks me how things are going. I tell him I'm fine. And of all the people who come over to hang around he's the only one who really gives a shit about either of us.

'Hey man, you wanna smoke a joint?' Carl asks.

I nod at him. Smile. I think he knows I'm on edge. Wants me to feel better. And this is why I like having him around. He's necessary at this point. He's as much of the apartment as the walls. The floor. My roommate or I.

And I think without him the situation would crumble. My roommate and I would run out of things to say. We wouldn't get along as well. And there'd be more nights when we end up trying to kill each other on the living room floor.

So when Carl does decide to go home I'm always sad. And a little scared. Which usually resorts in begging when he gets up to go. Even though there's no use and I know it. Because at home he's got his comforts. And no end to hot meals.

Carl pushes a few empty containers out of the way on the coffee table.

Rolls the joint without saying a word. His older brothers taught him when he was a kid. The kind of thing that defines the rest of a life.

My roommate sits in a plush blue chair. The arms worn and dark with sweat and grease. He's been staring into the screen since I sat down. And even though we drink and take drugs I think that video games are his favourite escape.

Hey, I yell over at him. Ask him how far along he is in the game. I was watching him the night before. I want to get caught up on the story. But he doesn't answer. He's locked into another world. His fingers pushing the control stick in configurations lost on me.

Carl passes me the joint and I stop caring about the game. Or what my roommate's doing at all. I sit back. Deep in the couch. I kick some empty bottles and a box of old wires off the coffee table. Stretch out my feet. No one notices as the wire spills across the floor.

I tap my roommate on the shoulder. Blow some smoke in his direction. He pauses the game and turns to me. Notices me for the first time since I sat down. He takes the joint and tells me where he is in the game.

I nod along trying to give a shit.

He passes the joint back to Carl. Says, 'Ok. Here we go,' and shakes his torso like he's a warrior going into battle. I laugh at him. And that's the one thing I don't like about being stoned. I don't know if I'm stoned and laughing for no reason. Or if I'm just beginning to think he's a jackass.

Carl and I smoke the rest of the joint to ourselves. My roommate doesn't even notice when we give up passing to him. Carl reaches into his bag and pulls out a couple of beers he stole from his dad. He gives me one.

And I remember that not all of our guests are terrible mooches.

The two of us settle into the couch. Watch the game unfold on the television in front of us. Carl asks me if I'm excited about graduation. Which isn't too far off. And of course I am. I'm sick of going to that place everyday. Sitting in those classrooms.

But I tell him I'm a little worried about passing all my classes. I never know. Some of my teachers don't like my lazy attitude. And all the homework I never do goes toward the final grade. Plus, there's my lackluster attendance.

I've been pegged as a delinquent.

Carl tells me I should be fine. That they'll be looking forward to getting rid of me. And I like the sounds of that. Like I'm some local fucking terror. The kind of hoodlum rock and roll songs are written about. Instead of this useless mass of shit on the couch.

'But man,' I tell Carl, 'I'm really just looking forward to getting a job. Making some money. Live the high life.'

And Carl says he's jealous. Because his old man has guaranteed him a job in the same factory he works in. And the sad part about it is the two of us sitting here. Together. Can't come up with a better idea about the future than this.

Spending our days in some awful shithole. And it's really the fault of our fathers. That they'd been beaten down too much. They had no more belief in life. What you could be if you wanted to work for it.

They taught us that the best future we could have was standing at an assembly line. Or pulling a lever. Or pushing a button. The less work the better. That's what life was about.

So neither of us thought about going anywhere. You just didn't hear about it. Or if someone got the balls to move. To some big city. Like Toronto or Montréal or Vancouver they always came back. A failure. Looking for the job in the factory.

Totally giving up.

And I'm only a few months from this. Staring down the end of my future. But I can laugh in the face of being almost 18 and knowing that I won't have to ever think again.

Which looks pretty nice. Not having to think and having all the money to eat like a regular person. I close my eyes for a minute. Think about the big Sunday dinners my stepmother would cook. Roast beef. Gravy and mashed potatoes. Hot buns and butter.

I never stop to think about the boredom. Or how my father never really looks that happy. And he never talks about how his job is stimulating. Or challenging. And how long the days in that prison must feel.

But Carl and I don't talk about that. We just talk about the good things. Like the stability. The salary. And the ability to become just like our fathers.

After a couple hours Carl says he should be getting home. I do my best to convince him to sleep on the couch. And I don't blame him when he says no. After he leaves I go back to my room.

I lie there listening to the sounds of the video game in the living room. Thinking about getting up in the morning. And how maybe I'm not so sure about this getting a job in a factory.

11.

On the surface I don't have any idea what's going on. As graduation gets closer I have a harder time making it to school. I wake up in the morning on time. It's not a problem. But putting on clothes. Making the effort of the walk. I can't be bothered.

I must be scared though. Because a large part of me, even though it won't admit it, wants nothing to do with getting a job in a factory. And a lot of my friends still have a year or so of school left.

And I probably don't want to graduate.

Because it'd be a lot easier to just keep doing what I'm doing. Which is nothing at all. My father's advice of the least amount of work possible guiding my decisions.

But it's hurting me. I have to keep up my attendance. It's Friday and this week alone I've missed 2 days and left early twice. And the way it's shaping up it doesn't look like I'll have enough attendance until 2nd period.

Plus I keep missing the free breakfast in the mornings. My primary source of food. It's getting harder and harder to concentrate. These terrible headaches I keep getting. They cut right through whatever the teachers are saying.

I try and hustle when I get out the door. But about two blocks away I slow right down. Like I don't have anywhere to be. And just as I walk up to the school grounds the bells rings. Over half the students pour out the doors looking to smoke.

So there's not really any reason to sign in now. I light a home rolled smoke. The thing stinks like shit. Rolled from the old butts. But it's all I have. It's getting to be the end of the month.

Some of my friends from the beach town come over. They ask me how 1st period was. I tell them I just got there. They tell me how lucky I am. How cool it is. How they wish they had my life.

All they see is my freedom.

They don't see me coming undone.

They don't see me starving.

And at lunch they don't notice me looking at their lunches. Thinking how cool it is. How I wish things could've worked out. How I wish I had a normal life.

They don't see how I've stopped caring about anything. How I'm bored by everything. How it's so fucking tough to get up in the morning. And how all I want to do is sleep or get fucked up just to forget that I'm alive.

And that how my 17th birthday is only a couple months away. How I should be driving around in my old man's car. Looking for girls. Instead of all the worry I have over things like how many maggots are in the bottom of my sink. And how am I going to get some clean clothes.

They don't know it. Because I won't let on. But I'm jealous of every one of them. Because they still get to believe in the lie. That life is a wonderful thing worth looking forward to.

When the warning bell rings I go in. I figure I can make it to the office. Sign the late sheet and make it to 2nd class on time. Look like I give a shit. But when I get there the secretary tells me to sit down. That the vice principal wants to talk to me.

I knew he had it out for me.

Sitting there I can feel the secretary's eyes on me. She's a nice old woman. The kind that's incapable of giving off any other impression than kind grandmother. And I know she feels sorry for me.

I'm there about five or ten minute before the vice principal comes into the outer office. He must've been out walking the halls. Making sure every last straggler made it into class. And when he sees's me he smiles. Like he's been waiting for this.

'Well look who decided to show up?' he says.

I sit there and look at him. I want to tell him to fuck himself. Spit on the ground directly in front of him. They way they do in old movies. A real insult. But I keep my mouth shut. I can't risk getting kicked out. I have too much riding on this.

He tells me to get up. To go into his office. I sit down in the chair across from his desk. When he comes in he shuts the door behind me. Sits down. It's his turn to keep his mouth shut. Instead he just stares at me.

I look around his office. His desk is a mess. Which I can't help but think sets a bad example. Pencils. Papers. Student's permanent records. Photos of his daughters.

Which I end up taking the time to look at. They're good looking girls. The oldest looks to be about the same age as me. But she looks well fed. Lean. Has long blonde hair. And a perfect smile.

And I stop to think about my own teeth. How they hurt. How they're chipped and crooked. How I need a new toothbrush. And how I spent the last money I had on a hamburger. Now I pick bristles out of my mouth every morning.

But I can still remember the way the grease ran down my chin. The taste of meat. The memory of that alone can keep me going.

The vice principal is a monstrous giant. Soft pink flesh. Dutch through and through. He's six and a half feet tall. Two hundred and seventy-five pounds. A fat gut. It hangs over the top of his tan pants. It swings in the folds of his tucked in shirt.

He wears thin wire-framed glasses. Which make him look like a witch. His hair is even thinner. It barely covers his head. He combs it back. It falls in his face. He always looks a little sweaty in his polyester suits.

To me he looks like he was a football star when he was my age. That he never wanted those days to end. And that's how he ended up here. Trying to relive the glory days of his youth. And I probably smirk a little thinking about how he looks from this side of the desk.

Because his face creases. His forehead pushing his eyebrows down. The beady little dark eyes receding even farther into his face.

'It says here that you've been late every day for the last two weeks,' he breaks the silence with. He's smug. Waits for my response. But I don't have one. 'Well?'

'Yep. I've been late,' I say.

'That's all you got.'

'What am I going to do. Argue? You're got the proof.'

'Don't you have anything to say for yourself? A reason? Some explanation?'

'Not really. I'm just late.'

'You're just late? That's it?'

'Yeah.'

'Well what do you think about me calling your father?'

'Not much.'

He pauses. He isn't used to this sort of defense. He comes from somewhere where boys live in fear of the vice principal. Their fathers. He wants me to start sweating. He expected me to break into a cold sweat. Start coming up with excuses.

'Well, I guess we're going to have to see what he thinks.'

And by the look on his face I know he thinks he's already won. In his head he's been privy to hearing my old man scream me stupid. He's seen me break. He's seen me scared.

He picks up a folder on his desk. Flips through a few pages. And I have to assume it's my records he has in his hand. Because he stops. Points at something in the file. And then I watch him dial the number of my parents' house. He pushes the button for speaker phone. Puts down the receiver.

He's trying to live out his daydream. He thinks he's in store for some come uppence.

I have no reason to tell him otherwise.

After a couple rings I hear my old man's voice. It's been awhile. Three or four months. It's strange. Then again, I think, I might cry. But for different reasons.

'Hello'

'Yes, Mr. Acker. This Mr. Van Doren. The vice principal at Forrestside.'

My old man responds. Sounds like he can't even imagine why he might be calling. Mr. Van Doren tells my father about my recent shitty attendance. How I've been late and missed an alarming amount of days. He asks if my old man knew.

'Sorry. I can't help you,' my old man says,' he hasn't lived here for months. I'm not sure what he's up to.'

Mr. Van Doren is stunned. His whole fucking scenario is crumbling down around him. He sits a moment. Silent. Tries and regroups. 'Well, who's in charge of him then?' he asks my father.

And my old man gives him the best damn answer he can. That I'm the one Mr. Van Doren should be talking to. And I have to use every little bit of strength that I have to stop myself from crying. Because I miss him. And his attitude. And I wish he'd married another woman.

'Oh, well I'm sorry for bothering you sir.'

'Oh, it's not a problem. Tell him I say hi.' and just like that my old man hangs up. Before Mr. Van Doren has a chance to say goodbye.

The old man never did like the phone.

Mr. Van Doren has no idea know what to do. His plan backfired. He expected to see me crying. Terrified of the beating I'd get when I got home. Or at very last the lecture.

He leans back in his chair. Chews on the end of his pen. Looks for words. He stares at the pictures of his daughters.

'You know sir, those are some beautiful daughters you have there. Real nice teeth.' I blurt out. I knew I couldn't keep my mouth shut forever. And I'm sure I hit a nerve. Because he just looks at me. His pink skin quickly turning red.

'Listen here you smug little shit. You think I can't do anything to you.

That you can come in here and act like a big man. Well. You're wrong. I can cause you all kinds of trouble. What the hell is your problem?'

'I don't know.'

And it's not a lie. I really don't.

'I've got a prediction for you. You want to hear it?'

'I suppose I don't have much of a choice.'

He tells me that I don't have much of a future to look forward to. He cites years of seeing it happen. That there's only two options for a kid like me. And both of them involve government institution. That if I'm lucky I'll get dubbed crazy. Locked up in a mental ward.

And if not, I'll surely be put in prison.

I laugh at him. I can't help it. But who the fuck does he think he is. This washed up gym teacher. And I tell him that either of those options couldn't be any worse than this dump.

Which is a mistake. Because he promises me that this is only going to get worse. That from now on I have to personlly report to him first thing in the morning. That this is my first class. He'll get the work from my teacher. I'll do the work on the bench in the outer office.

And that if I miss one fucking second he'll kick me out. And my whole year will be a waste.

'Do you understand?' he asks me at the end. And get that urge to spit at his feet again. But instead I just give in. And admit that I comprehend everything he just yelled at me. 'And I'm going to be watching you every other second of the day too. Got it?'

I pushed him too far. Now I have to come in. Or else I'm going to lose my benefits. Lose my chance at a diploma. Lose the only future the city can offer me. Other than his less than favorable prediction.

'Yeah I got it,' I say.

'Now get out of here and get to class.'

'Yes sir.'

I open the door to the office. Start to walk out. The vice principal comes from his office. Calls the next kid in. I laugh. That poor fucker's in for it. I've warmed him up for him.

Unless he's there to receive an award he's going to get shit on.

When I get to my class I stop outside. Look in the door. See the other kids sitting there. Looking half asleep. The teacher blathering on. I figure this is it. My last chance. That old piece if shit is going to be all over me from here on in.

So fuck it.

I go outside. Walk just into the woods. Just out of sight of the school. I light a smoke and think about what just happened. How this is going to be a good thing. Now I have to get up in the morning. I can make it in time for the free breakfast.

A couple more months, I tell myself as I stand there smoking. Then I'm out of here. And that old asshole will never get to tell me what to do ever again. And I wonder if it's even worth finishing. And that maybe I'm trying to fuck up on purpose.

Because the prediction he had for me wasn't very pretty. Being locked up somewhere. But what's the difference with a job. Or going to school, I think. Because from where I'm standing. This building looks the same as the mental institution down the highway.

And for the first time I admit that I might want more from my life. That maybe there's more out there than just giving up directly after high school. Because there's a feeling of dread in the air. That none of this is going to work out for me.

So maybe the psych ward isn't a bad place for me. At least there there's always a bed and a meal. Which is more than I can say for myself at the moment. And the trajectory that Mr. Van Doren is so sure of might be the right one for me.

Right now, I think, welfare ain't all that bad. It gives me just enough. And I'm learning something none of my friends are. About poverty. About losing your shame.

It's teaches me about things like having. Like wanting.

It teaches me about going without. Getting creative.

It teaches me about a strength. One I didn't know I had.

It teaches me that I need to be tough.

And as I daydream about all the options laid out in front of me my smoke gets smoked and I light another. The bell rings. Kids come running out. Books under one arm. A smoke in one hand. A lighter in the other. Every one of them smiling.

I don't have a clue how they do it.

I take the last haul off my smoke. Crush it under my boot. I get up. I don't wait to see any faces I know. I turn in the opposite direction of school. I start the slow walk home.

This is my last chance after all.

12.

Right up until I left home I was seeing a girl. I was delusional. I thought that she was a part of the puzzle. That as soon as I graduated I'd get the job. Then I'd ask her to marry me. We'd buy a house. She was the first girl I slept with.

I believed this was how things worked out.

But when I moved in with my roommate. Went on welfare. She decided I wasn't so cool to be dating anymore. She knew better than to be the girl fucking the guy who's one step from being a bum. She had sensible parents. She came from a good family.

Which isn't something I can blame the girl for. Yet I do.

And I refuse to believe it's over. I think I can show her that I'm still desirable. And I'm sure that one of these days I'll open the door and she'll be standing there with tears in her big blue eyes. And everything will go back to the way it was when she used to say she loved me.

I tell myself things are going to change. I'll get out of this fucking school. Get a job in a factory. Somewhere where the starting wage is $18 an hour. I won't be the loser anymore. I'll show up in some fancy car. She'll swoon. And we'll drive off into our happy life.

Or at least that's what I keep telling myself.

Because there aren't any other girls out there for me. She was the one. Now I've gone and fucked up the only chance I've been given to have happiness. And I begin to get desperate.

I start calling her house. I know it's the wrong thing to do. But I can't stop myself. She hangs up on me. Frequently. Or gets her folks to tell me she's out. And I see red. Then one night I tell her stepfather that he better put her on, or else.

A couple days later he catches me coming home from school. He pulls his car over in front of me on the sidewalk. He gets out and corners me against a fence. Lets me know it's best if I leave his daughter alone.

He's not a big man. Or even a frightening looking one. But he's a hunter.

'You know Stan, I'm pretty good with a knife. Carving up all them bucks over the years,' he says with a wink as he gets back in his car.

After that I give up calling. He got his point across. But he can't stop me from obsessing. And I spend most of my time thinking about her. Pathetic daydreams of our future together. Us having children. Vacations to hot climates. Growing old together.

And the funny thing is, I don't see how far out of my mind I am.

. . . .

I figure my big chance is on its way. Her best friends' mom is getting married. It's at the city hall in next town over. Not many people have been invited. Just friends of the bride and groom. But I know Sam will be there.

So on the day of the wedding I get up early. And when I leave the apartment the fucking grass is still wet. And as I walk across this shitty little town I barely see a soul.

I think about how nice it'd be if the place was deserted. Like in the old westerns my dad likes so much. And I wonder if that's what he likes about them so much. All that space. So little people.

I get to the far end of town. And when I hear cars coming from behind I turn around. Walk backwards with my thumb out. Hoping I get picked up quickly. My spirits are high.

It takes a while to get a ride but I don't care. It's a nice day. And I'm certain that by the time I go to sleep I'll have won her back. We'll be in love and my life will be back on track.

When I get dropped off I thank the driver. Get out of the car and light a smoke. I'm nowhere near city hall. And I've got a long walk ahead of me. But it flies right by. I'm too jacked up to notice the sidewalk rolling beneath my feet.

And I when I get to the steps of city hall I'm more than an hour early.

And it's time to admit to myself I'm sweaty and starving and tired. Across the street is a park. I find a shady place under a tree. Lie down.

Then I smoke away the time and the hunger and the fatigue. A smile on my face. Dreaming of her blonde hair. Her soft skin. And the way she used to tell me how life was going to be okay.

I don't know what happens. Maybe I fall asleep or I'm too relaxed. But I'm late now. I missed everyone showing up to the wedding. So I jump up. Shake the grass and dirt from my clothes. Walk through the front door. Look around.

When I find where I'm looking for, the procedure is under way. So I don't open the door and go in. I'm satisfied looking through the glass. There's only a handful of people. Friends of the bride. Drunks. Friends of the groom. Bikers.

And up front. Standing with Julie. Is Sam. Just like I thought. In a short tight dress. Her hair clean and long and flowing down her back. And I stand there remembering all the times I ran my hand through it.

I watch the bride and groom. But I start to see Sam and I in their place. Nervous and shaking and holding hands. Going through the motions to spend the rest of our lives together. Getting ready to throw in the towel.

And I never stop to think I'm only 17. And there's still a lot of time to pass. Things to do. Other women to convince I'm more than I am. But I don't believe in myself. And she's my only chance.

Before the ceremony is over I turn around and leave the building. I don't want her to see me here. Yet. I don't want to look like a creep. Some fucking stalker who got up early and hitch hiked here just to see her.

I have to look more suave than that.

So I go sit on the steps. Come up with a story. Something that I'm sure she'll swallow. Something I can tell without batting an eyelash. Something that sounds believable.

And when the bride and groom come out of city hall I stand off to the side. They don't notice me. Too wrapped up in their own happiness I guess. The selfish bastards. But I stop caring when I see Julie and Sam come through the doors.

I look down at myself. And I know I look like shit. My clothes are wrinkled from being sweaty and lying in the grass. And the both of them look so beautiful. Hair and make up and youth. How the fuck am I ever going to do this?

I think about running away.

But of course I'm too late for that. Because now Julie's noticed me. She waves and smiles. I smile back. Ashamed of myself. And knowing this was a big fucking mistake. Because Sam doesn't do the same. She looks at me like she just slid her high heel through a wet shit.

There's nothing I can do though. It's all over. I'm stuck here. Looking like a god damned maniac. Creeping out from behind the corner. Jesus. What was I thinking?

This is the kind of thing the other kids parents talk them out of. And I sure could use some advice from someone better at not fucking things up all the time.

When they get close I say hey. Julie gives me a hug and asks what I'm doing here. To me she looks genuinely excited to see me standing here. But I'm an idiot. And I'm paying attention to Sam.

Who's not paying attention to me.

'Shit, I'm here, um ah, 'cause I'm thinking of moving here after school.' I hear myself saying, 'So I figured I'd come by and wish you're mom the best.'

Which is such a huge lie I'm surprised I got it out without laughing. Or rolling my eyes. But from the smile across Julie's face I get the idea that I pull it off. That I didn't come across like the prick that I am.

I ask Julie how the wedding was. She goes on and on about how beautiful things were. How lucky her mom is. To have found such a gentleman. I do my best to listen. But I keep looking over at Sam. Remembering all the good times.

'Are you coming to the party, Stan?' Julie asks me. Later. At her mom's house there's a reception. All of her mom and her husband's friends will be there. Everyone I know will be there. Sam will be there.

'You bet, Julie. I was wondering. Did you guys drive? I kinda need a ride back home.'

'There's your reason,' Sam breaks her silence towards me.

While smirking at Sam, Julie says it's all right. That they'll give me a ride. And I don't get it. I'm too excited maybe. But that little smile is every conversation they've ever had about how pathetic I am.

Sam lights a smoke. We all walk to the car. Me a little behind the two of them. Even being here is pushing my luck. But I can't help thinking that by the time we get out of the car I'll have won her back.

Maybe I'm just confused by the sequins in her dress.

We get in the car. Sam turns on the radio. Cuts off the conversation. I sit in the back looking out the windows. Watching buildings pass as we zoom through downtown. And to me this town feels like somewhere famous. From books. Where big things happen.

And I can forget that I'm in the middle of nowhere. And nothing happens here. Except lives beginning and ending. I light a smoke and roll down the window. Sure that Sam is up in the front thinking about how much she still loves me.

· · · · · · ·

Julie tells me she'll drop me off at home. I offer to come back to her mom's place. Maybe help with getting things ready for the reception. I have no idea about what I can do to help. But it's as good as an excuse to stay real close to Sam.

Without turning around, and before Julie can say a thing, Sam says no. That they don't need any help. They'll drop me off at home. That's the end of it for her. And I don't say a thing.

We pull up out front of my apartment building. I get out. Bend over. Look in Sam's window. Tell her I'm looking forward to seeing her later. She lights a cigarette and exhales. And I've worn her down. Because she admits it'll be nice to see me as well.

Julie pulls away. I stand in the parking lot. Things are going to work out. I'm finally going to win. And when the two of us leave the party tonight we'll be back in love. I tell myself this delusion as I watch them drive away.

I turn around. Look up at the ugly blue aluminum siding of the building. This place looks like shit. I spit on the ground. Inside is not much better to look at either. The floors are filthy. The super's been letting things go. I should go down and complain. The lazy bastard.

I open the door to my hall. Walk past all my neighbours doors. Think about how I don't know any of them. We just nod to each other. Never say a thing. Barely make eye contact.

Things are working out well.

I go into the apartment. My roommate and Carl are sitting on the couch smoking a joint. I sit down. Carl passes it to me. I smile. And I'm sure they think it's because I'm getting stoned. But I'm still floating from being so close to Sam.

My roommate asks me where I've been. I don't even think. I tell them that I got up early. Hitched out of town. Ended up at Julie's moms wedding. My roommate chokes a little. Asks why the fuck.

'I thought it'd be nice,' I say.

Instantly I know it's not the kind of lie I can pull off. I don't have a history of getting emotional over weddings. Or anything really. And my roommate says bullshit. That there's no way he's buying that.

'Was Sam there?' he asks while passing the joint back my way.

I take a drag. Hold it in then blow out a large cloud of smoke. I tell him I'm not sure if she was. That I don't remember seeing her there.

'You weren't invited were you?' Carl asks me.

'No.'

'That's getting creepy, man.' he says while laughing at me. Which hurts me a little. I look at my roommate. His eyebrows are raised. Like he just heard something awful. A tragedy. And all I can think is that neither of them understands love.

'Nothing is getting creepy. I'm gonna win her back tonight. You'll see.'

'Yeah. Good luck with that. If I were you I'd leave her alone,' my roommate tells me.

I tell him that everything's fine. She offered me a ride home. The whole time we laughed and reminisced about all the fun we've had. He asks me how I got a ride home with her and can't remember if she was at the wedding.

'You know how these things work,' is the best answer I can come up with. Carl asks me how it was. If there were a lot of bikers. I say I couldn't be sure. That from where I was standing I couldn't see. But when I tell him the room stunk of whiskey he seems happy.

After that, we go out. Walk over to the closest beer store. Wait around the side until we convince someone to buy us a dozen bottles of beer. When we get back to the apartment we open it up and dive in.

Carl and my roommate play video games. I roll another joint. The two of them talk about all the girls that'll be at the party tonight. The things they want to do to them. I agree with everything they say. Just so I don't come across as an outsider. But I can only think of Sam.

When the sun sets I tell them we should go. I'm anxious to set my plan in action. But I keep that to myself. I say that we'd better be moving. That there's only one keg of beer. And who knows how much those drunks and bikers will consume.

They agree. Julies moms place isn't that far. But still. In our state it takes us about 45 mins to get there. It's in a newer subdivision where all the houses look the same. And I'm certain that if I was alone. I'd be stuck wandering these streets all night.

From the end of the driveway we can hear music. See the shapes of people dancing behind the curtains. Carl and my roommate stop. So I follow suit. I figure maybe we're going to smoke another joint. Get loose before we go into the party.

Instead my roommate looks at me. Asks me if I plan on doing anything stupid. Like make Sam's night terrible. And I can 't believe what I'm hearing. Who do they think I am?

'What are you talking about?' I ask him. And the two of them stand there under a streetlight. Looking at me like I'm a lunatic. Like they know things are going to go south.

'You know what I mean, man. You're drinking. She's here. You're a piece of shit. And then I have to drag you home. It's not fun,' my roommate says.

'I told ya man. This is my fucking night,' my confidence at a level I'm not accustomed to. And I'm not sure. But I might even be standing up straight. But instead of believing in me, my roommate scoffs. Tells me that's what makes him worry.

And my blood boils a little when he says that. So I jump down his throat and tell him to give it a fucking rest. And if anything goes awry he's absolved of me. That I'll drag my own ass home.

He grumbles but doesn't say much. Because he knows me. And he knows that this is best he's going to get.

The three of us walk up the driveway. Which is full of cars. Just like the whole god damned street. I'm surprised there's not people falling out into the yard. This isn't a large place. Just some crummy little one floor dump. The same as all the others in this subdivision.

We try knocking on the side door. But it's fucking futile. And I'm not sure why I suggested it. Because there's no way someone is manning it. Waiting for guests to be checked off a fucking list. So my roommate opens the door and walks right in.

We're on a landing between the basement and the main floor. The kitchen is through the door to the right. I can see that it's full of people. They laugh. They toss back drinks. Pick at platters of food off a table in the middle of the room.

And I know I'm not ready for all that. It looks like the kind of situation that's impossible to navigate without getting stuck. Being dragged down into some awful conversation. Like listening to someone's life plan.

I don't wait to see what my roommate and Carl decide to do. I make my way into the basement. Where I can't see anyone. I hear voices and laughter. But it's more subdued. And I picture an easier transition starting from there.

At the bottom of the stairs I turn left. And in front of me is an unfinished room. Cinder block walls. Boxes of useless crap stacked around the perimeter. People are sitting around on makeshift chairs and benches. And in the middle of the room is a keg of beer in a large plastic tub of ice.

I make myself at home. Walk into the middle of it all. Grab a red plastic cup and fill it to the top with cold beer. I take a long drink off of it while shutting my eyes. It feels so good. I'm as relaxed as I've ever been.

I still haven't acknowledged a single person in the room. So I take a look a round. Smile and nod at everyone I know in the room as I do. I don't see Sam down here. But there's no way I'm going upstairs right away. Because Carl and my roommate followed me down here. And I don't want them to know what I'm up too.

Those assholes and their judgment. I'll show them. This night is going to end like a beautiful fairy tale. And it'll have nothing to do with the recent bride and groom. They can go to hell. Today is about Sam and I, our endless love.

I drain my beer foolishly celebrating something that hasn't happened yet. Then I pour another.

I wander about the room for a while. Looking through boxes. Getting stuck in conversations. Which end pretty quickly. And I'm so happy with the result that I don't notice why.

Because I'm not paying attention to anything anyone says. I just grin and gulp down the beer. My mind a thousand miles away. Twenty years in the future. These shit days nothing but a memory. The rough patch before everything worked out.

And every time there's any mild amount of disbelief in this all working out I take another drink. Drown the voice in my head. Convince him he's being irrational. That the world is on our side.

I never think for a second that I'm the fool.

There's nothing down here for me, I tell myself. Just these one way conversations. I want to see Sam. Get the ball rolling. I fill my cup one more time. Make my way to the stairs. My roommate looks at me with a cocked eye. I tell him I have to take a piss.

And I know he doesn't believe me. But he can go fuck himself. He should worry about his own damn behavior. And by the time I make it up to the top of the stairs I'm half down my drink again. I can feel it now. I need to take a second and catch myself.

I stand there in the doorway. Watching people move around. Laugh and talk and drink and eat. There's bottles of booze and buckets of ice and large platters of deli meat and cheese and buns and deviled eggs and salad.

It's the answer to all my problems.

I stumble up to the table. My feet are a little heavy and I bump up against a man I've never seen before. He's got a rough face. Long hair. And when I push against him he looks at me with anger. But I couldn't care less. Not in the face of all this food.

So instead of apologizing I grab a paper plate. He walks away with his. And I spend some time piling mine high with sandwiches and salad. I drain my beer. Take a small clear plastic glass. Fill it with ice, then whiskey.

I move up against a free spot on the counter. Lean against it. Put my drink down beside me. Ignore everyone in the room. Start shoveling forkfuls of macaroni salad into my mouth. I eat a sandwich in two bites.

There's probably crumbs and salad all over me. But I don't notice. It feels too good to be eating. I can't remember the last time I had access to so much food. And every one of the three sandwiches I have has at least a half-pound of meat stuffed into the bun.

I pick up my glass. The ice has melted a little and I'm able to pull back a mouthful. I swish it around my mouth. Dislodge pieces of ham and salami and turkey and mustard soaked bread from my teeth.

Christ. It sure feels good to be alive for once.

Julie walks up to me as I'm chewing back the last half of my third sandwich. I curse her timing. There's nothing I want more than to head back over to the platter. Make another one. Just in case I don't get another chance.

'Hey Stan, you came,' she says to me with a smile on her face. And I don't take the time to think how nice it is to have a pretty face looking at me like that.

'I wouldn't miss it. I ain't seen your mom yet though. I want to say congrats.' I tell her because I think its what she wants to hear. I think about Sam. And how now that I've eaten I feel like a fucking champ. I take another drink. And I feel even better than I did a second ago.

Julie tells me they left already. That all of their friends were going there soon. That there was a better place to party somewhere else. That they'd just stopped in here to eat. She points to my face. And says she can see that I did to.

I wipe my bare arm across my face. And when I bring it down there's a streak of mustard 3 inches long down the top of it. Julie laughs at me. And I do to. I don't have anything to wipe it up with so I just rub into my arm with my hand.

'Hey, is Sam around?' I ask. And she stops smiling. She tells me that Sam isn't looking forward to seeing me. That I should leave her alone. That it's not worth all the bullshit.

And for a minute I can't say a thing. I'm too mad. I can't believe that Julie would lie to me like that. As calmly as I can, which isn't that calm at all, I tell her to go fuck herself. And that she should watch what she says.

I down the rest of the whiskey. Go to the bathroom and take a piss. When I come back out I go back to the basement. I need a minute to think. To figure out what I'm going to do. Because a small part of me believes in Julie's words.

It's a little livelier than before. The beer is flowing more freely. More people have shown up. I pour a beer and go stand with Carl and Mitch and Greaseback and my roommate. Carl looks at me like he knows everything that happened already. Like he could see me fucking up through the floor.

I don't say much. Just half listen. Laugh when it feels appropriate. I'm too lost in my head. The plan is unraveling. And if I fail here then I have to think about failure elsewhere. Like graduating. Like getting a good job.

And standing there in a room full of people smiling and laughing and drinking and talking about their bright futures I can see mine just in the distance burning down into a smoldering pile of steaming shit.

When I hear my roommate ask if anyone wants to go outside to smoke a joint I'm the first one to say fuck yes. I say I could use the air. That I'm sick of being in this basement. Under this ceiling. I'm not done with my drink but I fill another glass before I go outside.

Outside everyone is in the front yard. The last of Julie's mom's friends leaving. There's no need for us to be out there. We go into the back corner of the back yard. We stand there smoking in silence. Listening to cars starting. Voices bidding farewell.

I walk away from the circle without saying a word. I tell myself I'm in a moment of perfection. That I can't waste it. That I have to find Sam right away. That this is the instant I'll be able to regain control over where it feels like life is pushing me.

When I come around the side of the house Julie and Sam are walking arm in arm towards me. Their heads are down and they're laughing. And when I say hey girls they jump and squeal a little in fear.

I ask them how they're doing. Apologize to Julie for earlier. Tell her I flew off the handle. Then I ask if I can have a minute alone with Sam. She rolls her eyes and sighs. But agrees. Julie asks if she needs her to stay. But she shakes her head and I'm relieved.

I don't know if I have the balls to say what I have to say in front of her. And when she walks away and we hear the side door close behind her I ask Sam how she's doing again. And she just tells me to cut the shit. To say my piece.

And I let loose with it all. About how much I still love her. And how soon things are going to change. And how soon I'll have a job. How then I'll be the person she's always wanted. We can have the life she's dreamed of. And how without her my entire life's plan will run off course.

When I'm done she stands there. And she looks hurt. Which is the opposite effect I was looking for. And when she opens her mouth she doesn't say I love you like I imagined. Instead she asks me if that's all I see her as. As a piece in some fucking puzzle.

And I don't see what's wrong with that.

But before I can tell her as much she looks up at me. Her beautiful eyes a little glassy with drink and smoke and what I mistake for undying love. She says, 'Stan, I have something I want to tell you.'

And I think this is it. She's going to tell me that she wants me back. That in a couple of minutes we're going to be in each other's arms. Making out. Back in love like we were a year ago.

'Stan,' she says, and I'm about to explode with happiness, wishing there was some way to preserve this moment, 'I'm dating Matt,' she says without any concern for me, 'We've been going out for a couple months now. It's going great. And I'm sick of having to hide it.'

I take a step back. I need to sit down. And I let go of gravity. Fall backwards. Land sitting up in a bush. Its branches jab into me from the back of my knees up to the middle of my back. I drop both cups of beer I was holding. The full one spills down my leg.

But I don't notice the physical pain or the damp denim.

And I know that she's standing there. Not a meter from where I'm sitting. But all I see is a swirl of colour. Feel a nausea that gets a hold of me. One that lets me know it's not letting go for a while. I rub my eyes with the heel of my hand until I feel like I can handle it again.

I look up and I'm alone. The only one sitting in a bush. The only one on the front lawn. The only one on the street. And I can't argue the situation doesn't reflect my own black hole growing inside me.

There's no way for me to tell how much time passes. It might be a minute or an hour. But Carl comes out. Which I take as a godsend.

Instead of seeing it as him already knowing what's happened. And that Julie or Sam or whoever asked him to come out here. And check on me like a child

He asks what I'm doing. I don't make a peep. I want to. I want to tell him I'm not doing great here. That a lot of the things I believed in are beginning to lose meaning. And I'm not sure where I see myself going.

But I just sit there staring. Thinking about how long I've known Matt. And how I thought good friends didn't do things like this to each other. And how in the fucking world could Sam go and pick one of my friends to fuck behind my back.

And I guess Carl gets worried when I don't say anything. Because he shuffles back and forth on his feet. Tells a couple of jokes I don't hear. Anything to get a response out of me.

'You're looking thirsty there bud, how about I get ya another beer?' and for the first time since I fell down into the bush I feel my lips move. And sound come up from my throat.

'Yeah, I think that just might do the trick.'

He tries to get me to get up. But I'm not ready for that yet. I still need some more time. I ask him to go inside. Bring me one back out. He says sure. Happy to have gotten any response at all.

When I hear the door shut behind him I get out of the bush. Lie in the grass looking up at the sky. It seems like the right position to properly think things over from. The right angle to see how pathetic my happiness was earlier.

And how I maybe should've listened to Julie. Instead of telling her off. And I see the hallucination I was operating under all day. The way I walked around with my head in the clouds cashing in on a gamble I hadn't even bet on yet.

Against the backdrop of the night sky I see them. Sam and Matt. Lying in bed together. Her curled up against him under a thin sheet. Their sweat still fresh on their skin. Laughing at me.

And I realize I'm angrier than I thought. So when Carl comes back out with four cups of beer and sits down beside me it's a relief. I gulp down the first glass and I feel better. I can tell myself that everything is fine.

I tell Carl what happened. What Sam said. He hangs his head when he tells me he's known for a month or so. That everyone has. Which doesn't help the visions of their laughter escape my mind.

He says he's sorry he didn't tell me before. That my roommate and him had planned to before we got here. But they chickened out at the last minute. At the end of the driveway only a couple of hours ago.

And there's no way I can blame either of them. If they'd tried to tell me that story earlier I'm sure I wouldn't have taken it well. I would've laughed at them. Told that there was no way Matt would do something like that behind my back.

But it seems the longer I live the more I realize I'm wrong all the time.

Carl matches me gulp for gulp on the beers. Even though I don't I tell Carl that I'm feeling a thousand times better. That he's been a big help. But I'm already thinking of tall buildings on the way home. Ones I could easily climb. Ones I could easily fall from.

But I must do a convincing job because he agrees when I say we should go back in. That I'm ready for it. He has to help me get up from the grass. My legs aren't so sturdy. All this drink is finally getting on top of me.

Before we go in I tell Carl that I think I should eat a sandwich. Do something before I'm too far gone. There's still a lot of booze left. And I want to do my best to put a dent in it.

Carl goes to the basement when I tell him I'll be fine by myself. And he either believes me or is sick of having to deal with me. Because he doesn't even look over his shoulder to see if I make it.

I climb the three stairs into the kitchen. I'm suddenly conscious of the fact my left leg is damp. That I reek of the beer I'm covered in. I don't know with any certainty. But I'm convinced I'm covered in dirt and grass and sticks.

But I'm in here now. And I keep moving with my head down. I don't want to make eye contact. I believe if I don't I can stay invisible. I'll be able to quietly eat a sandwich and slither back into the basement. Like the vile creature I am.

I rip open a bun with my hands. Stuff it full of meat and cheese. A heavy dose of mustard. I stand there eating it. Hoping it has the desired effect. A sobering one. Because I'm not so sure I won't vomit everywhere.

The sandwich is dry. And I'm having a hard time chewing. I look around for something to drink. A coke or some water or something. I fill a glass with ice. And before I know what I'm doing I've filled it with whiskey again.

I stare down at it. I know it's not a good idea. But I've made my move I tell myself. There's no backing out now. I pick up the glass. And before I have a chance to finish chewing. To take my first sip. I hear a familiar voice.

'Hey Stan, don't you think you've had enough booze for the night? You're looking a little rough.'

And that's when everyone starts to laugh at me. Because I do look a little rough. And I stand there. Still avoiding eye contact. Thinking of course I look like shit. And cant you just shut you're mouth and let me have my quiet misery.

I tell myself to just give up. Don't look up. Finish the damn sandwich and the drink. But I can't. I want to stomp whoever's deciding to take this opportunity to shit on me.

I finish chewing the mouthful I have. I knock back the rest of the drink in the glass. I wipe my mouth along the back of my hand again. I don't have to look down to know I'm covered in crumbs. Bits of meat.

It's probably embarrassing. But I don't look down. So instead I look up. And I see where the voice is coming from. And who's laughing at me. It's Mike doing the taunting. His brother Matt is standing with him. His arm around a laughing Sam.

'Is that right Mike? Well you know what…'

'C'mon Stan, settle down, he don't mean nothing,' Sam says.

'You know Sam? I've heard plenty from you tonight. So why don't you shut your mouth,' I say while pointing at her face from across the room.

'Watch it Stan,' Matt says

'I see, Matt. I get it. You're the big protector now. Big tough man.'

I pour another glass over my remaining ice and drain it. I take a few steps towards them. A little farther down the large kitchen table. They're still on the other side. Closer to the door to the living room. Still too far away to start strangling any of them.

I place my glass down beside a giant punch bowl in front of me. And that's when my brain goes slow. I see what I'm doing. From different angles. So I don't believe it. Like a dream. And I let go. Watching myself. Feeling sorry for Julie. Because I can she her standing there. Horror all over her face.

I reach in front of me. Grab the ladle like I'm about to spoon out a cup of punch. But instead I drop it on the table. Matt says what the fuck. But I don't stop I pick the punch bowl up over my head. It spills all over me. I throw it as hard as I can. It misses them all by a wide yard.

It explodes against the wall.

Everyone screams.

I pick up a bag of chips. A bowl of dip. Walk as calmly as I can. Soaking wet. Dripping down the stairs. I don't stop until I get to the keg. I pour off a glass. Drink it down and pour another. I sit down with my back against the wall eating chips and dip. Watching where the stairs end.

I smile.

I feel good.

Someone asks me what went on up there. That they heard the crash and screams and why the fuck am I so god damned wet. I take a drink. Eat a couple more chips. Think about it for a minute. Then I calmly tell the room that Matt went crazy and threw the punch bowl at Julie.

'Of course, I'm wet I because I was protecting her,' I tell them. And it might only be 30 seconds, but I get to know what it's like to feel like a hero. Because it's not long before the angry voices upstairs are accompanied by footsteps on the stairs.

And lucky for me it's Julie when someone comes into the room.

'Stan,' she said. She doesn't want to do what she has to do.

So I don't let her.

I tell her I think it's about time I leave. That I've had a hell of a good night. But I could use a walk. And I can see she's glad she doesn't have to ask me. Because cleaning the kitchen is going to be bad enough.

When I get up I fill my glass before I start moving. I shrug and say one for the road. Wink at Julie. When I go to hug her she pulls back. And tells me she'll owe me one. I nod my head. Climb the stairs without saying goodbye to anyone else.

Matt is standing in the door to the kitchen. His brother is behind him. And another big brute behind him. I don't look at their faces. I don't need to. I know they all hate me. I know they all wish the same thing as me.

That I might not live through the night.

'Well, thanks for the good times Matt,' I say with a wave and whole lot of sarcasm.

He winks at me. Tells me 'They're just beginning, Stan.'

And I understand what he means. I'm not going to get to leave all that easy. That I'm not just going to be left alone with my misery and the long lonely walk home. That won't be good enough tonight. And I can't disagree. I owe them this at the very least.

I walk outside. They follow close behind. Just far enough away for me to hear them and their wishes for me. Their hopes for how the next few minutes go. They wait until I get out into the street. I ask if I can put my beer down. Save it for after.

They're good guys in the end because they allow me that.

His buddies hold me. Matt punches me for what seems like forever. I look at the house. Sam's on the lawn. And so are a lot of other people. They watch every last punch. They look like they enjoy it. And I can smile because I know my actions have made others happy.

But of course smiling isn't the right response. It only makes Matt more angry. I can barely stand up. It's clear I'm not going to put up a fight. His brother and the brute drop me. I crumple on the ground. My hands over my head to protect me from their kicks.

When it's done they walk back in the house laughing. I roll off the street and sit on the edge of Julie's lawn. This time no one comes over to find me. To coax me into drinking more beer. So I finish the one I brought out alone.

By the time I get home the suns almost up. I fall asleep curled up in the tub. And when I come to several hours later there's not a part of me that doesn't hurt. It takes a minute to get out of the tub. When I do, I look in the mirror.

And I wish I hadn't.

I can hear the sounds of the television from the living room. It must be my roommate. I splash some water on my face while I give in to knowing things between Sam and I are dead forever.

When I go into the living room my roommate and Carl are both there. Neither of them looks free of a hangover. I look at my roommate. 'I told you you wouldn't have to drag me home.'

13.

I finally get the call. A monotone voice informing me of a meeting with my caseworker. In place of any form of goodbye, I'm informed that if I miss the appointment I'd better have a good excuse. Or a job lined up.

The city's bus system leaves something to be desired. There's only two routes and neither of them is a straight shot to the downtown terminal. Instead they twist and turn through barren areas. Around the outskirts of neighborhoods.

I'd be on it all morning. And there'd go the rest of the change I have jangling around in my pocket. I pull it out. And I don't even think there's enough to get on. So my decision is made. I guess I have to walk.

Which is better than when I had to hitchhike I tell myself. As I stand in the morning sun. It's early and the air is thick. And I know it's going to get sticky. And that the walk is going to probably take me all morning.

Or at least feel like it. Because there's nothing to look at. Just long roads of houses that all look pretty similar. That I've already seen a hundred times before. And the boredom of life creeps into me.

Because I just want to see something happening. I'm sick of this sleepy little town. I want crowded streets and beautiful women. I want restaurants and flashing lights. I want options. Not just the inevitability of what will come to pass.

But it doesn't take long before I forget about boredom. The humidity starts to cause problems. I'm sweating through all my clothes. I'm out of shape. Been subsisting off bowls of white rice for too long.

I feel like a fat fuck. I look down past my shaking heavy gut. To where my thighs are rubbing together. They burn. Without being able to look I imagine a cigarette pack sized red rash on either leg. Just below my balls. I curse the sky.

I keep my morale up for a couple of blocks. Telling myself that I can't turn around. That I have to get to this meeting. I can't afford to have my money cut. Because I'm sure if I tell them that I had a rash it's not going to cut it as far as excuses go.

But as the burning gets worse I have a harder time believing I'm going to make it. I'm thirsty as hell. I wish I'd brought a bottle of water. Or if there's a corner store anywhere close to here. Then I could go into their air conditioning for a minute. A bit of reprieve from it all.

Instead, I give up on the edge of someone's lawn. Sit in the shade of a tall bush. I spread my legs out as far as they'll go. Wave my hands above the problem area. Try and create a breeze. But the burning continues.

I try and think of something. Anything I can tell the welfare people. Because I'm not even halfway there yet. But any excuse I can conjure up I need corroboration. Someone of authority to back me up. And that's when I realize I have no options.

'The story of my life,' I say while standing up. I wipe the back of my arm along my forehead. I sigh. Wish that something could just step in and take my life away. Spare me this trial. But I've never been one full of luck.

I walk bowlegged. Do my level best to keep my thighs from touching. But it's tough. I've put on more weight than I thought. They still gently rub up against one another. And every time they do I wince. Tell myself not to cry.

A car drives passed. Honks. Another one slows down to call me Tex. And asks if the rodeo is in town. I don't have the energy to tell him to go fuck himself while he laughs. Because I'm losing my will to live.

And this walk is taking forever. And the sun just won't give up. And I have to make this appointment. And all I want to do is lie down. Maybe on the strip of grass between the sidewalk and the gutter.

It seems like the best place to give up.

Another truck drives up. Ladders and buckets and tools fill the back of it. Two men sit inside. They're tan. One of them hangs a dust covered forearm out the window. It looks like it's made of steel. And I think about my own pudgy body.

They slow right down. Drive alongside me. They must be on a coffee break or something. And this is what they do to relax. The driver leans over. Yells across the bench seat and out the window.

'Hey fat ass, you shit your pants or something? You're walking pretty funny.' They laugh at me. I look at the ground. The only thing I can do to better my situation is to keep my legs apart.

And anyways. There's two of them.

'Look how sad he is,' the passenger points his tanned hand at me.

'If I were that fat and shit my pants I'd be depressed too,' the boss adds.

More laughter. More humiliation. There has to be something better for these fuckers to be doing. I pray for another car to veer off. Hit their truck head on. Obliterate the two of them permanently. Into oblivion and away from me. But I'm not that lucky.

Instead they continue to drive beside me. Yelling out profanities. They call me chubs. Shit pants. They laugh more. Throw an empty coffee cup at me. They tear off down the street. And I wonder what I did to deserve this.

At least that's the end of it.

· · · · · · ·

When I get to city hall my crotch is a nightmare. The first thing I do is go inside. Make my way to the basement. The welfare office is down there. But I still have an hour to kill before my appointment. And I need to get to the bottom of what's happening in my pants.

It's cool in here. And I instantly feel better. Have the energy to tell myself that things aren't going to be that bad. But each step causes me to wince. Even with my legs as far apart as I can get them.

I go into the first empty stall. Pull down my pants. My inner thighs are red. Scaly. When I touch the left one with my finger I can't help hollering in pain. My pants had been soaking up most of the sweat.

And now with them off. It pours down my thighs. Burning my friction burns.

I unravel a wad of toilet paper. Start trying to pat myself dry. But it only sticks to my legs. Makes things worse. I want to give up. I want to lie down and go to sleep. Maybe I can wake up and my life will be completely different.

But I know I can't. That the only life I'd wake up to is getting yelled at by a janitor or security guard or cop. So I pull my pants up. I leave them undone. I open the stall door. I'm the only one in here.

At the sink I pull them back down. Run cold water and gently rub it into my legs. At first the pain of it makes me pull back. But once I get past the initial shock I feel my whole body relax under the relief.

Standing there like this. Hunched over. Massaging my inner thigh. A man comes in whistling. One with a haircut and a nice suit and full stomach and a college degree. When he looks at me he ceases his walking and his whistling.

We make eye contact. And I'm certain the emotion I read from his is confused disgust. So I look down at the floor. Lowering my entire head. When I hear him walking to the stall I imagine him shaking his head.

I pull my pants up. Rub a little cold water into my eyes. Walk out into the basement of the city hall. It's open like a square. The permit and welfare offices look out on to it.

It's small. So it seems busy. Mainly dusty, paint covered men coming and going from the permit office. The odd employee from the higher levels come down for a piss. And bums like me. People in dirty clothing coming down to collect a check.

And I feel the eyes of them all on me. Judging me. Knowing that I'm not one of them. Here for a permit. But I'm a fucking bum. Someone their taxes pay for. And in most of their minds that gives them a right. To not hide their hate.

So I stand there. Feeling like an outsider. The same way I did when I lived at home. How that if I just fucked off and disappeared then everyone's life could be better. But this is life I tell myself. And there's nowhere to fuck off to. Except death. And I don't have the balls for a move like that.

The worst part about it is the town's so small. There'll be moments of desperation. I'm going to end up applying for jobs from these men. And I'll have to hope they think they've seen me in one of the bars. Instead of in this air-conditioned basement. Looking for a handout.

I walk over to the water fountain. Lean over and drink. This is some of the best water I've ever tasted I tell myself. It's ice cold. Hurts my teeth. It's nothing like the water at home. I can run the tap forever at home and it's always luke warm. Tastes like metal.

And as I'm telling myself to remember to bring a container next time I have to come down here I hear someone laughing. It's a laugh that I recognize. But I don't have a clue from where. So I stop drinking. Wipe cold water from my lips. Turn around. And there they are. By the doors to go outside. The guys from the pick-up truck.

Fuck, I think. I don't need this again. That cold water had almost pushed all the bad thoughts down. To somewhere I leave them and forget about them until the next time I scrape together the money to get drunk.

So I lower my head. Make slow movements. Try and take up as little space as possible. Will myself to blend into the cinder block walls painted grey like some chameleon. Anything to keep them from noticing me slinking into the welfare office.

I make it to the door. Get my hand around the heavy brass handle. Give it a pull. But it's heavier than I remember. And I have to give it another try. But just as I do I hear them. And if they'd noticed me walking through here it would've been better. Just passing through. Using the facilities.

But now they know what I am.

'Hey bud, check out who it is? The kid who shit his pants,' the guy I remember as the driver says in a voice loud enough for everyone to hear. And except for a synchronized head turn in my direction all movement stops.

'Christ, Dougie. He shit his pants and he's going to the welfare office. Doubt he works there.' And now it's not only the two of them laughing. But other contractors join in. Others just look at me the way you look at something pathetic. Like a skinny dog short on time.

'You should've asked, fatty. We could've given you a ride,' the driver says. More laughter.

'Hell no, he's too fat. Over the limit. Not to mention his shitty pants,' Dougie replies.

'He's not walking so bad now. Maybe he changed his diapers.'

These pricks. They think they're so much better than me. Them with their fancy job. Their money. Their homes. Their families. That's not good enough for them. They have to run me down too.

And there's nothing I can do. But give the door a good heave. It opens this time. I'm fueled by the laughter I guess. But when the heavy door shuts behind me it blocks out the teasing. And I hope that it doesn't follow me in.

I know I'm supposed to check in. Tell them that I'm here. But I need a minute so I sit down in one of the six chairs in the room. I put my head in my hands. Breathe deeply. Think about my friends. Sitting in class. Money in their pockets for lunch. A very small chance of them being harassed by grown men.

When I'm ready I stand up. Walk over to the chest-high counter. The three inches of plexiglass. I'm pretty sure that the woman sitting on the other side hasn't noticed me yet. She talks into a headset. Looks at her nails. Eats a potato chip.

Basically anything she can do to ignore me.

I listen to her conversation. But her words come through the plexiglass like underwater voices. And the only thing I can make out with distinction is her braying horse laugh. Which makes me shudder. I have to close my eyes as a means to survive each outbreak.

The plexiglass has a yellow tinge to it. A dreamlike lens over the situation. And maybe that's what keeps me from more drastic measures of garnering her attention. Like banging my fist against the space directly in front of her face.

That and the handwritten sign taped on the inside. The one that says anyone who even touches the glass will have their claim immediately terminated.

So I just stand there, waiting. Wondering how many clerks had been threatened with weapons. Or knew the feeling of angry hands around their throats before this scenario had been implemented.

She puts down the phone. Picks up another chip and eats it. Looks at me like it's the first time she's seen me. Like she honestly didn't notice until this second. And I start to have fear about the human capacity for feigned ignorance.

'Can I help you?' she says leaning over her side of the counter. Speaking into the circle of holes and the slot used for receiving checks and submitting proof of identification. I bend over to tell her my reason. Give her my name. Pull my student card from my wallet in anticipation of the steps.

Once she believes I am who I am she tells me to wait. That my caseworker is very busy. I sit in one of the six chairs in the tiny waiting room. The clock says I'm right on time. I wonder what in the hell she's doing and why I have to wait.

So I look around the room. Everything is old. Heavy like the door. And if it weren't for the bulletproof glass and posters on the walls and the woman behind the counter and my reflection in the glass of the door across from me I'd swear I'd slipped through time. Back to the 50's.

I amuse myself by looking at the posters. They all have a thematic meaning. One that's easy to grasp. That committing welfare fraud is an instant termination of your claim. Punishable by law. And if you know of anyone involved in this disgusting offence they offer up numbers to call. A vague implication of being rewarded.

And I lean back. Count the people I know on welfare. And the ways in which they're all guilty. Working under the table jobs. Selling drugs.

Tattooing. I think about the reward implied. I try and commit the 1-800 number to memory. Just in case my situation gets dire.

But I also wonder what the fuck is wrong with me. Why I'm not doing something on the side. Anything for a couple extra bucks a month. And I know the reasons. I'm too scared. I think there's welfare agents everywhere. Watching me. Making sure I'm not generating anin world income of any kind.

The door I can see my reflection in opens. A senior citizen stands there. His security guard shirt as white as the hair on his head. He looks brittle. I can't imagine him settling any violent disturbances.

He calls my name and I get up. Nod at him and smile. He holds the door open for me. I follow him down a long hall. The walls are white. And the only windows look into offices. Most of them have their blinds pulled shut. It's damp. And I feel like I'm thousands of kilometers below the surface of the earth.

He stops at another door. Knocks politely. Leans and listens with one of his ancient drooping ears. He must hear an invitation. Because he swings the door open and ushers me into the room. I nod a last time to him. We never said a word to each other.

I walk into the office looking at the ground. I'm trying to walk as normal as I can. But when my thighs rub together I wince. I don't want her to see me do it. I don't want to have to explain myself to her. After everything already today I don't have the energy.

What gets me to raise my head is her voice. It's soft. And compassionate. And even before I see her I can imagine the owner of this voice. Telling me everything is going to work out for the best. And I of course I believe her. Because it's tough to distrust the songs of angels.

When I see her it's all over. She's the most beautiful woman I've ever seen. From three feet away her skin glows. Her large blue eyes sparkle. Her long blonde hair falls on her narrow shoulders. Her slim body fitting into her blouse and pencil skirt with perfection.

My knees wobble wondering how she manages to look so good under this flickering fluorescent light.

I grab hold of the chair in front of me. She comes around the front of her desk. She's in high heels and from the knee down her legs are bare. She shakes my hand. Smiles at me while introducing herself. Her hand is softer than anything I've ever known. And I squint as the room gets brighter.

She invites me to sit. I watch her walk back to her own side of the desk. Sit down and put on a pair of glasses. She laughs a little. Says she apologizes for looking like a nerd. I mutter some noises. Nod. Imply it's no concern.

A strand of hair falls in her face as she looks over my open file in front of her on the desk. When she raises her hand and runs it back behind her ear I imagine doing it myself. Being that intimate with her. And I forget about the rash. The men and their laughter. And the long walk home.

She starts talking about how I'll be graduating soon. How after that my claim is going to change. But I'm somewhere else. In a different universe. One where we met under different circumstances. Ones that didn't end up with us talking about my future. But instead ones that ended up with her unbuttoning her blouse.

I get startled back into things. She asks me what my plans are after school. The same thing everyone keeps asking me. And I tell her the same old story. Follow in my old mans footsteps. Get a job in a factory. Become a man.

It's the right answer. She keeps smiling. Tells me that that it sounds like I know what I'm doing. That I'm young and I still have a chance.

And I think about asking if I can just come home with her. Because this is the nicest I've been treated in a long time. And I don't think I could ever take for granted the way in which she says things.

Then she tells me that she wants to talk about how my claim will change when I'm out of school. How I'll have to start going to meetings. And workshops on how to make a resume. And how to search for work. That I have to hand out a minimum of 15 copies of the resumes I'm taught how to make a month. I have to record them all. Hand it in to them. And if I don't I won't receive a check.

It's all bad news. And this is beginning to sound a lot more like work. I'm scared that I'm not responsible enough to keep up with the demands. But all my fear disappears when I look at her. And it's the first time I see how a woman can change you. Make you feel like a giant.

'Are you fine with all this?' she asks me. And without even thinking I tell her she can count on me. And that she shouldn't worry. I'll have a job in no time.

'That's what we're hoping. You're so young. You've got a whole lifetime of potential ahead of you.'

She tells me that she'd like to see me once a month until school ends. Get a feel for me. How she can help me get back out there. Become a member of society. She's full of optimism about my life. About the factory job I'll get. About the family I'll one day have.

I just wish I cared.

She looks on her computer. Makes an appointment for three weeks from now. She wants to keep up to date on my grades. I have to bring my last report card. There's a knock on the door. The old man in the security uniform comes in. She stands up again. I try and get a glimpse between the buttons of her shirt.

Any amount of skin.

Something to jerk off to later.

The old man ushers me back down the hall. Opens the door for me. I tell him goodbye. He answers by shutting the door in my face.

There's a dirty looking couple in the waiting area. His hair is almost as gray as the sweatpants he's wearing. She's not much better. And her hand is stained from smoking. They're yelling at each other. The security guard shuts the door behind me. The receptionist doesn't give a shit. So neither do I.

I leave as quickly as I came in.

There's no one in the basement this time. I walk bowlegged. Uncaring of who sees me. I take a long drink of cold water from the fountain.

Revel in its superior quality. Stand up straight and tell myself that the walk will be fine. I won't even notice the pain.

I walk across the street from city hall. There's a small concrete parkette. It's empty of people like it always is. So I get my pick of the benches. I sit down and light a smoke. Tell myself that the more time I give it the better.

I lean my head back. Look far off into the sky. And thing about the curve of my caseworker's breast beneath her shirt. How soft her skin was. And with thoughts like this I can forget about the rash. I get up. And walk home without complaining once.

14.

The next couple meetings with her go pretty much the same way. Her talking and me sitting there dreaming. But she brings things up over and over. Like how I have a three month grace period. And after that I have to be involved with the mandatory workfare program.

And the only reason I don't leave there with an erection every time is because of how depressing it's becoming. She asks me why I don't want to continue my studies. I tell her I don't have the money. She tells me to get a loan. And I ask who gives out loans to bums.

I start going to school more. With the end nearing I need to kiss some ass. The last time I got a report card things were right on the edge. I think about if I fail. And how life would actually be easier. I could just coast through another year of school.

No obligations.

But I've already taken my time getting through it. And if I take another year I know I'm going to look really pathetic. People will ask questions. They'll begin to think I'm stupid. That there's something wrong with me.

So I know I have to pass everything. Because I can't take the humiliation. I already suffer enough of that. Mostly at the hands of my peers. Other students. As the days become memories there's a feeling in the air. It makes your hair stand erect. It's the beginning of the end.

And as the days count down I have to avoid the questions. The hopeful looking eyes staring at me. Expecting me to have some plan. A good idea of what school I was going to end up at. Or what country in Europe I'd start my backpacking journey of self-discovery in.

So all I can do is lie to them. Say I want to work a year. Save some money and then decide what to do. And maybe a part of me wants to go to school. To read books for four years. To learn how to do something. Or to get a passport. Hop on a plane. Hitchhike my way across a series of countries where I don't speak the language.

Familiarize myself with being uncomfortable.

But I don't even know what the steps towards those would be. And neither of those things feel like what the son of a factory worker does. Even though some of the kids in my class. The ones with bright eyes asking me the questions. I know their fathers work alongside mine. Yet still they dream.

And I wonder what advice I've been missing out on.

. . . .

When the last day of school comes it's the end of June. The sky is as blue as it gets. Perfect wisps' of white clouds float through it. The air is crisp and feels good to breathe. The teachers are smiling. Students ecstatic.

I feel like shit.

By the time the bell for lunch has rung I'm hanging my head. From a kilometer away I look depressed. All morning it's been final bits of advice from teachers I never listened to in the first place. I never had the energy to care.

And all the goodbyes full of forced importance. Kids walking around with yearbooks under their arms. A pen in hand. Making sure they get all the signatures they need to feel complete.

I didn't have the money for one. So I have no scrawled names and final farewells to collect. One more thing in life I'll miss out on. And the funny thing is. No one comes looking for me either. No one wants Stan Acker's name in ink. No one wants me to taint their future, I tell myself.

And I see the logic in it.

So when I walk out the doors after the bell I don't stop at the smoking pit. I just keep going. One foot in front of the other. Like a sleep walker, I light a cigarette. I disappear into the woods that separate the school grounds from the park on the other side.

And even back here there's more kids. The ones with the same idea as me. Fuck the rest of the day. But they'll stay here. Pull out bottles of booze stolen from parents' liquor cabinets. They'll smoke pot. Take acid. Celebrating the end of something they weren't ever interested in anyways.

I walk slowly. Take my time. Because that's all I have anymore. Time to do whatever I want. When Monday rolls around I have no obligations. And that goes for every Monday after that until I die.

Which is a pretty heavy weight on my shoulders.

The trees are competely full of leaves. And the sun has a hard time getting through them. So that only small patches flicker on the ground. When I step on them I feel like I'm crushing something beautiful.

When I come out the other side of the woods I'm hit with the sun. And I notice how cool it had been in there. It reminds me of sitting on the couch in my parent's basement. Always a little cooler than the rest of the house. Drinking a cold can of coke.

And how I could go for a can right now. But I don't have a penny on me. And there's nothing I can do. So I wander through the park. Make my way through a gazebo where I tried too hard to impress a girl once. There's a small lake near it. I sit on the edge. I don't get up for hours.

And when I do get up I take my time. Because there isn't a fucking thing waiting for me. Just a bunch of parties I don't want to go to. And the endless summer staring at me. The one I should be excited about. But seems more like a curse.

By the time I get home it's twilight. I know my roommate's there because I can see the lights on from the road. I cut across the large grass area in front of all the three-story walk-ups. Families have their screen doors open wide. They're on the lawn. Children playing. Hot-dogs sizzling on dirty black grills.

And I know that most of them are on welfare too. Not just because of the buildings we live in. But as long as the sun's shining then they are out there. White plastic lawn chairs trying not to break under their weight.

But look at them, I say to myself. They've got it all. Kids. A place to live. A barbeque. It's more than I'm going to be walking into in less than a minute. Because at best, I'm half the rent to my roommate.

And these assholes out here have smiles and love and hotdogs. So can it really be that bad on their side of the fence? I don't know it as I'm standing there wondering. But this is about as close as I've come to packing it in. Giving up.

· · · · · · ·

I open the door to the apartment. I can hear the television. But no voices. I expect it to be a little livelier in here. What with the end of an era closing today. And when I come around the corner it's just my roommate sitting there.

Shit, I say in my head. I wanted Carl to be here. I wanted anyone to be here. I wanted to sit on the couch and listen to other people talk. Let them go on and on at length. Their excitement fueling whatever ends up happening.

He smiles when he sees me. Asks where I've been all day. That he doesn't remember seeing me all afternoon. I tell him what I did. How I feel like I've lost my purpose. And he looks like my words hurt him.

'What the fuck are you talking about? This is what we've all been waiting for,' he says to me. And I'm not sure I've ever seen anyone so confused. He shakes his head and changes the subject. 'I've been waiting for ya, look what I got.'

He pulls out a huge joint. He's smiling like a maniac. And for a second I think about declining. But after he takes the first few puffs and passes it over there's no way I can refuse.

I sit there in a cloud of smoke. Thinking that my roommate isn't all that bad. And I shouldn't be so quick to be angry with him. But I know that it's not really me thinking. It's just this fucking haze.

He gets up and turns on the video game console. Gets himself ready. Goes to the kitchen and pours himself a large glass of water. Puts a small ashtray already full on the arm of the chair he's sitting in. Lights a cigarette. Sinks into the chair.

I tell myself he's right. That I've been looking forward to this all my life. This is when all the movies and books say life starts. When you get out there in the world. Get dirty with it. Clean yourself out a little space in all the shit.

These are the good times I'm staring down at, I tell myself. This is when it's all going to get better. At the end of the summer I'll start handing out resumes. I'm certain I'll get a job in one of the factories. I've seen it work out for dumber people than me.

I sit there confident. That this'll be a fucking breeze. That someone is going to give me a job and start throwing money at me. And then I can buy homes and cars and boats and all kinds of shit. And it'll last forever. And I'll never have to worry again.

Maybe it's how stoned I am. Or how depressed I am. But I look at it from the other side for once. That a factory is going to be no different then what I just left behind. The same break everyday. The same lunch everyday. Teachers replaced by dirty goons breathing down my neck.

And the only difference is it lasts for life. No easy four-year stint. The only thing I could hope for would be an early death.

I still have the roach in my hand. So I drop it on the table. I get up and walk across the room to the screen door. It's dark out and all I can see in it is the reflection of the room I'm trying to leave.

I slide the glass open. Step through and take a deep breath. The odor of blackened hotdogs is in the air. I can see the shadows of people. Hear their voices out there in the courtyard. But I only get glimpses of them when they come within the range of other patio doors.

My hands are on the railing. I lean back and stretch my arms. Pull myself straight. Let go and light a cigarette. Sit down on a stack of empty beer boxes. They shift under my weight, the glass tinkling. It's a feat of balance to keep them from falling.

I stare out into the darkness of the courtyard. Listen to voices come and go. Wondering what's going to become of me. Where the fuck I'm going to end up. And what's going to happen at the end of the summer.

I think about my friends going to university. And a part of me wants to learn more. To go and read and learn about books. Spend my days lying in the grass. Skipping class and drinking wine. Meeting more girls.

The acceptable way of not doing anything with your life.

Which is what I want more than anything. To do nothing. To have no responsibilities. To ask nothing of anyone and have nothing asked of me. I might be a kid still. But I'm smart enough to know that isn't real either.

So I stare. And smoke. And think of ways to prolong things. To stave off having to work. Or go to school. Or make any fucking decision at all. Because I'm sure I'm going to fail.

And that's probably why, when I had the money, I never put it toward college applications. And instead bought booze and boxes of frozen hamburgers. The cheapest ones I could find. Which tasted like shit.

But every bite of those fried up atrocities reminded me of something. That people like me aren't meant for fancy educations. Boys like me grow up to be drunks in dirty overalls. Just like our fathers.

I sit there on those old beer cases. Resolved to do just that. Become the man my father became. For no other reason than I think I have to. Like I owe it to the universe to give up. Let life push me along. Right into whatever early grave it sees fit.

Some rotten brat down in the courtyard starts crying. It's mother chimes in with a list obscenities. And by the time I hear some deep-voiced man start yelling I decide I've had enough fresh air.

And that it's time for a drink. That it's time for a celebration.

I go back inside and head for my room. There's $15 under my pillow. Just enough to get drunk. To forget for a night. To give myself some peace. I lift up the pillow and smile when I see the purple and blue bills there. I get ahead of myself. And in my mind I'm already drinking the whiskey it'll buy.

I go in the living room. 'Hey man,' I say to my roommate. 'You wanna walk to the liquor store with me?'

He looks over at me. Looks back at the TV. He makes a sound that I take for no. I shrug my shoulders. Close the door behind me when I leave. The closest LCBO is about 45 mins away. I'm happy for it. It's a nice night and I'm stoned and I like the sky above my head.

Life could be worse.

I cut through a gully behind a church. Walk through wood lots. Hop over chain link fences into the backyards of people I don't know. They all have lawn furniture sets nicer than the couch in my living room. I sit down on one. Put my feet up. Walk over to the pool. Cup my hands and wet my hair.

A taste of the good life. And all the things I can buy if I land that factory job. And standing there. The pool water running down the back of my neck. I ask myself a question. Why do I even want this?

Because I'm beginning to feel like I don't. That I can't see the point in it. That I don't want a family. Living with mine was a nightmare. I left for a reason. And here I am. Dreaming of walking down that path.

I just wish I knew another way.

Another way to spend my nights like this. A little loose and roaming. A clear sky overhead and enough money in my pocket to keep feeling just as free. Instead of chained down. To the job and the wife and anything else that demands you show up on time.

I walk out of the backyard. Down the long quiet street the house is on. And every home is the same basic place. And they all have the same things in the driveway. Two cars. And a boat.

By the time I get to the LCBO I'm sick with anger. Anger because after I get some one to buy me a bottle. And after I drink it and wake in the morning I'm still not going to know what to do. Or where to turn to.

I stand around the back of the parking lot. Watching guys in great big rumbling trucks roar up. They hop with a swagger. The ones that come from having a fat paycheck and a sweet smelling girl in the passenger seat.

And I know what it is I hate about these factory workers. With their confidence. Their belief that they have it made. That this sweet ride is going to keep on chugging along. Like it has for so long. I hate them because they don't have to think anymore.

I wait around. Stewing. Getting thirsty. I ask a few bums to buy me a bottle. I figure they're down on their luck. The kind of guys who can use the extra couple of bucks. They can buy mac and cheese with my change. It still tastes fine even without milk and butter I tell them.

But they all refuse. They say it's too big of a risk. That they hear the cops are sending underage kids around. Looking to snag them. I say it's just a rumor. But they don't want to trust me.

Rough night. I can't catch a break.

Keep thinking what the hell am I going to do.

Give up?

Go down to the factories. Hand in my resume. Beg whoever takes it to consider me. Tell them I'll do anything for a chance. But I know that doesn't work. It's a job for men, not grovelers.

Just before closing someone takes pity on me. Takes my money and comes back with whiskey for me. The first gulp burns. It helps. I'm appreciative. I slide it down into the paper bag it came in. Put it in my back pocket.

I walk down the main street of the city. Take a drink from time to time. All the stores are closed. Empty for years. Nobody walks down the street. Just me. Cars pass. Freshly graduated kids yelling out the windows of their dad's sedan.

They never miss a chance to call me faggot.

The bottle is still three quarters full when I get home. The lights in my place are off. My roommates gone. I'm glad. I don't feel like talking. I stand at the door for a minute. My key in my hand. Across the hall I can hear Greaseback and Mitch. The laughter of girls. It comes through their door.

I turn the key in mine.

Walk into the living room. Turn on a lamp. There's a note on the table.

My roommate is at a party. Says I'm invited. There'll be girls. Booze. Good times. I put the note back where I got it from. Turn off the light. Walk down the short hall and go into my room.

The streetlight coming in the window is nice. I take my sleeping bag and pillows and push them up into the corner. I get down on the floor and lean against it. Light a cigarette. Take another drink.

I sit there like that for hours. Never getting up. Only moving to readjust my weight. Or light another smoke. I look out the window and through all the years. And I wonder if things will ever change. Or if I'm destined to be sad forever.

It's late when my roommate comes in. I can hear Carl's laughter mixed with his. My roommate calls out to see if I'm home. Carl says I'm probably sleeping. I don't correct them. I just sit here. In the dark. Waiting for the silence to come back.

15.

Since welfare's not on my ass I take my time. This is the end of it. Until I have to face things. And admit that I'm adult. So I lay around. Take advantage. Act like my life doesn't terrify me. Like I don't lie awake sweating pure fear most nights.

Because things don't sound good. That most of the factories around her are going to start pulling out. Moving their operations to climates where people are hungrier. And expect less from life.

And the companies that aren't moving out are scaling back. Dropping production from 24 hours a day to 8. 1500 men out of job in one place. 800 at another. Now there's all these middle-aged men crawling through the streets. Desperate. Because they have families on their backs. Payments.

A lifestyle they've surely grown attached to.

So how can I compete with that kind of incentive? Which is a lot more than I've got going on. Because when I think about it, I'm not really ready to give in like that yet. I just want to sleep late. Wander around free. Like a bum. No worries or cares. Maybe I'll even grow my hair long. Maybe I'll stop giving a shit altogether.

And I already feel lighter.

Although it doesn't feel like an option.

In the end I convince myself I don't have the balls to pull it off. I'm too weak and scared. And I'm not even sure of what. The shame of it. Because I don't have the things I'm supposed to have. Or won't ever. That I'll lose all the people in my life. That I won't be making my parents proud.

But the fear wins out. And the ease of my father's life sounds appealing. He's got a boat and a house and two cars and four weeks paid vacation. All the amenities. The American dream we keep seeing on cable television.

Also it's what I'm supposed to do. I have expectations to live up to. And even though they're not very high, I don't think I have what it takes.

So instead of giving up completely I just bide my time. One last summer I keep telling myself, Live it up while you can. Because come September I'm going to have to start marching into personnel departments all over the city. Application in hand. My head held high.

And I'm certain the head of personnel will notice it right away when I walk in the door. That I have the stink of mindless labour on my skin. And that factory life is the only thing I know.

It'll be a breeze, I tell myself. And I enjoy my summer. Most of the people I know are all around. So there's always someone over at the apartment. Bringing booze. We sit on our porch in the evenings. Drink until early the next morning.

Some of them are working fast food jobs for the summer. Trying to save for school in the fall. Others are like me. Bumming around and banking on the same jobs in the same dwindling industry.

They tell me they've handed in applications at all the big places. And the look of hopeless desperation on their faces as they tell me how they get up every day dreaming of the call. The one from a cold voiced secretary asking you to report for an interview.

It makes me sick. And I don't want to be like them. I don't want to be some desperate fucking kid looking to become his father. I want to go see places. And live in other cities. And I need to explore before I get settled into dying.

And as the summer races on more often the news of lay-offs trickles into my apartment. And I don't know what I'm going to do. Things aren't looking as easy as I thought they were going to be.

I get worried. I stop sleeping. I only leave the house for the most basic of things. Food. Something to drink. Most of my time is spent in front of the TV. Unsure of the images flickering in front of me.

In the second last week of August when my caseworker calls, I crack. Because she tells me she needs to see me. That I have to sign some documents. And she wants to go over my claim. Seeing how it will be changing as of the September 1st.

She says words like job hunting. Resume building. Workfare. I don't think I have what it takes. And I decide that I'm going to go back to school. Do another semester. I'll tell her I want to apply for university. That I want to get some of my grades up. So I call a school and make an appointment.

I don't want to go back to the one I just left. I'd have to answer too many questions. Like what in the hell are you doing back here? So I pick one on the other side of town. One that's not going to be easy to get to.

They tell me that I need to get my transcripts. So I call the school. They tell me it's no problem. But I'm going to have to wait until school starts. They're understaffed at the moment and have too much preparation to do.

Which is fine by me. Putting things off is my specialty. And when the day of the appointment with my caseworker comes, I walk there slowly. Taking every second I can.

When I see her I sigh to myself. Her beauty. The kind manner she treats me with. It's currently the closest thing I know to love.

We sit down and she asks why I want to go back to school. I spit out some half lie about wanting to get some of my grades up. That I think now is the best time to do it. Then in January I can get a decent job. Start saving. Then maybe apply for university next fall.

Her smile lights up the room as I'm blathering on. I almost lose track of what I'm saying. Feel faint several times. Imagine a perfect life where we met and fell in love.

She tells me that she's happy for me. That it sounds like I'm getting my life back on track. And I wish I felt the same way. Instead it feels more like I'm spinning around in the mud. Sinking. And too dumb and panicked to come up with a way to save myself.

I tell her I can't get things going until the school year starts. She says that it's fine. She'll extend my claim as a student. But the second I get the confirmation I need to call her. Give her some kind of proof.

When I leave I'm not sure what I've done. If it's for the better or not. I like the idea of going to school. Getting an education in something. But I know it's not going to happen. That I just can't sit in a classroom anymore.

And before I get home I'm sure I'm doomed to fail.

· · · · · · · ·

On the first morning of school I know it's a mistake. That I shouldn't have done this. How hard can looking for a job be. At least then I could roll out of bed at my convenience. Make my way as I please.

I think I'm afraid to not have a schedule. I didn't exactly do anything constructive during the teachers strike. And I wasted away a summer. When I could've had all my applications filled out. In line with all of my friends.

The long, hour walk there I berate myself with insults. You goddamned coward, you idiot. Are you capable of thinking things through? There's no wonder you have no one in your life. You're shit.

I get there early enough to stand around out front of the school. Mitch is still going here. I have some other friends here too. Most of them are huddled around a set of stairs near an entrance close to the automotive and wood shop departments.

For the rest of them this is already their fourth week of school. There was trouble with my transcripts. It took longer than expected. So I was starting with a handicap. I listen to my friends laugh. I think about how useless it all is.

And my buddy George asks if I want to go get something to eat. He's buying in celebration of my first day. I can't resist. I'll just sign in after first period I say to myself as I'm getting into the front seat of his shitty car. Smoke in mouth. I'll tell the office I had some trouble judging how long it'd take to get there.

It's my first day. It's the only chance I'll get to use the lie.

But before I realize it we're driving down to Lake Eerie. To sit on the edge of the coast. Our legs dangling over the edge of Hawk's Cliff. Passing back joints and a bottle of whisky. Smoking cigarettes and enjoying the last days of summer.

It takes another week before I even try going in again.

I get lost in the halls. The place is like a maze. And the students are cramped in. I get to class just after the bell. I stand in the doorway silently. The old woman at the front of the class eyes me with suspicion. I don't know what to do. So I wave.

'Well, what would you like?' she asks. And even though she's polite, I can tell the rumors I'd heard this morning from friends when I told them my teacher's name were probably true. That she was horrible.

I tell her my name. She feigns excitement. Throws her bony hands in the air. Tells me the whole class has been wondering if I was real or not. Have been speculating on whether I might ever show up.

Through it all I just stare at her. Until she asks me to take a seat. The only one open is in the back. Some relief. I sit down. Wonder how many more times I'm going to have to go through this again today.

The old woman starts her lesson. I'm lost from the beginning. She's talking about some book the rest of the class has read. I do my best impression of someone who's listening.

By the time the bell rings I fell like I've aged a million years. And before I get to leave I'm asked to stay back a minute. I need to be issued books. And lectured on how hard I'm going to have to work.

And I wish I was back home. Rolling cigarettes from the butts of my roommates stubbed out ones.

At least there I feel like I have *some* dignity.

When I get outside most people are coming back in from break. Making their way to the next class. I see George. I stop him and bum a smoke. He asks me how it went. I tell him this is a huge mistake. Before he hustles off to class, he laughs at me. Tells me I better not be late.

And the whole day continues like that. Me, just behind the rest of the world.

When the last bell rings and I'm given my last set of heavy books to lug around, I'm exhausted. Walking home becomes my worst nightmare. My feet and my back are killing me. It takes me forever. And by the time I turn the key in my door the sun has set and I'm wondering what it's going to be like to get old.

My roommate is sitting on the couch. His feet are on the coffee table. Partially obscured by several plates and bowls stuck together in the centre. I don't have the stomach to verify my suspicions. But I think the top one has moldy beans in the bottom.

He looks up at me. Nods his head and asks how school went. Just behind him I can see two large garbage bags leaning against the inside of the patio door. Neither are tied shut. And both are overflowing.

I ignore it and answer his question. Tell him it was shit. That the workload I have to catch up on is tremendous. That even now. Instead of relaying my day to him I should be in my room. Reading at least three books.

He laughs at me. Tells me he thinks I'm crazy. That I shouldn't have gone back. That I should be enjoying the good life. Read some books or something. And what makes me want to strangle him is that he's right. And he was right when he told me the same thing weeks ago.

I sit down on the couch. He starts to roll a joint and I have to admit he's a pretty good guy sometimes. When he's not gloating at my continual bad choices. He asks if I have any money. He's thinking about ordering a pizza.

And there's nothing I want more in the world. But my pockets are too full of lint to keep any money in there. So I decline. Get up and boil some water for rice. He doesn't stop rolling to call the closest delivery place.

We smoke the joint. His pizza comes just as I'm fluffing my rice. He eats his and enjoys every bite. I'll continue to live another day. But there's not a chance in hell I'm going back to that school I decide.

. . . .

A week or so goes by. I don't tell my caseworker that I've given up. My claim is going to change the second I do. I'll have to face things. Make a resume. Go out into the world to try and make something of myself.

Which doesn't sound appealing to me at all.

And I don't want to shatter the image of myself I've created. I can't stand the thought of her frowning with disappointment. After my big speech about how I was going to go to university. Was going to be something.

But I can't keep it to myself for long. Because the principal keeps calling me. Harassing me really. Trying to get me to tell him that I'm not going to come in anymore. So him and his staff can forget about me.

But I refuse to answer the phone. Instead, I listen to his messages. Laugh when his voice sounds pathetic. But one morning I fuck up. It's early and I'm not thinking. I pick it up and answer.

He tells me who it is. I realize what I've done. Another check mark beside a long list of every imaginable fuck up possible. He tells me it's over. That I've missed too much school. There's no way of getting caught up.

And I hear myself pleading with him. Telling him that I think I'm up to it. That I just got off on the wrong foot. That I was planning on showing up today.

He tells me to face the facts. And I can see there's no chance of convincing him otherwise. 'Well, Mr. Ottawa,' I tell him, 'it's been fun. You run a hell of a school and I thank you for your time.'

I hang up before I have a chance to hear what he has to say.

Slumping down into the couch I see an open pack of smokes on the table. It's neither my roommates or my brand. So I pull one of them out. Light it. Stick the pack in my pocket as I hear my roommate open his bedroom door.

I stare at the wall. Smoking. Listening to my roommate take a piss down the end of the hall. The toilet flushes and he comes into the living room. A dirty afghan around his shoulders. His eyes are bright red. Looks like he's forgotten to take his contacts out again before falling asleep.

'Who the hell was that?'

'Mr. Ottawa.'

'Who's that?'

'The vice principal.'

'What did he want?'

'Kicked me out of school. '

'Surprised it took so long.'

'Me too.'

He doesn't say anything. Walks back to his room. Shuts the door.

I light a cigarette with the end of the one I finish. Get up and open the screen door. It's cold out. The air feels good. I leave it open when I go sit back down. By the time I finish the smoke I decide I have to call my caseworker.

She doesn't answer the phone so I leave a message. Briefly outline what happened. Leave out how I've only gone one day. Sit back and wait for her to call me. Which only takes about an hour. Her voice sounds disappointed.

I knew it.

She tells me that I'm going to have to start handing in a job search sheet by the 15th of every month. If I don't, they hold my check. Then I starve. She also tells me she's going to get in touch with the unemployment office. Sign me up for some job finding workshops.

If I miss one they hold my check.

And then there's workfare. She'll get me on a crew as fast as can be. I'll have to volunteer somewhere once a month. Forced manual labour. I resented the idea of. But if I was even a second late they they'll hold my check.

After I agree with everything she says I hang up. And from now this is it. Before I could lie. Tell people I was a student. Which implies that I'm going somewhere. That I'm doing something with myself.

But not anymore.

It's official.

I'm the high water mark of what failure feels like.

16.

One afternoon I'm sitting around. Doing nothing. Just staring at the wall. There's a knock on the door and I'm thankful. I haven't said much the last few days. Since my roommate got a job in a restaurant I don't see him as much. Our lives are different.

When I open the door Greaseback is standing there. He doesn't have a shirt on. His long black hair down to his shoulders. He has a box of beer in his hand. So I invite him in.

He sits on the couch. Opens a beer. And passes one to me. Both of us flick our caps somewhere into the apartment. A habit that started one night I no longer remember. But the ritual carried on. And now the things are piling up all over the place.

He tells me we're celebrating. That Mitch and him are moving out of this fucking dump. That they found a nice old loft downtown. Cheap rent. Lots of space. And, as Greaseback tells it, he's in with the superintendant.

Some man he used to do odd jobs for.

So of course I beg him to get us a place as soon as he can. His only answer is a wink and long drink off his bottle.

I sip my beer. Light a smoke and listen to Greaseback bitch. Says the landlord came down hard on them. That the place was ruined. That all the carpets were going to have to be replaced.

I laugh. Remembering that I've never seen them with their shoes off. Or that night I spent making fun of the black paths worn into their living room and hallways. And both Mitch and Greaseback dismissing me with a wave of the hand.

'We fought the fucker though,' Greaseback says. 'We'll save some money by installing it ourselves,' he laughs.

'Really?' I ask. Not knowing what's so funny. To me it sounds like a lot of hard work. I'd let the landlord do it. Just another bill to skip out on.

'Yeah fuck, I've installed a million carpets.' He holds his body in a casual posture. But there's so much confidence in him it's hard for me to not change my opinion. And before I know what I'm doing I tell him I'll come over and help.

So the next two months I spend hoping he'll forget. I've seen him lose track of his apartment for Christ's sake. So I figure I've got a good shot of weaseling out of it. I just have to keep my mouth shut. But I'm wrong. Like always.

And when the time comes Greaseback is there at my door. So all I can do is hang my head and follow him across the hall. Like some fool. But I tell myself this will show him. He'll get us a place in his new building.

Then things can stay just similar enough where I can convince myself nothing has changed at all. Because I don't like the idea of them moving out. I've become attached. And I can't admit it to myself. But this is my family.

And I took losing my real one all right. Though I'm not so sure I'm going to handle this as easily.

Greaseback and I walk into the apartment. Mitch is standing in the middle of the empty living room. His hands on his hips. Taking it all in. He smiles when he hears us come in.

He tells us he has it figured out. He's going to start at the bathroom down the hall. Rip up that end and then slowly walk backwards to the living room. Then the 3 of us can pull the rest of it up in one great big piece.

I like the way he talks. And I begin to feel like this is going to be a snap. My level of confidence rises when he gets a good grip on the edge. And the next thing I hear is long ripping sound. Like a large strip of Velcro coming slowly undone.

As he walks backwards I start to feel like I should cheer him on. Shout slogans at him. Pump my fist in the air. Whistle. All manners of degenerate behavior. I'm getting swept up in the moment. And everything seems possible.

By the time he gets to where the hallways opens up into the living room there's a full cascade of sweat running from his hairline. I wonder how it's even possible to see through it. And I remember that he's at least five times as strong as I am.

Greaseback is wiry. Has the strength of a guy who's never known anything but physical labour. He'll manage. But I'm a fat lazy fuck. I've ballooned up under the pressure of all the rice I eat and the long days of doing nothing.

So this might kill me.

Mitch keeps at it. And when the first corner of the living room is pulled up Greaseback dives in and starts pulling. He grunts as he yanks. I step backwards. Waiting my turn to grab a hold of this dust-filled carpet and start sweating.

And when I get my chance I'm soaked within seconds. I'm huffing. Expelling air like a steam engine breaking down. I can hear my heart beat in my temples. And I can't recall the age limits on having a stroke.

By the time we finish with our backs against the opposite wall we're all beat. But Greaseback offers to pull the last strip up by himself. I look at Mitch. He's already lighting a cigarette and leaning against the kitchen wall.

Greaseback I and roll it up when he's done. I ask how in the hell we're going to get it out of here. Mitch points his thumb in the direction of the balcony door. The three of us pick it up and heave it over the railing. A light brown cloud of dust is spit out into the air when it hits the ground.

We smoke while Mitch and Greaseback decide how to go about this. They figure it'll be easy. The roll of carpet they have is the width of the living room. So all we have to do is spread some glue and roll it out.

Greaseback takes the bucket of glue and dumps it out onto the floor. He laughs while he creates a small yellow lake. Saying the poor fool who tries and tears this up next time is going to have a hard go of it.

And I don't disagree.

Mitch and I position the new roll along the wall. And when Greaseback is done spreading out the glue we kick it. And walk slowly behind the unrolling carpet. Underneath we can feel the glue. It squishes. We slide.

Mitch cuts it to size. We stomp the thing down as best we can. Some of the glues pisses out the edges. Greaseback takes an old striped towel. Wets it in the sink. Starts sopping the glue up. His left eye tightly closed. His cigarette smoke threatening to blind it.

I begin to wonder what the building will be like without them here. The rest of the neighbours don't want anything to do with us. The one night we got invited over to our neighbours place, by the time we left we'd been accused of stealing a Kiss CD.

He swore he didn't do it. But I'll always believe it was Greaseback.

I take a look around at their place as we stand there. The white walls are more of drab grey. Stained. The ceiling begins to feel lower than normal. I tell myself it's just the fumes from the glue. All this smoke. And not a single window open.

But I can't shake the feeling that I'm living in a nightmare.

I remember the beach house. And how the days there were better. I could walk out the front door and be sitting by the water in less than 5 minutes. I could look out on Lake Erie. And everything would feel better.

At least for a while.

I have no escape here. And I admit to myself that the apartment is beginning to feel like a cell. That the days are beginning to feel longer. It's getting easier to never leave. I'm surrounded by suburbs. A shopping plaza that's best attraction is an over-priced pharmacy.

There's no life here, Stan, I tell myself. The place is a wasteland. Filled with brain dead bags of flesh and skin. You're better than this. And these bums. You must get the hell out of here. Before you become the same kind of degenerate as those in the courtyard. Barbequing hot dogs at all hours.

Mitch takes some initiative. Measures the hallway. Then takes the bucket of glue and a shitty old paintbrush with him. Starting at the bathroom door he draws out a huge cock shooting a load of jizz all over the landlord's name.

We laugh. Thinking about the next people pulling up the rug. This message left for them. And whether or not they'll know the landlord. His name. But the three of us are all sure of one thing. That there's no room for disagreement.

They leave the bucket of glue open in the middle of the kitchen. Mitch tosses the paintbrush out the screen door. Down with the rest of the carpet. Greaseback grabs a 12-pack from the fridge and we go back to my place.

We all sit down on our couch. Mitch has to kick a few magazines and a sub wrapper off before he can sit down. Little bits of lettuce and Italian dressing go all over the floor. I wonder what I'll draw under the carpet when we have to replace it.

Greaseback hands out some beers. The three of us flick our caps. We hear them clink against others. Mitch takes a look around and says that he's glad to be getting out of this dump.

I watch Greaseback nod his head and laugh. I tell them that they have to put a good word in for me. That I can't stand living in this shithole another second.

Mitch takes a drink. Looks at me out of the corner of his eye. And I'm not sure what he's about to say to me. He looks like he could kill me or start laughing. His eyes make me uncomfortable. I look down at my beer. Anywhere but at him.

'You know Stan,' he says, 'I'll put in a good word for you. But not your roommate. The guy's an obnoxious prick.'

I laugh a little. But he doesn't. I look at Greaseback and he nods his head along. And I wish I was better at knowing if people are joking with me.

Sitting here on the couch like this. Them looking at me. It reminds me of every interaction I had as a kid. With people at school. My parents at home. That I just didn't fit in. That I was somehow always being left out. And the whole world was laughing at me.

And I thought these guys were my friends. That I could trust them. And I'm beginning to get a little sick of always being wrong.

Greaseback drains his beer and says they should be going. They have a lot to do he says. Mitch agrees. Before they walk out the door Greaseback gives me a couple more beers for my trouble. And tells me he'll put in a good word for us.

I sigh.

After they leave I open another beer and go on the balcony. There's four families already out there. Barbeques blazing. The familiar smell on the air. I light a smoke and take a sip. Tell myself that I'm not like these people. Yet.

But I'm on the same road. That's for sure. I just need to gain a few more pounds. And completely give up. If I stay around here too long it's going to sort itself out.

Numberless chapter

My beautiful caseworker follows through with her threats. She sets up an appointment with a councilor. Some woman whose job it is to make me look employable. She knows all the tricks, my caseworker tells me, and if you weren't on welfare her services would cost a lot of money.

The night before I have to go see her I pick up all our empty cans and bottles. They've been piling up forever. It takes me over an hour to drag them all back to the drop off. I get $12,50 in return. The first thing I do is buy a pack of smokes. And I walk home smiling. Feeling like a king.

In the morning I go over to a coffee shop nearby. It sits in the center of a parking lot. The drive-thru window snakes around the building and I almost get crushed between two cars navigated by anxious drivers. Scared of being late.

I smack the hood of the car facing me. It's loud. People inside the place look out at me. And I know I should just go inside. Get my coffee and leave. But instead I point through the windshield. Right in the driver's face. And call him a prick.

Which makes me feel pretty good. And I stand a little bit taller as I stride up to the door. I hear the driver behind me say Hey. And I turn around. His head is stuck out the window. He calls me a faggot. Says I'm lucky. That if he weren't late he'd be over here breaking my teeth.

I laugh and wave him off. I have an appointment to keep. Most of the people look at me when I walk in. None of them probably saw me almost get crushed. And think I've been acting irrationally. They expect more of a show.

But like usual, I disappoint. And after I get my large coffee I leave without saying a thing.

The walk is long. And I can start to feel the winter cold in the air. I look down at my shoes and know they aren't going to cut it. And the jacket I'm wearing is too thin for the awful days in January.

I think about the appointment as I walk. What the hell this woman is going to do for me. I don't need her to tell me what to do. It's pretty straightforward. Make a resume. Hand it in. Lie to the person who interviews you. Tell them you love working. That whatever the place is this is where you want to be.

But I just don't want a job. The idea scares me to death. Because I don't want to throw my life away like that. I want to bum around. Spend time in the grass. Read books. Smoke. Enjoy my days.

Not buy things. Like houses and cars and pools and freezers full of meat and six different flavors of ice cream. I don't see how I need all that to be happy. But every conversation I end up in about the future, the vision is always the same. All the things they'll one day own.

Which feels like a bone in my throat. Cutting off my oxygen. And I can't see why people waste so much energy on it. And I guess this is what my parents and teachers and guidance councilors meant when they said I have a bad attitude.

I'm relived when I finally get to the unemployment office. My feet are freezing and damp. I'm tired from the walk. And all I want is to sit down. But first I walk up to the counter. Announce myself. Sign in.

The woman behind the counter smiles at me. Tells me I have to fill out some forms. She hands them to me. Points to a collection of round, communal tables. In the middle of each one is a cup with pens in it.

I go over and sit at the one with only one other person sitting at it. To me he looks old. But he's probably in his mid-30's. He's filling out a collection of forms as well. And I feel united by our poverty. I smile and nod at him as I sit. All he does is stare.

Which is kind of unnerving. But I do my best to ignore him as I look over the forms in front of me. I fill in my name and address. Birth date. My education. And then it asks me for my work history. Which isn't very long.

For the first one I write in fishmonger. And under duties I write down shoveling ice. Because after that I draw a blank. The only other things I ever remember doing is hiding between the large tubs filled with pickerel and ice to smoke a cigarette. Or sneaking to the bathroom to jerk off.

Both of which I felt were better left out.

In the next space down I write tobacco picker. And under duties I write down picking tobacco. I put the pen down. Look over at the man across the table. And he's still staring at me. And I can't tell if he's dead inside or full of rage.

I don't really want to ask either. So when I hand the forms back to the secretary I go and sit somewhere else. In a row of single chairs along the wall. And out of his line of sight.

I take a look around. The whole place looks like it's been painted the same colour as a cold rainy day. Which makes the experience even worse. And I can feel myself becoming more and more dejected. I'll never get hired by anyone I think. I'm a piece of shit. I should probably just slit my wrists in the tub tonight.

And maybe that's what the government wants. The reason they paint the place like this. To get us thinking the kind of thoughts that lighten the load on taxpayers. And create easy work for county coroners.

I look over at the secretary. Sure, she smiles. But I wonder how many nights she spends in front of the bathroom mirror. Her eyes red from crying. A bottle of sleeping pills in her hand.

I hear my name called. And I look up. I see a woman with short hair in a grey polyester suit. The suit's a shade lighter than the wall. She has glasses. And in her hands are some papers. Probably the ones I just filled out.

I stand up and walk over. I introduce myself and try to be polite as possible. I want her to think well of me. I want her to tell my case-worker that I was agreeable. I want this to go as smooth as possible.

She signals me to follow her. And I do. We weave our way deeper into the unemployment office. At the entrance to a cubicle she stops and asks me to seat myself. I look over the top. Into the next one. Another caseworker. Another bum.

I sit. She walks behind her desk and I look at the ground. There's something I don't like. A feeling in the air. This place stinks of failure. From this woman in front of me to people sitting in the reception area. We're all fucking doomed.

And with an attitude like that it's hard to see how they're going to help me.

But of course the woman in front of me blathers on. I nod and nod. She tells me everything I already know about myself. That I graduated high school. That I'm on welfare. That I I've been told I need to get a job.

She asks me if I brought a copy of my resume with me. I tell her I don't have one. Her eyes go dinner plate big. She's shocked. She looks like I'm the first person to have ever said this. I ask myself what's wrong with me. I ask myself what have I been doing with my life.

'Well, do you have any work experience?' she asks me. I shrug my shoulders. Roll my eyes. She's got it all right there in front of her.

But I give in. And I go over my work history verbally. She nods along. And when I finish I can tell she's waiting for me to keep going. But I don't have anything left. I don't have the confidence it takes to start lying on the spot. So I just stare at her. Hoping she'll take some initiative.

Which she does.

'What kind of job are you looking for?' she asks me. And I get the feeling she expected some guy to come in with a bunch of experience. And skills. And training and all the shit you need to get a job. She expected to not have to do a thing.

'I just want to work in a factory,' I tell her. And the words come out of my mouth like lead. It's not what I want. What I want is to be back at home. Smoking cigarettes and thinking about girls.

But it's the right thing. Because her face takes a new turn. Like this is the kind of goal she can easily achieve. She'll be going home some day soon with a smile on her face. And feeling she's done some good.

She tells me first thing first I need is to make a resume. No one is going to hire me without a resume. Not even a fast food kitchen. Let alone a mighty factory. So when she gets up I follow her. Back out into the reception area.

When we get to a row of computers we stop. She explains to me that I can come here anytime I want to work on my resume. That that's what they're here for. She asks if I know how to write a resume. I tell her no. She says it's easy.

'Just pick a template and fill it in,' she tells me. And I wonder how hard it is to get her job. Because so far she hasn't had to do a thing. There's no way she's going home with an aching back tonight.

She sits me down. Opens a computer program and shows me where to get a template. I'm told to pick the one I think best represents me and my intentions. That a resume is how I'll be judged. That I need to make the right choice.

'When you're done let the receptionist know, I'm going to need to check it over,' she says over her shoulder as she's walking back to her cubicle.

I stare at the screen. Lean back in the chair. Contemplate getting up and walking out. Down the street and out of this city. And this life. But I don't. I scroll through the templates. I pick the one that asks for the least amount of information.

I type in my name where it tells me to do so. And there it is. Stan Acker in bold black letters. It gives me nausea. I want to lie down.

I put in my address and telephone number. Which is easy enough. But the next section is goals. I type in 'to not starve' and 'pay the rent' but it doesn't look right. I know that woman back in her cubicle is going to give me that look again.

So I delete it. Think about what this woman is going to want to see. What is some asshole sitting at his desk in the personnel office going to want to read. And I think I have it. I write in the space provided.

'I'm looking to get a full time job in your company so I can start my life. Buy a house and start a family.'

If only my guidance councilor could see me now. He'd be so proud. It's all the advice he ever gave me wrapped up into a couple short sentences. Even though I think I could of gotten the point across even quicker.

'I want to give up.'

I move down and start filling in the rest of it. Jobs and my duties. I try and spice it up a bit. Make it sound flashy. But it's not easy. Especially since most of the tasks I've had to perform involved some kind of awful mess and me doing a third rate job cleaning it up.

I look over what I've written so far. And I have to admit that it's pretty fucking sparse. It doesn't do a thing to dazzle me. Grab my attention. And I can already see it being crumpled into a ball. Thrown into a garbage can without a second thought.

At the end of the template there's a hobbies section. A little spot to give the employer a glimpse into your life. Here's my chance I think. I'll tell them I'm a big reader. That I like to draw. I'm a man of culture.

And this is what I write down. My innocence getting the better of me. Not realizing that factories don't want someone who's doing a lot of thinking. And I should've written down watch sports. Barbeque. Scratch my ass.

Because then at least it might seem like I'll fit in. And I won't shake the boat.

I print out my resume. I close the file. When it asks me to save it I click on no. Get up and collect my sheet of paper from the printer. Look at it. And think this is it. It's concrete. I'm going to get a job. I'm going to have to do something with myself.

When I tell the receptionist I'm done, she smiles at me. And I think I could get used to this. I don't even mind sitting there 15 minutes in a shitty chair. My legs stretched out waiting for the councilor to come and approve of my resume writing genius.

But when she comes out she looks it over for longer than it should take. I tell myself she just needs to read it a second time. To take in the precision I employed to describe all my former duties.

'There's not much here is there?' she asks when she looks up from it, 'I think what you need is to take our resume writing workshop.' She goes on about how it'll really help me. And that she'll sign me up. Let my caseworker know.

I sigh a little. She asks me if I'm alright. I tell her yes. That I'm just relived to be getting the help that I need. It's tough to say without gagging. But I must pull it off. Because she looks at me like I'm one of the good ones.

'One last thing before you go today, Stan,' she says to me. I follow her over to another corner of the office. There are a bunch more computers. But these ones are housed in wooden casings. They look like boring arcade machines.

She tells me this is the job bank. That all the available jobs in the city can be found here. And that each morning it gets updated. So the more I come down the better chance I have of finding employment.

When she's done with her spiel she asks if I have any questions. I tell her no. And that it's been a pleasure to meet her. She says the same thing to me. And adds that she thinks I'll have a job in no time. That things are going to pick up.

She takes her leave and I sit down. Look at the screen. Want nothing to do with it. There's a man a few places down from me. When he notices me looking at him he gives me a dirty look. Positions himself so I can't see his station.

Like I'm going to go steal his job somehow. Or even care.

I spend some time scrolling through the jobs. Every one that asks for unskilled labour always has a catch. Like it's so far out in the middle of nowhere that I could never get there. Or the position is only open to those on unemployment benefits.

A lot of the other ones are in fast food places making hamburgers and mopping up grease. But I tell myself that I'm better than that. That's a job for some teenage brat. I'm a high school graduate. I'm out on my own. I need something a little more respectable.

There's a couple ads for factories. The pay is good. Full medical benefits after three months. I take down the information. Write it on the back my resume. Convince myself that that this is it. My chance.

I get up and go over to the photocopier. Make a few copies. Fold them neatly and slide them in my back pocket. Walk past all the circular tables. In my head I call the people sitting there fools. Sure that any day now I'd be a big man with a good paying job.

When I get outside it's midafternoon. I'm feeling better than when I went in. I'll get a job and then I won't have to go to that stupid resume workshop. Fuck that woman and her bullshit. And to prove her wrong I pull out my résumé. Read it over.

But when I'm done I'm not so excited. Because the thing is full of spelling errors. I sound like a moron in it. All the copies are already beat up. Dog-eared. And if there's one thing I know. Is no one trusts a man with a filthy resume.

I stand in the street. Hang my head. Pull all the copies from my back pocket and stuff them in the first garbage can I see. I start walking home. My feet drag along the pavement. I'm in no rush.

I'm still cold. And I could use another coffee. I don't have enough change left to get one. I think about begging people on the street. But the last time I tried that I got a rude awakening. Small town people aren't all that kind.

Instead of being showered with change and offers to come home for dinner. They called me names. Like lazy piece of shit. Gave me advice like get a fucking job. So I learned my lesson. And decided to look for empty bottles.

I wander around looking in garbage cans. Dumpsters. It takes me until late in the day but I gather up a pretty good haul. And when I take it to the liquor store for the refund I get about $7. Which is more than enough for a coffee.

I walk down the main street. Through the downtown. Passed all the empty businesses. And for the time of day there's barely any one out. Even the road is basically empty.

The restaurant my roommate works at is just up the block. It' not open yet but I push my face up against the window. Look in. I can see him in the back. So I bang on the glass. He sees me. Comes over to let me in.

'How was your meeting?' he asks.

'Shit.' I tell him.

'What do you mean?'

I tell him all about it. How it went nowhere. How it wasn't that much help at all. How I ended up throwing the resumes I wrote in the garbage. I tell him I'm destined to be a failure. That I have to go to a fucking resume writing seminar.

And I must sound pretty pathetic. Because he offers me a cup of coffee. And I take it without hesitation. There's some buns on the counter nearby. I take one. Rip a hunk off with my teeth. Follow my roommate out a door.

The two of us sit down on some greasy milk crates. My roommate hands me a smoke. I take it with one hand and stuff the half eaten bun into my coat pocket with the other. After my roommate lights his smoke he holds out the flame to me. I inhale. I feel good.

My roommate and I sit there without saying a thing. Just smoking and drinking our coffee. And I think to myself that I don't need much more than this. And that life is pretty good. And who needs a job anyways.

17.

The resume writing workshop is just as bad as I imagine it. They hold the thing far in the back of the unemployment office. Past all the cubicles filled with polyester-clad councilors. The women as sweaty and dejected looking as the men.

We're stuffed into a long, narrow conference room. The lights hurt my eyes. Everyone else showed up with a pen. A notebook. Copies of their current resume. I don't have a thing.

And for a second I regret throwing my resumes in the trash.

There's six of us here. Another man and four overweight ladies in their 30's. The man keeps his head down. Doesn't make eye contact with anyone. But the women strike up a conversation. Start laughing. It makes me feel sick.

I don't know how they're having a good time.

A disheveled looking man comes in. His suit is crumpled. His tie loose. And what hair he has is wispy and sticking in the air at all kinds of angles. I think to myself, He must be pretty good at writing resumes, because he looks like hell.

The seminar is exactly what I thought it would be. Him telling us what employers look for. How to word things to make yourself sound like you're worth something. He has an overhead projector. Shows us some examples of what he's talking about.

One of the women keeps interrupting him. Asking questions. Or just running her mouth. Telling boring stories about job interviews she's had. I look around the room. I want the rest of the people there to be as bothered as I am.

Instead they all look like they like listening to her. And I wonder what is wrong with people.

But I suffer through it.

When it's done I go back out to the reception area. Sit down at one of the computers. Pick the same template as before. But now I take my time. Make sure that everything looks perfect. By the time I'm done the secretary is looking at her watch and ushering me out the door.

But for once I leave there feeling like it's going to work out.

I believe everything I'm told. That the resumes are the only thing I have going for me. And I have to make sure they get into the right hands. Given to the right people.

My handing out of the resumes has to be all meticulously recorded on a sheet if I want to get my check. The check gets delayed if I don't have the thing handed in on time. A task I can never seem to manage. Because every month I fuck up. And by the time I get off my ass and down there, it's already the 29th.

So another month and I'm behind on the rent. I tell Joe and he understands. But I know I'm pushing the limits with the landlord. And I wonder when Greaseback's going to call. And say there's a place available.

I don't have time to worry about this though. I have to actually go hand the things out. Which is another feat. None of the factories I apply to are anywhere near where I live. It's the stupidest thing in the world. Because even if I do get hired. I have an hour and a half walk just to get there. And the same coming home.

But I tell myself it's what I have to do. I'll just walk as long as I have to. I'm tough. And I have my youth. I'll get my driver's license as quick as possible. I'll buy a big fucking truck. And who knows, maybe I'll even begin to fit in.

So I get up early. Walk across the city. Out past where anyone lives. Along roads never meant for pedestrians. No food in my stomach. And knowing full well that I won't be getting home before sundown.

When I walk along the highways I think to myself, Jesus. It doesn't look too good. And I easily become depressed. So I pray that one of the cars or trucks that's screaming past can just veer to the right a little. The driver maybe looking for something under the seat. And roll right over me like a wayward raccoon. A bump in the road.

But I'm not a lucky kid that way. And they just blast along beside me. Sometimes yelling out insults that I only ever catch a syllable of. But I don't need to hear any more. I'm quick. I get the gist of things.

I'm a loser.

I don't have a car. Or even a clean shirt. So I can see their point. But I wonder how'd these assholes giving me shit get their cars. Their jobs. Didn't they ever have to walk along the shoulder of a dangerous road with nothing more than a little hope to keep them going?

And if they didn't, fuck them and their entire lives. I get worked up. And I'm convinced they all got jobs with ease. Did well in school. Eat great big hot meals every night. Fuck all the best looking girls.

I take pride in the fact that I don't do any of that. And when I go home I'm going to eat another pack of instant ramen noodles. Sleep alone. And remember how I barely scraped by.

Each place I apply to has a long driveway leading up to it. Usually a kilometer back from the road itself. And as I walk down here cars drive much slower. I look straight ahead. Pretend they're not there. The drivers looking at me, laughing at me from open windows.

And when they call me shithead and faggot and dick-licker I never break my line of sight. Because I know they're trying to get a reaction. A reason to pull over just ahead of me. Get out and slap me around. Something to laugh about in the break room.

I think about my old man. And how he said all he had to do was walk up. Then there it was. A job handed over just like that. But maybe he left a part out. Like why it was going to be so fucking humiliating. So degrading. Is this how he was shaping me to be a man?

When I get close, some one from the security booth usually meets me. They don't like when I get near to the building. And at every place they treat me the same way. Like some gentle retard. Or mental case. Someone to be placated. But never considered.

And month after month I go to the same places. So naturally I start to develop anxieties. I picture these fat oafs from places all over town. Getting together after their shifts. In the sports bar. Sitting on stools.

Devouring chicken wings. Gulping back light beer and laughing at me.

Thinking they're better than me.

And there's nothing I can do. But act polite. And humble. A silent form of begging for their acceptance. While underneath I'm boiling. Focusing all of my strength on not acting out of turn. Being a god damned gentleman.

Which keeps getting harder and harder. Because I'm certain that these fuckers are all in on it. And are out to get me. And all my hard work is for nothing. That I never have a chance from the beginning.

So when I hand over my resume and turn around, I make sure my heads up high. So they don't know they have me beat. I don't think I keep coming back because I want the job. I want to show these damn security guards something about persistence.

Not to mention I never know when welfare might look into things. When they might call up some of the numbers on the sheet I hand over. And when they do they need to hear that Yes, I have come by groveling for work.

I run into people. They ask what I'm up to. I'm too dumb or honest to lie. When they hear what I do they look at me like I'm crazy. Like there are easier ways. But no one ever offers up a solution.

In between going to places in person I routinely have to make my way to the unemployment office. Always making photocopies. Always scrolling through the hundreds of shitty listings in the job bank. Always being disappointed.

Most of the postings are looking for someone with experience. A few years in a relatable field. It doesn't make any sense to me. Because things like cutting lawns and painting sheds isn't that hard.

I wonder what happened in the world. I'd always thought that after high school things were going to be easy. I'd just jump right into it. Have the job in no time. And then my life would play just the same as everyone else's.

Rolling along as expected.

But it's not. And sitting in front of these computer screens is a sad affair. I usually leave without any hope left. And a few tears in my eyes. Not knowing what I'm going to do. And where my life is going to go.

I find a job listing for once. A nursery. Manual labour lugging pots of flowers. Sacs of dirt. It doesn't ask for anything other than that you show up. They're desperate. Or the job is so easy an ape can perform it. So I figure I'm fully qualified.

It's a good hike. But nothing like going out to the industrial section. It's just outside the edge of the city. By the high school I just graduated from. On the side of the highway towards the village I used to live in.

On the walk over I tell myself that I have this in the bag. That there's no way I won't impress the manager. He'll hire me and start thinking of me as his son in no time. I'll be running the place by next week.

But it's a long walk. And by the time I get there I'm sweaty. And disheveled looking. My hair is matted to the side of my head. I smell terrible. Did I even wear deodorant this morning?

I walk up from the shoulder of the road. A man in a green shirt and khaki shorts eyes me as I do. Since he's in the uniform I go straight over to him. Introduce myself and ask if I can see the manager.

He looks at me suspiciously. The same look I get from the security guards when I walk up to a factory. Like I'm crazy. But I just want a job. Just like every one else. And I don't get what I'm doing wrong.

Or this attitude. That I already have to be on my way to be trusted. And how the hell am I going to get things on track if cant find someone to trust me.

He tells me that he's the manager. And I can just give my resume to him. He'll take a look over it. Reluctantly I do. Because this isn't how I thought it was going to play itself out. Why haven't I been invited into his office for a cool drink and a place to sit?

When he takes the resume from my hand he does so like he's touching someone's stained underwear. He holds it with the least amount of his thumb and pointer finger. So far away from his body that I'm skeptical on whether he can read it or not.

'What did you say you're doing right now?' he asks me.

I tell him that I don't have a job. And that since I graduated high school I've just been out there hitting the bricks as they say. Trying to find somewhere that I can completely abandon myself to.

But I don't think my lie sounds that convincing. And from the way he looks at me I can see he doesn't either. He's nice enough though to tell me they've had a lot of applicants. And that they have a long and laboring decision ahead of them.

I nod my head. Smart enough to know this is a polite way of saying get the hell out of here. I smile at him. Say thanks. Although I'm not sure for what. And I walk away. Feel like shit. My head down. Not really paying attention to the cars going by. Or having any destination in mind.

But I end up back home. Because while I'm walking I can't help but have fits of tears. Shortness of breath. I catch the attention of people in cars. I notice them crane their necks. And I don't want anyone to see me breaking down like this. Or even worse. Ask if I need any help.

When I get in and lock the door behind me the place is quiet. There's no one here. My roommate must be working. Which gives me some relief. But not much. It just means I don't have to walk all the way to the end of the hall to my room. Instead I can feel like hell right here in the living room.

The building is silent. For once I can't hear the woman upstairs. She's always crashing around. My roommate says she's trash. That she's a whore. But I like the way she looks. And I wish I had the courage to introduce myself.

Which adds to my crushing defeat. I can't get a job. I can't make conversation with the suspected whore upstairs. I'm going to be on welfare forever. Or at least until I starve.

I get up and go into the kitchen. Look through the cupboards. Push aside empty bags. Shake a cereal box. Dump the dust and crumbs into my palm. Lick it clean. Behind that I find a pack of noodles. I start to boil some water.

All the dishes are in the sink. So I root through them. Find a bowl that looks like it will require the least amount of work to clean. Dig deeper through the mess. Find a sponge at the bottom. I pull it up. It's slimy. Covered in something grey.

I look through the cupboards and under the sink, which is all just wishful thinking. There was never a chance of a fresh sponge, still in its packaging waiting for me. That just wouldn't have made any sense.

So I close my eyes and sigh. Run the hot water until it starts to steam. Pick up the slimy grey sponge and lets the water run through it. I squeeze it repeatedly while telling myself that this will have to do.

When my hand can't take the heat any longer I decide the sponge is as good as it's going to get. Sure, it's not optimal but at least the slime isn't oozing from it anymore. I squeeze some of the watered down dish soap from the bottle. Scrub away the hardened bits of macaroni and cheese.

My water is boiling. I dump the dry noodles into the bowl, fill it with water and the accompanying spice pack. Walk back to the living room. Push aside all the junk on the coffee table, put down the bowl and wait for my dinner to cook.

This is it Stan, I tell myself. Your whole future. This damp couch. The filthy apartment. The shitty food. The disappointment. You better get used to it. And I figure what choice do I have.

I swirl my fork through the noodles. There's little resistance. I hunch over. I can smell the ashtray over my food, but I don't have the energy to move it.

Another chapter, maybe.

I get home from a long day. I'm beat. There were more insults hurled out of car windows today. More rocks in my shoes then normal. And every step in the direction of home made it feel like I was just adding another.

The whole day I had to fight the urge to lie down. Right there on the side of the road. Just let the dust slowly cover me. I know it might take years. But at least I'd be working towards something.

The first thing I do when I get in is take a shower. There's no one home. I leave the door to the bathroom open. So when the phone starts ringing I can hear it. I think about hopping out. Running down the hall. Water soaking carpet. But in the end I say fuck it.

Even though it seems like it's never going to stop ringing.

I take my time. Waste all the hot water. Hope that maybe my room-mate has an early shift. And is going to walk in the door any second. Expecting a hot shower. And get disappointment instead.

Then I could smile from the living room. Knowing that I fucked him over. Which would make my whole day seem a lot better. And the fact that it's super selfish would make it even better.

When I get out of the shower I look in the mirror. There's not much condensation. But I can't see much through all the caked on tooth-paste. Popped zits and smears of god knows what.

I get dressed. Go into the kitchen. I boil some water. There's no food but there's a tin of instant coffee. I hate the taste of it. Even with cream and sugar. And those aren't luxuries I can afford right now.

While the water boils I go sit on the couch. Pull an ashtray close to me. Start looking through it for large butted out cigarettes. I pick out all the ones I think are the most full. When I get a bunch I start gently rolling out all the tobacco of them. Catching it in the crease of an old newspaper.

When I'm done I have a pretty good-sized pile in front of me. Enough tobacco to last the rest of the night. And maybe even have a couple left for the morning. That's if I can control myself. Before I roll up a smoke I make my shitty coffee.

I pick up the home rolled cigarette. I sit back. Rest the cup of black liquid garbage on the arm of the couch. Inhale. Take a drink. And know that there's not many more combinations that taste quite as bad. But I just can't stop indulging.

I notice the light on the phone flashing. I remember the call. When I was showering. I pick up the receiver and dial the number for voice-mail. It's Greaseback's gravely voice.

'Hey shithead,' he says, 'I did it. There's a place opening up and it's all yours if you want it. Just get back to me quick.'

I can't believe it. We can move out of this dump. I yelp out loud. Roll up another smoke right away. I want to celebrate. I think about how I can get some booze. Or something.

I scour the ashtrays looking for some old roaches. A forgotten piece of hash. Anything to lighten the mood. To give the evening the air of festivities. God damn it. It deserves it. And I need it.

Of course I find nothing. So I take a look around the apartment. There's some empty bottles on the coffee table. A few more over by the large, bulging, black garbage bag in the corner. I get up and find a few more out on the terrace. In my bedroom. Even one in the shower.

But when I round them up it's pretty pathetic. I do the math. It's not even worth the fucking walk over. After I cash them in I'll still be short. Not enough money to get even the cheapest bottle of sherry.

So I sit back down. Beat. But still feeling on top of the world. The place where Greaseback and Mitch live is right across the street from city hall. Where the welfare office is. I'll never be late with my job search sheets again.

The unemployment office is just a few blocks away. Those meetings won't take up my whole day anymore. I can be right up that job bank's ass now. I'll be the first bum down there every morning. I'll finally get the worm.

The industrial section is still pretty far. But with the move I'll be able to shave off at least half the time it takes. Which is half as many insults. And half as many blisters.

My roommate works just up the street from the place.

This is going to be the best decision we've ever made.

I sit on the couch the rest of the night. I wait until early in the morning. When my roommate finally gets home. He's surprised to see me. I just point at the mug half filled with the third coffee I tried to drink. He nods.

When he sits down in his chair I tell him the news. He sighs with relief. Complains about the walk he just did. At two in the morning. Something he's been getting sicker and sicker of.

He rolls a big joint to commemorate the evening. When I take the first puff I think, ah finally. And know that now the night is complete.

In the morning I call Greaseback. I tell him we're in. And ask what we have to do. It's nothing he tells me. You just have to come see the place. Meet the superintendant. Which I say is no problem. And I tell him my roommate and I are both free the next day.

We go see the place at two the next afternoon. We all meet up in Greaseback and Mitch's. The super is a guy in his forties. He has a huge fat gut. And the skin on the back of his hands and neck and face looks cracked. Like some great big desert lizard in sweat pants.

He shakes our hands. Tells us that as long as we have the money we can have the place. And that any friend of Greaseback is a friend of his.

We follow him down the hall. Around the corner. He goes on about the person who just lived her. A single woman. How she was such a sweet heart. And how he was going to miss looking at her ass when he came by to do repairs.

I laugh along with him. Because as a man this is what I'm supposed to do. But it makes me feel sick. Getting stuck in a conversation like this. With some old greasy pig of a man.

He stops in front of a door. Fucks around with his keys. Finds the right one and unlocks the door. When we walk in I can't believe it. It's fucking huge. One long box the size of our current place. Two large 3 meter windows. Sunlight streaming in. A staircase leading to a second floor.

My roommate and I look at one another. And we know we're going to be signing a lease before we leave.

The first thing we do when we get home is go to the super's office. I let my roommate do the talking. He tells him we'll be moving out as soon as possible. That we've found a better place to live.

Which are harsh words. Considering this is what Joe considers perfectly good for his wife. And I can see he's a little hurt. But I'm just glad I'm not doing the talking. Because I'm notorious for fucking up. I don't know how to act around people.

Joe says that it's no problem. That the only thing is that the landlord is going to have to do a walk through. An inspection. He needs to make sure that we'll be leaving the place in a proper state.

I start up with the cold sweats. Worried that he's going to find something wrong. Something expensive. Like Greaseback and Mitch. Even though they replaced the carpet themselves it still cost $300.

And we still owe for that window. He's going come down real hard on that. I can see it now. Joe telling him we're on our way out. Him sitting in some great big chair. A ton of rings on his fingers. He's going to smile. Knowing that this is the moment to recoup all his loses.

By the time we get upstairs to our place I'm a god damned wreck. I have to pay first and last at the new place. Which is already more money than I know how to come up with. And now this. Fuck it I say when I sit on the couch. This is the end.

My roommate tells me to give it a rest. All we have to do is clean up. The place will look great. There'll be nothing the old piece of shit can say or do. And about the window. I bet he'll just be glad to get us out of here.

Like always, I admire his conviction. And I imagine he has some trick up his sleeve. Because he usually comes out of things untouched. But I'm not so cool and easy. I think that everything is going to blow up in his face.

And I'll just be there for the ride. Expected to pay half the bill.

Over the next two weeks I pack up all my stuff. Which still isn't very much. I can fit most of it into a couple of boxes and a backpack. The only thing I've really picked up is a mattress. Which was a hand me down. From a distant aunt who died.

My roommate does the same. We clean the place up. Scrub the floors and wash all the windows. I pick up all of the beer caps. When I'm done I count them. There's just over 200. And I view this as an accomplishment.

By the night that the landlord comes over I have to say that the place looks pretty good. But it doesn't matter. I'm still scared shitless. And about two hours before he's supposed to show up I tell my roommate I just want to go out. Get some fresh air.

He barely acknowledges me from behind the remote control.

I put on my shoes and walk out the door. Glad that he didn't say he wanted to come with me. Because I have no intention of coming back before the landlord shows up. I can't do it. I can't face him.

I walk around the neighbourhood. I've never done it before. Nothing about it interests me. I hop the chain link fence behind our building. Walk down the dead-end street that runs up to it. This is where our buddy Carl lives.

It's been awhile since I've seen him. These days not many people stop by. I guess it's lost its edge. And I wonder how he's doing. So I walk up to his house. Stand at the end of his driveway. Look at the lights on in the windows.

And I can't walk up to the door. Because I don't feel good in people's homes anymore. They look at me differently. Like they need to pity me. Or that as soon as their backs are turned I might steal something.

So I just stand there. Wondering what it'd be like to be like to live at home again. Things would be easier. I'm sure I could call up my old man. Tell him I'm starving to death. That I'm sick of the poverty.

But they expect that. Which means that I can't. Instead I'll make do with standing in the shadows. At the edge of the lawns of my friends' houses. Trying to imagine what it's like to get along with the people you're related to.

After a while I begin to feel like a pervert. A creep. Not because I'm trying to see some college girls firm tits. But because I'm spying on them. Hoping that some of their love might wear off on me. And I'll know what it feels like.

I keep walking in the direction opposite of where I live. I follow my way around the wide suburban streets. The ones with no sidewalks. Because everyone has a car.

It makes me feel like I don't belong. Like at any minute the cops are going to drive up slowly. Ask me what I'm doing. Where I'm going. My name. My address. My telephone number.

But I don't really know where I'm going. Every time I take a street in the direction I want to go it veers off just out of sight. Drags me deeper into the subdivision. And before I know it I have no idea where I'm going.

It takes awhile but eventually I see the lights of a larger street up ahead. I walk towards them. I start to see cars crossing. A good sign. I haven't seen a soul since I hopped the fence. I was beginning to wonder if I'd fallen off the map.

I know where I am when I get to the corner. It's about a half hour walk back home. I figure I can take my time. Maybe stretch it out. I should be good. It feels like I've been out forever. And the landlord has surely come and gone by now.

When I get home my roommate is sitting in the same chair. In the same position. The remote control held just as it was when I left. I wonder if he even moved. If the landlord has been here or not.

So I ask. And my roommate laughs. He tells me I've been gone three hours. I don't believe him. But when I look at clock I can see that he's right. I tell him what happened. How I got lost. The twisting and turning streets got the better of me.

He says it all went off without a problem. It was the nicest he'd ever seen the landlord act. And he didn't even mention the broken window. Or the money we owed. I asked my roommate if he was joking. And he convinced me he wasn't.

Well, I say to myself sitting on the couch, at least for once things are working out in my favour.

18.

Now that we live downtown I stop handing out my resumes. I figure at this point I can just forge the sheet. I'll write down the same places I've been going for months. If welfare calls, every one of them has a stack of the things with my name on it.

There's no way I can lose.

So I spend my days like a true welfare bum. Wandering around the downtown. Sitting on benches. Hitting up the Salvation Army for stale, molding bread and the odd can of beans. But I rarely make it there in time for those. Hungrier and more industrious poor people don't sleep as late as I.

I find a place where the coffee is still just 50 cents a cup. I get it to go in a Styrofoam cup. Sit on a bench across the street from our place. Watch people with jobs hurry around. Laugh to myself. And think for a second that I might have life figured out.

Some days I go down to the high school nearby. The one I tried and failed to go to after graduating. I still know people that go there. Casual acquaintances. I meet them on their breaks from time to time. Bum smokes. I try not to go often though. I need to be special. Or they'll never give me a thing.

And I start to understand my station in life. My poverty. What it means. I start to operate in survival mode. Other people lose their humanity in my eyes. I see them as an extra smoke. A can of beer. Some change. An uneaten pizza crust.

Which is rare.

And I transcend the shame of it. All the years of being taught that you support yourself come untangled in my mind. I no longer care. Because this is better than running to and from a job everyday.

So I come up with an idea. A way to supplement my income. I figure if I show up on someone's doorstep around dinnertime. Looking as pathetic and hungry as I can when they open up. It's hard for them to refuse. Because I'm a face they know.

It works. I go around the homes of kids I went to school with. Ones who still live with their parents. The one's I hear complaining about having to be home for dinner every night.

I show up around four o'clock in the afternoon. Get myself in the door. Show no signs of leaving, as the smell of food gets stronger. Ingratiate myself more in their living room. Make it impossible not to get invited to stay.

The first time is easy. But by the third or fourth time everyone is on to me. They know my pathetic little game. All the moves that I make. Fed up fathers get short with me. After that I feel some shame. But not enough to not keep trying.

And for the first time in my life. I wish I had more friends. Was popular. Then this would be breeze. I could just cycle through them week after week. Eating like a king. I'd be the best fed bum in three counties. And I'd never worry about wearing my options out.

But that's not who I am. And I know that it's coming. That every time someone lets me in the door with a sigh it could be my last chance to savor real food. So I take huge portions. Eat second helpings. Gorge myself on the kindness of others. Which is probably my downfall.

One night I go knocking at Mark's. I've been showing up here weekly for a little over a month. His mom makes good food. The kind of things I didn't know I missed about living at home.

She makes pasta. And meat with mashed potatoes and corn on the side. She buys real butter. Not the plastic-tasting margarine I've become accustomed to. And she never looks at me like I'm a nuisance. Or a deadbeat.

Which is more than I can say for some other mothers.

But tonight when I get there I'm a little too late. Just in time to smell cooked meat. Hear the clatter of dishes being done. I curse myself. I should've gotten off my ass sooner. Now I'm going to have to walk home listening to my stomach.

Mark asks if I want to sit on the front porch with him. Have a smoke. So I do. He looks content. Well fed. I take the cigarette he offers me. In my head I curse him and his easy life. His full belly.

We sit there in silence for a couple minutes. Staring across the street. Then Mark opens his mouth. And the way he talks to me. I know he's trying to figure out a nice way of putting it.

He tells me his mom heard about a truck that parks out behind the Salvation Army. Gives out hotdogs to other dead beats and drunks every Wednesday night. That maybe I should go there some time. It could probably help.

And I know that I've had my last free meal here.

But I couldn't care less. They threw me a bone at least. Pawning me off on some do-gooders. Some kind of charitable organization that was better suited to deal with people like me.

I laugh. Mark looks at me like he expects a sour response. But he's got it all wrong. This worked out pretty good. Standing in line at a food truck with other down-n-outers has less shame. I won't feel like I'm dirtying someone's house just by standing in it.

Because that's how it is now. Families are beginning to make my skin crawl. And when I get invited into a house I don't know how to act. Eat like a pig. Crumbs raining out of my mouth onto my lap. The floor. I spill things. Make feeble attempts at cleaning up after myself.

I'm losing my etiquette. If I ever had any.

I tell Mark how this couldn't be better. That this is a guaranteed meal every week. One I can count on. If I can just hold out to Wednesday. Then I've got it made. I feel like I need to get on this. Do some preparation. I get up. Tell Mark that I have things to do. Places to go.

I barely wave good-bye.

Because how can I. My head is filled of fevered visions of hot dogs. I imagine a fat man leaning out of a window cut crudely into the side of shitty old VW bus. I walk home lost thinking about soft, steamed buns stuck in my teeth. The sugar rush of green relish. The bite of mustard.

When I get home I sit on the stairs at the front of the building. My roommate has the night off. And I know he's not going anywhere. I want to watch the city get dark. I want a few more minutes alone. I smoke a cigarette. Sure that the world is a good place.

· · · · · · ·

Tuesday night I can't sleep. I just roll around in the bed. Anxious. Like when I was a kid. And Christmas morning was waiting for me. I'd lie awake all night back then. But that was nothing compared to how my entire body is tingling right now.

In the morning I get up. Do as little as possible all day. I lay on the couch. Read. The only time I get up is to refill my glass with tap water. Something to keep the hunger pains from getting to be too much.

The hours crawl by. I can hardly concentrate on the book I'm reading. I keep putting it down. Giving up. Staring at the ceiling. I close my eyes and try to sleep. But I can't. The promise of a full stomach. The excitement.

Mark's mom said that the truck pulls up around 6:30. But there's no way I can wait that long. So at six I put on my shoes. Look through the mess. Find my keys on top of the stove. Underneath a collection of ripped, plastic shopping bags.

I grab the keys and leave the bags.

Out on the street I feel good. I stop at the bottom of the stairs. Take it all in. There's not many people on the street. A few cars pass. Probably on their way home. To their own hot cooked meals. To their families. To their nice big house.

Shit, I think. This would be the perfect night for a stroll. Something to work up an appetite. If I wasn't already starving that is. Preparing to gnaw off my own arm. Or boil up one of my roommate's old boots. Just in case Mark's mom isn't 100% correct.

I stroll down the main street. My stomach growling the whole damn way. I'm sure people walking by can hear it. I'm embarrassed. I don't want anyone to think I'm not doing all right. When I think no one is looking I make a fist. Hit myself in the abdomen. But it offers no relief.

The pain of hunger is all I feel. And it gets hard to walk. I feel light-headed. Giddy. Like I'm just floating. But it's not the case at all. I'm doubled over. Clenching my teeth. Holding my midsection and softly groaning.

And I'm glad that I left early. Because it takes me 20 minutes to walk there. Which on a good day takes about five. When I get out behind the Salvation Army I find a curb. Sit down. Feel a little better. But faint. Hope for a bottle of water. Look around.

There are a couple of guys standing behind the Salvation Army. Over beside the dumpster. Smoking a cigarette. I can't tell if they're like me. Here for food. Or if they work inside. The difference in appearance is subtle.

I lean back on my elbows. Hope that I'm not just here for nothing. That there was no miscommunication between Mark and his mom. And that a big truck or bus or whatever is going to pull up any second. Start throwing out hotdogs like old women feeding bread to the birds.

And my fears don't last for long. Because other men in shabby looking clothing start showing up. They shuffle up alone. Or in pairs. With their heads down. Hands in the pockets of dirty looking pants.

As the parking lot fills up with them there's a feeling in the air. Like the static before a storm. And it could be caused by all kinds of things. Like our collected depression. Or hunger. Or the excitement in knowing tonight we have it figured out. That we don't have to worry until tomorrow.

I mimic the men around me. Sit upright. And I pull out one the few smokes I have left. I light it. Pull my knees up to my chest. When a big bus pulls into the parking lot I'm staring between my feet. At the asphalt. And all the tiny rocks that make it up.

The bus is a beat up piece of shit. Covered in rust. Rumbles and rattles like it's going to explode. And except for the windshield all the other windows are blacked out. It looks like the kind of thing a bunch of rotten hippies would drive around the country in.

But who am I to judge?

The other men butt out their smokes. Form a line at the back of the bus. They know the routine. And all I do is watch. I smoke my cigarette down to the filter. Then get up. Stand at the back of the line and wait. And at this point I'm not even sure for what.

The back door of the bus opens. 1 man hops out. He's in filthy white pants, shirt and apron. Another man in the exact same outfit passes down a wooden staircase. Once that's fixed in they start lugging out everything they need.

And in no time the two of them have set up tables. A couple of camping stoves. Pots. Several giant water bottles. Packages of hotdogs. Buns. Mustard. Ketchup. Relish. The line starts murmuring. Shuffling back and forth on weary feet.

Two cheery faced women come out of the bus. Start dumping water in the pots. Opening packs of hotdogs. Buns. Set out the condiments. The sight of them working gets me excited.

My stomach starts screaming. I double over to mask the hunger pains. Knead my hands in my gut. Whisper assurances to myself. Like things are going to be alright. That food is close at hand.

It feels like forever. Like I've aged while waiting. But it's most likely only been about ten minutes. And the line starts moving. I see men walking away from the table. Two hotdogs in one hand and a bottle of water in the other. Smiles on their faces. My vision wavers. My weakness getting the better of me.

When I get to the front of the line I can't believe it. I'm finally here. This is happening. The two women look at me. Smile. I stand there like an idiot. I can't speak. It's like meeting the god you never believed in.

I want to get down on my knees and weep.

One of the women says she hasn't seen me before. Asks me my name. I stutter when I tell her it's Stan. I just want to eat. And I'm having a hard time being pleasant. But when she introduces herself and the other woman as Nancy and Louise I pull out my best fake smile.

Which seems to work. Because they keep smiling back at me. When

Louise asks me how many I want I ask how many I can have. They laugh. And tell me I can start with three. But to feel free to come get more if I'm still hungry.

I take the hotdogs from her. She gives me a bottle of water. And I feel good. Like someone's mother is proud of me. Or I did the right thing for once. And I might have to be outside, and sit on a curb, but this is going to be the best dinner I'll have eaten in a long time.

I walk over to the curb where I was sitting before. Put the bottle of water down. Sit on the edge. I bite into the first one. Mustard and relish squirt out the end. Land on the pavement. It's hot. I chew as fast as I can. Like a dog.

I eat the first one in two bites. Then I slow down a bit. It takes me 3 bites to eat the other ones. I get back in line. Which moves pretty fast since most of the men have gone back for seconds. I ask for another three.

'That good, huh?' Nancy asks me with a little laugh. I nod my head yes when she hands them to me. I tell her it's the best thing I can remember eating in a long time. And she blushes.

I sit back down and eat these one a little slower. Sip my water. Which I forgot about. No more men go back up. It seems they're all full. Nancy yells out. Makes sure no one wants any more. I think about getting another three. But decide I don't want to press my luck.

Some of the men start to wander off. I figure there's going to be a religious sermon. There usually is when strangers hand out free food to bums. We have to pay somehow. I try to get up. But I can't. My stomach is killing me.

What's a little Jesus bullshit now and again?

The two men come out of the bus. Take in all the heavy things. Nancy and Louise walk up the steps. Wave goodbye. One man walks up the steps. Pulls them in. Then helps the other up.

The engine starts. They drive away. Holy Christ. This is my lucky day. Six hotdogs and no sermon. I pull out a smoke. Light it. Inhale. Smile and watch the other men leaving. One comes up to me. Stands where my feet are stretched out. I look up at him. Nod.

'Hey, you better get moving. After the bus leaves the cops show. Hand out tickets for loitering.'

'Oh, thanks man.' I get up. I shake his hand. Tell him my name.

'I'm George. D'ya think I can bum a smoke?'

'Yeah. Sure.'

He gets his smoke. Shuffles off. Waves when he gets about twenty meters away. A big smile on his face. A trail of smoke going up to heaven. I turn around. Walk back to my place. Doubled over again.

Happy I'm not hungry.

19

I never get any calls for an interview. Which isn't really that bad of a thing. But welfare doesn't like it. They think I have potential. That I'm going to be one of the cases they turn around. But I mainly disappoint.

So instead of offering a warning I tell myself they'll find out eventually.

When I go in for my next appointment my caseworker has some good news she says. I get excited. Think the best. A rash decision on their part. Maybe an increase in my monthly payment?

But instead she says I've been accepted into a crew for workfare. A government program just installed. An effort to get some kind of return on the money paid each month. And to stifle the public complaint that we're living some kind of high life.

When she tells me I feel like puking. It's a shock. I shake my head. I tell myself I must've heard her wrong. That I was right in the first place. That they've been wrong all along. They've been shortchanging me. And I'll get a big fat check.

But yeah right. She starts telling me how I have to be in a parking lot as the sun is rising. Waiting for a van to drive me and a bunch of losers out into the country. To help out at some conservation area.

And I find the idea degrading. That the people who have real jobs at this place are going to know that we're all bums. Just puttering through the day to get our handout. So we can all just go back to watching television.

I know what people think about me.

When I leave the office, I'm pissed. I angrily smoke a cigarette out front of my apartment building. Telling myself that I have to be able to get out of it. That I'll call in sick or something. But then they're going to want to see a doctor's note. Which I couldn't afford even if I was sick.

My only other option is to get a job before next week. When I have to subject myself to this public humiliation. But that's not going to happen. At least not without the help of a miracle. Or a favour.

And since I'm a bum I owe a lot more favors than I can call in. So all I can do is do it.

So when the first day rolls around I get up with the sun. Walk down the main street a few blocks. I'm the only person out. Not even a car passes by me. I wonder what the hell I'm going to have to do today. How hard I'm going to have to work.

I get to the vacant parking lot I'm getting picked up at. There's already a few people standing around. I walk up. I don't want to ask if they're standing there waiting for the same van as me. I don't want to admit what I am.

But I get lucky. An older man asks before I have a chance. I nod yes. He introduces himself and everyone around him. I forget their names quicker than I hear them. I sit down on a parking curb while they chat.

I want nothing to do with them. Because I look at them like they're bums. And this is just a temporary stop for me. Soon I'll have a good job I tell myself. Even though I have no evidence to support it. But I believe in it. And that's what matters.

At two minutes to six a van pulls up. The driver tells us to get in and wait and that at exactly six we'll be leaving. And anyone late will be left behind. And then they better have a damn good excuse for their caseworker or they're going to get kicked right off.

Which he barks out like a threat. Like we're the ones who are late. But I get it. He's trying to scare us for next time. And the time after that. So we'll never be late.

I sit in the back of the van. When the driver calls out my name I make sure he hears me say present. I don't want any misunderstandings. When the driver's done his role call he starts the van and tears out of the parking lot.

I stare out the window for the next 45 minutes. Until we pull up to a conservation area way out in the middle of the country. We drive down a long gravel road lined with tress. And for a little while I'm glad to be out of the city.

At least until I have to start working.

We pull up at a large building. It looks like a rich person's cottage. We're told to get out and that he'll be back at five to pick us up. And we better not be late. Or he leaves without us. Which I find a little harsh.

A park ranger, or whatever she is, comes over. She smiles and tells us to follow her. That she'll be the one coordinating all the work today. And that she's happy to have us. That she hopes we all have a good day.

Which I have a hard time believing. Because she knows we're deadbeats. And that the only reason we're here is owing to the fact that we can't find work. Or just aren't good at it. Or just too lazy.

We follow her over to a couple other groups of people the same size as us. They look just as rundown and hungry as we do. And that's when I get it. It's welfare day here. Groups bussed in from all the neighboring counties.

The park ranger is joined by five others dressed in pale grey and green outfits. A short sleeved military style shirt. Some tasteful knee length shorts. They all went to college to wear that uniform.

They line us up like cattle. Tell us that there's a lot of things to do today. That we'll be picked for certain jobs. And that if we have lunches there's a staff room we can use.

No one has a lunch.

They come down the line. Tell us where to go based on physical appearance. I get paired up with some kid around my age. But he's fucking huge. Strong looking. Like he grew up on a farm. Is used to hard work. But here he is. With us. On welfare. Smiling from ear to ear.

An employee tells us to follow her. Get in a pick up truck. We still haven't been told what to expect. She tells us her name is Kate. The kid pipes up. He looks happy to be here. I suspect he's slow. Not right in the head. He asks what we'll be doing.

Kate smiles at home. Tells us that there was a storm the other night. That it knocked down a bunch of trees. She says they cut up the big ones. Dragged them all to one place. But now it was going to be up to me and this kid to clean the mess up.

'Ah great,' the kid says.

He sounds sincere. The sick fuck. I look out the window. Watch the trees pass by. It's a beautiful day. I wonder if I can hide in the woods. Get left behind. Live off stolen lunches from the staff room.

And just as it begins to sound pretty nice. Kate pulls into a clearing. Turns off the truck. Gets out. We follow.

In the clearing is a trailer. A pile of fresh cut logs. Sawdust ground into the forest floor. The sun is shining down. It's beginning to get hot. I'm already sweating. I don't have any water.

Kate explains things to us. It's pretty easy. We have to take all the logs and put them on a cart. Make sure that they're not going to all fall off. She tells us that she's got some other stuff to do. That she'll be back in a couple of hours.

She turns around to go. But I stop her. I ask what to do if I get thirsty. She tells me to have some water. I ask where the closest fountain is. She looks at me like I'm retarded.

'You don't have any?' she asks.

'No.' I reply

She sighs. Annoyed. Goes over to her truck. Gets a bottle of water and hands it to me. Tells me it has to last. Go easy on it. I nod. She gets in her truck. Drives off. I stand and watch. Take a long gulp of water from the bottle.

This is never going to last until she comes back I tell myself.

I turn around. Ready to start working. And the kid has already gotten into it. He's already got three good-sized logs up on the trailer. I can't fucking believe it. He's going to have a heart attack. He's sweating like a pig. The back of his shirt already drenched.

Christ. What kind of welfare bum is this? He must be crazy. Or stupid.

They don't expect much of us. And why give them a reason. I walk over. Introduce myself. He tells me his name is Kevin while carrying a log.

After that we look at each other. We're strangers. We're alone in the woods together. No way of getting back to camp. I'm anxious. I know I should just put my head down. Pick up a log and get at it. But I can't. I start asking questions.

'Um, have you done this before?' I ask him

'No, this is the first time I ever put logs on a trailer,' he says.

'No, I meant done workfare?'

'Ah naw, I've done it a bunch. It's nice.'

'It's nice? How old are you?' I ask him. I must've been right. He's got to be slow.

'I'm 21, you?'

'18.'

'Are you married? Kids?'

These words freeze me. I'm a fucking kid. I'm on welfare. That's the last thing I want. A wife. Some kids. People who depend on me. People I can let down. I tell him no with a bit of laugh in my voice.

I ask him. He says yeah with a big fucking smile on his face. Tells me he has 3 kids too. They all live with his folks. Same as his brothers and their wives and their kids. I must make a face. Show my shock. Because he explains himself. They're Mennonites. Part of a large community close by.

That's it. I thought he was dressed a little weird. Also explains why I thought he was retarded. Plus his brute strength. He's been picking up hunks of wood as big as my torso. Weights that would cripple me.

He stops working for a second. Tells me that his whole family is on welfare. And that every summer they pick tobacco. Get paid in cash. Since they live out in the middle of nowhere, in some rundown farmhouse, welfare never checks up on them.

He tells me this while smiling. And I feel bad for thinking he was slow. Because by the sounds of it the fucker probably has all kinds of cash hidden away. And here I am starving most nights. Looking through ashtrays for something to smoke.

The son of a bitch. I should turn him in. This is why people hate welfare recipients. Picking tobacco. That's good fucking money. You can live the whole year off of that. Plus that many people in the same house. Their bills must be nothing. They probably live pretty high on the hog.

I'm doing this all wrong. I'm the one who's retarded. I need some dishonest family to join. Perhaps he has a sister. Maybe I can marry into his. I think better of it. Don't ask.

I put my head down. Start working. Picking the smallest logs in the pile. I'll let this grinning asshole grab the big ones. I watch the sweat build up on his forehead. And I tighten the cap of the bottled water. There's no way he's getting a drop of this.

The morning goes by. It's nice to be in the forest. I sweat. I take small sips of water. Sit down for a little while. Watch the Mennonite work for a while. A cigarette hangs from his mouth the entire time he does it. I wonder when he's going to have a heart attack.

Just as time stops moving I hear the sound of a pick-up truck in the woods. I figure it's Kate come to see how we're doing. And thanks to this fucking ape chugging along the whole time it looks like we've both been working hard.

She gets out of the truck. Looks around. Nods with approval. Tells us it's time to go back to the main building. It's lunch. That's great, I think. Some time to lie around in the grass. Enjoy the day in the country.

I ask Kate if I can sit in the bed of the pick up. She says sure. I put my foot on the back wheel. Grab the top edge and hop up and over. I'm not graceful. My knees just make it over. And I land with a thud.

'You alright back there?' Kate asks. I wave her on. Mutter yeah yeah. Imagining the two of them yucking it up. Laughing at me. I sit with my back against the cab. Watching the forest run away. Feeling like the world's biggest fool.

When we get to main building I hop out. When Kevin comes out of the truck I ask if I can bum a couple smokes off of him. I have a pack in my pocket. But fuck him. He's got the money. He can afford to support my bad habit.

He pulls out a pack from his breast pocket. Gives me five of them. Tells me he never runs out. Him and his older brother go out to the Indian reservation. Buy them buy the sack. They cost next to nothing.

I tell him thanks. Walk around the other side of the truck. Light one of the cigarettes he gave me. And I instantly know why they cost next to nothing.

Kate is standing beside the truck. I ask her if I'll be going back out to haul logs after lunch. She says most likely not. I thank god. I don't think I can keep it up all afternoon.

My legs are already tightening. I'm sure I'll be bedridden tomorrow. They should know better. I've been slowly settling into atrophy. My muscles aren't used to all this.

I take a walk around the main building. I find a hose. I turn it on and soak my head under it. It's cold. And after all that lifting this morning it feels good. I take long drinks from the hose. Fill up my bottle. By the time I leave, the ground around me is a three foot puddle.

I find the people who I got a ride in with. They're sitting at a picnic table in the sun. I don't know why. Because I don't like a single one of them. But I feel like I have to sit with them. That these are my people.

So I walk over. Sit on the end of the bench. I don't say a thing. My hair is dripping down the back of my neck. I couldn't be more relaxed. I light a cigarette. And this time the hard burn doesn't bother me as much.

A fat woman beside me notices me now. She asks if I have an extra smoke. I tell her no. That I got these ones from a Mennonite in the woods. The look on her face says it all. She's picturing some asshole in a house drawn buggy with no zippers. I look at her and smile from the side of my mouth.

She doesn't believe me.

The loudmouth from this morning is sitting across from me. I take a good look at him. He must be in his fifties. Graying hair. A fat gut. His fingertips are stained yellow. He smokes and talks. Tells stories I don't listen to. Until he looks at me.

I can feel him getting ready to ask me something. I roll my eye in anticipation. Which I guess is his queue. Because he immediately asks me what I've been doing all morning. I tell him.

He leans back a little. Takes a drag from his smoke. Says, 'Boy, you had it rough.' Tells me all he's done is sit in a truck. Get driven around from trashcan to trashcan. Take the full bags and chuck them in the back of the truck. Then put a new bag in.

'Hell,' he brags, 'guy even let me smoke in the truck.' and the look of self satisfaction on his face is too much for me. This old fuck. He's just trying to rub it in now. Like he's got it so fucking easy.

I look around the table. And the rest of these morons seem to be looking up to him. Him for fuck's sake. This asshole. And these are my people? This isn't for me. I have to make sure that I never to do this again.

Never see these degenerates again.

The only answer is to get a job. Employable people have to be better than this. That's the word on the street. That's gotta be the reason welfare bums are always looked down on. Their absolute stupidity. I'm glad I came here. I've seen the light.

I get up. Look at the guy across from me. And before I know it I'm saying words. Like 'Well, aren't you lucky' and 'Go fuck yourself you old fart.' He shuts up as I walk away. And I know I'm going to have a pretty bleak ride back home tonight.

But what am I supposed to do? Sit there and listen to him. Christ. I'd rather be out there lugging wood with that fraud-committing Mennonite.

As I'm muttering to myself, a park official walks by. Tells me it's time to get back to work. So I make my way back over to where we were chosen earlier in the day. When all of us are gathered, they pick us over again.

I get driven off with four other guys. I sit in the back of the pick up. It reminds me of being a kid. My old man tearing around the country-side. Me in the bed looking out at the sky. The tobacco fields racing passed. The summer sun on my skin.

And I forget about that old prick. About these people I'm with. And the shitty turn my life has taken. And by the time we drive through the woods for half an hour and stop at a small river. I've calmed myself down.

We all pile out. Listen as the ranger explains how to build a small damn. We get to work. The rest of the afternoon goes by fast. It's easy with so many people. I can slack some. With all the people working. It's hard to notice.

When we're done we get driven back up to the main building. Our rides are here. I get into the van. Sit in the back. Rest my head against the window. Watch as farm fields roll by.

The others talk. Not once do they try and include me. So I know I did my best when I mouthed off. When we get back to the city I walk away from the van as fast as I can. I walk home. I'm starving. I pray that there's some ramen noodles in the cupboard.

When I get home the lights are off. I yell as loud as I can. No answer. I tell myself that my roommate must be at work. Thank god. After today I don't think I can put up with anyone. It would've been unbearable.

I've spoke too much already.

I heat some water. Open two packages of noodles. Dump them into the biggest bowl we have. Light a smoke. When the water boils I pour it over the noodles. Walk it over to the coffee table. Wait.

I think about today. And about the Mennonite. Out of everyone I know on welfare he's got it all figured out. He lives in the middle of nowhere. His bills are nothing. And he makes a killing all summer.

But I don't have some big family to share my costs. And I don't want one either. My roommate is enough. There's no way I could do that. Have more people in here. I think I'd go nuts. Snap some night. Murder them all.

So I figure what I need is a job. Something that leaves no trails. No social insurance number needed. Just cash. And a willingness to do whatever's asked.

20.

I get a call from Greaseback. He tells me I should come over. I look around. I've been lying in bed staring at a television since I woke up. I tell him I'm not that busy. I'll be over in about 20 minutes.

Since we moved the four of us don't hang out as much. I don't know what happened. But there's not a good feeling in their place. Not like there used to be in that hellhole three story walk up. Over there they were my saviors. The big brothers I never had.

But now Greaseback's not around as much. And Mitch is getting a little too cool for me. Now that he lives downtown he tattoos more people. Doesn't collect welfare anymore. Gives me attitude when I go over. Like he's never been where I am.

When I knock on the door I hear Greaseback yell. I can't make out what he says but I take a chance. Open the door and walk in. He's at the far end of the place. Sitting on a couch in front of one of his large open windows. He's hunched over a coffee table rolling a joint.

I walk over. Sit on the couch opposite him. He leans back while licking the glue. Smiles. Showing crooked teeth. His eyes light up. We lock hands and he calls me brother. I laugh. It's good to see him.

He lights the joint. Tells me he just got a real job. One that pays well. I ask him what it is and he says he's going to be laying asphalt. So he'll be out there in the hot sun. Baking. Inhale the noxious stink of the stuff. And I think he's luckiest guy in the world.

I tell him I thought they only hired ex-cons to do that kind of thing. We laugh. But as he passes the joint to me he gets serious. Tells me that it's funny I said something. Because the only thing wrong with the job is the people he has to work with.

'It's a thousand times worse than working with criminals,' he tells me while I inhale, 'they're a bunch of fucking Portuguese.' There's nothing I can do but choke on the smoke as I spit it out. I've never met a Portuguese person in my life. I let the subject drop.

But I'll never stop wondering what Greaseback has against them.

Instead I pass him the joint. Give him my congratulations. Certain that this is why he invited me over. He wanted to do a little celebrating. And I'm the only one who's around at 11:30 in the morning.

But I'm wrong. Because he tells me that since he has that job. He doesn't need his other job. The one working for a man with a shitty van. A man who pays cash and doesn't ask questions.

I can't believe it. It's a piece of the dream coming true. My chance to fuck welfare for once. Just like Greaseback and Mitch and that dirty Mennonite with his endless supply of Indian cigarettes. Now it's my chance to live high on the hog.

And I don't know if it's just me getting stoned or if I'm so excited about the prospect of me coming home with cash in my pocket, a dozen beers in one hand, a bag of food in the other, just like Greaseback used to in the old building, but I feel like I'm going to explode.

'So I take it you want his number then?' Greaseback asks while laughing. All I can do is nod. My eyes more open than they've ever been in my life. I can already taste the hot meals I'm going to buy.

I grab the number from him. Stand up. Tell I'm going to go home and call him right away. Greaseback laughs. Tells me that I should wait a little while. Because I might come across a little frantic. And he's right. This weed really got on top of me.

When I get home I go right back up to my room. Lay down in bed. This is the perfect job for me. Greaseback's worked for him forever. He only ever needs someone about three days a week. And the jobs are always different.

It takes about a half hour. But I begin to calm down. Feel like I can handle a conversation on a phone. And by the time a woman on the other line answers I feel like I have it in the bag.

I ask for Trevor. The woman yells his name. Tells him to get his ass down here and answer the phone. I hear the phone being placed down somewhere. There's more muffled yelling. Some scratching as the receiver gets picked up.

A man voice asks me who he's speaking with. I tell him my name and that I got his number from Greaseback. He knows exactly who I am. Says Greaseback speaks highly of me. Asks if I can work tomorrow.

I say sure. But I was hoping for a day or so to ease into the idea. Then he asks if I have work boots. And when I tell him no he says I don't need them anyway. He says to meet him at a storage unit place on the other side of town. Hangs up without saying good-bye.

I put the phone down. Almost in shock. Unable to believe that I'm going to go to work in the morning.

. . . .

At a quarter to seven I'm standing out front of the storage unit place. There's a chain coffee shop next door. A gas station. Van after van pulls in. I watch each one as it make its way into the drive through. Then out again from the other side.

None of them stop for me.

I keep this up for a half hour. And I'm beginning to feel like an idiot. The gas station employee starts eyeing me suspiciously. I keep catching him staring. Watching me pace. Adding to the anxiety.

Has this fucker stood me up? I start to think. What is this some kind of fucking joke? Him and Greaseback laughing at me. But I can't see him doing that. And I can't walk away. Because I need the money. I want it. I've already promised myself so many things.

And when I've been standing there an hour a rusting blue van pulls up. The window rolls down. And behind the steering wheel is a scrawny man. He has long dark hair and a mustache. He looks me up and down. Spits on the ground. Asks if I'm Stan.

'Unh, yeah.'

'Well get the fuck in then.'

I walk around the front of the van. I'm scared. I don't like his tone. How he told me to get the fuck in the van. What the hell has Greaseback gotten me into now? Who is this psycho? I think as I open the passenger side door and get in.

He drives towards the drive-thru. Tells me that he waited at another storage place. One even farther from my house. He says that he needs me to meet him there in the future. I tell him I can't that it's too far away. I'll never get there.

I can tell that he doesn't like it. But there's nothing he can do. So he gives in. Says that this one will be fine. He asks me what I want from the coffee shop. I tell him I'm fine. I don't have any money. He says don't worry about it. 'When you work for me I buy the coffee.'

I tell him I'll take a large. He gets the same for himself. And a dozen doughnuts. Tells me to dig in. They're so fresh they melt in my mouth. I didn't eat anything this morning. And it's hard for me not to wolf back the whole box.

As we dive away I ask what we're going to do today. He tells me that some old bag needs some hedges ripped up. Says that she's redoing her yard and wants the things gone. He asks if I've ever ripped up a hedge. I tell him no.

'Ah, don't worry. It's a piece of cake.' He goes on into great detail. Tells me everything I need to know about ripping up hedges. I only half listen. Just enough to nod at the right time.

I eat doughnuts. Look out the window. Watch the town go by.

When we get there he has me unload the truck. Shovels. A couple of axes. He smokes a cigarette. Walks around the hedges. Looks them over. Crouches down. Gets both of his hands down into the dirt.

I finish bringing the things over. Light one of my own smokes. Stand there behind him a moment. Wondering what he's doing. How he's gauging things. Then I ask what he thinks.

'We'll be out of here in four hours.'

He sounds confident. I believe him. But then we start digging. The roots of these fuckers are strong. We have to hack at them. Trevor has me dig down. Then he takes a machete that he had under the front seat of his van.

The job seems impossible. But Trevor never gives up faith that things are going to go much smoother any second. I don't feel so good about it. I don't have gloves like he does. My hands are covered in blisters. The blood makes it tough to grip the shovel.

I'm sweating like a pig. It's not even noon yet. Jesus Christ. Theres's not a chance I'm going to make it to the end of the day. I want to cry. I want to throw down the shovel. I want to walk away.

But I can't. I'm in a different city. No way home. I'm stuck here. So I just keep going. Eventually he throws down his shovel. His machete. Tells me he's going to go get some lunch. Asks what I want.

'Anything,' is the only thing I can say.

He tells me to keep working while he's gone. But the second he's out of sight I sit down and light a smoke. My hands look terrible. They're covered in dirt. The skin is ripped. They burn.

I pick up the shovel. Try digging. It hurts like hell. But I have nothing to lose. I need the money. I hack like a maniac. I rip out two feet of hedges by the time Trevor gets back with a bag of burgers. Fries. Some large cokes. Tells me to stop.

The sweat is pouring off me. I'm soaked. I sit down on the ground with him. He passes me a coke. A thing of fries. A couple of cheeseburgers. I have to stop myself from eating the wrapper. I'm starving. I gulp down the coke. Shove fries in my mouth. Almost bite my fingers.

Trevor laughs. Says he never saw anyone eat like that before. That he's scared. Like I'm some wild animal. I laugh. Tell him to watch out. And he'd better hope I'm full. Or I'm going to gnaw off his arm.

I finish. Feel better. Lay on the grass. Smoke. Take the ice from my soda. Dump it on my hands. At first I want to cry. But the coolness helps. I close my eyes. I hear Trevor get up. Walk over to the truck. Rustle around. He comes back. Something lands on my chest. I open my eyes. A pair of leather gloves.

'C'mon, let's get this shit done.'

The gloves help. We finish a lot faster than I thought we would. I pack up the truck. Trevor sits in the front seat. Door open. His foot resting through the window. Smoking.

He's at peace with everything. His life doesn't seem all that bad.

We leave. Stop at a corner store. He sends me in for a couple of cokes. On the way back home we have the windows open. A breeze comes in. Cigarettes and a coke. I can get used to this.

I ask Trevor about his life. If he has kids. If that was his wife on the phone. He tells me that no. That wasn't his wife. But she might as well be. They've been together forever. And they don't have kids. Neither of them wants the responsibility.

Shit. That's not a bad life. Now all I need is my own van. A good woman who's too selfish to have kids. Then I'm set. It looks like a better way to make money than being in some factory. At least I get to be outside all day.

And sitting there. Driving home. I take a look at Trevor. Because he looks like the kind of person my parents told me to avoid. To not become anything like. But this man has some freedom. He goes as he pleases. And I wonder why people like my folks are so afraid of men like Trevor.

He breaks my silence. Asks if I'd like to work tomorrow as well. He doesn't have as much to do. But it'd really help him out if I could power wash the grease out of a local burger joint's drive thru.

I tell him sure. That I'm on welfare. That I'm always free and could always use the money. He laughs. Tells me that he thinks we're going to get along jut fine. I'm relieved. I'm going to be eating like a king soon.

He asks if I want to get dropped off at home. I take him up on the offer. When we pull up out front he hands me four rumpled greasy twenties. He tells me to have a good night. To not get too drunk. And that he'll see me at seven.

I stand on the curb. Holy shit, I think. Eighty bucks. I can't believe it. That's more than I'd spent on food all last month. I don't know what I'm going to do. I think of all the food I can eat. All the booze I can drink.

I go upstairs. Shower. Put on clean clothes. Comb my hair. Go right back out. Walk down the street. Smile. Feel good. It's the first time in a while. I go into the first convenience store. Say hi to the clerk. Buy a pack of cigarettes.

After that I go to the liquor store. Get a six-pack. Go down to the park. Sit at a picnic table. Drink the beer. Smoke some smokes. I think about what I'd had to do to get the smokes. The booze. I look at my hands. They've been beaten.

They stung like hell when I washed up. Even the condensation from the bottle hurts them. I tell myself that I wouldn't want to do this everyday. Like Trevor. He's a fool. I'm the one who has it made. I can work a couple of days. Get some cash. Then fuck off.

I'm not stuck there. I can still have my days filled with walking. Reading.

When the beer's finished I walk home. Stop for a piece of pizza. Eat it. Feel sick. My body isn't used to all this. Beer. Smokes. Hot food. It's too decadent. I do my best to get around the side of the building before I puke. But my best isn't very good.

I go home. Crawl into bed. Fall asleep in all my clothes. Sweaty.

The next day is a breeze. It only takes me a couple of hours. I try and drag it out. But it's impossibe. I chat with some of the girls working.

They lean out the drive-through window. They're young. Cute. Covered in the film of grease all people who work in fast food are covered in. But I don't care. They think I have a job. They think I'm something.

I don't tell them otherwise.

I only get twenty bucks that day. Trevor tells me to call him next week. He'll have some more work for me. But I never see him again. Or even hear his voice. I lose him number. Greaseback is never around. And then the phone gets cut off. I'm back to where I started.

Wishing I was as well off as that god damned grinning Mennonite.

21.

I wake up. Instantly something feels wrong. Under my left eye seems tight. I reach up and touch it. Half asleep. Where the bags normally are no longer feels like my skin. It's rough. Puffed out.

In front of the mirror I don't feel any better. In addition to being rough, it's bright fucking red. Looks scaly. Like this is some fucking cheap B movie. And in a few days I'll just be some giant god damned lizard in torn jeans and t-shirt terrorizing the neighbourhood.

Shot down by some handsome young cop.

And I start to get worried. I grab at one of the scales. Get my dirty fingernail underneath it. Try and peel it off. But I let go and yelp. The pain is too much. I instantly regret my stupidity.

Fuck. It's disgusting to look at. But I can't look away. What the hell is happening to me? Is this some kind of rash? Or should I seriously start to worry? I tell myself there's nothing I can do. But sit back. Hope for the best.

My roommate is still asleep. I don't want him seeing me like this. I don't want anyone seeing me like this. My levels of confidence are quickly draining. The other day I remember seeing some sunglasses on the coffee table. I pick through all the garbage. I find them under a greasy paper plate.

The glasses are dark. Cover my shame. I slip on my shoes and go out into the world. Thank god this city is a fucking ghost town. But standing at the foot of the stairs. On the edge of the sidewalk. I feel like the people who do walk past get a bad feeling from me. They know I'm disgusting.

In three hours I have an appointment at the unemployment office. Some kind of job search skills building workshop. Just the sound of it makes me offended. They treat us like kids down there. Like we're all too fucking stupid to find work. And the problem isn't the dying industry.

There's no way I can miss the meeting. They'll cut my damn claim. And I'm getting low on supplies. I need the money coming. And the damn landlord. Always up my ass. Sure I get it. I'm always a little late. But he has no delicacy.

So I give up. I'll just wear these sunglasses. I'm sure that'll go over great in the tiny little conference room we'll be stuffed into. No one will ask questions. Or give me a hard time when I refuse to take them off.

From time to time I catch my reflection in a window. And I feel like I can see the rash growing. Spreading down my face. But when I stop. And get a good look. It's all in my head. I'm beginning to lose it.

It's a small town. So when people walk by they look at you. There's no big city indifference here. And every time someone does my rash begins to itch a little. And after a few people and their politeness, I can't hold off.

I slide the tip of my finger under the dark glasses. Rub the rash. I can feel dry skin flaking off. It's too much relief. I should've been sitting down when I started this. My legs are weak.

To avoid people I stick to the side streets for over an hour. Criss crossing back and forth and up and down the streets. No one walks these streets at this hour of the day. I can be alone. To scratch and scratch and scratch.

And I don't know but I'm certain scratching at it isn't going to make it any easier to have on my face. I beg myself to stop. Pull my hand away. But before I know it. The finger is right back there. Scratching away.

My stomach is killing me. I need to put something in it. There's a small breakfast place close by. Back on the main street. It's been there so long that the inside looks like there's a fine coating of grease over everything.

There's never anyone under 50 in the place. All hard looking men and women. People who've been working in the factories all their lives. Who rarely wear clothes that aren't made by companies synonymous with labour.

When I come in I feel like I'm looking into my future. The one I'll have when I get that factory job myself. And I'll go to a place like this every day. Either before my shift or after. They'll know me. And I'll feel like I belong.

But those days are a long way off. And because of my age they look at me with caution now. People like me don't come in here. But it's the only place I can afford. Because just like the décor, the prices haven't changed in 30 years.

I can still get a coffee and a muffin for a dollar.

When I walk in, bells chime. There's three men at the counter. Sipping hot coffee. Eating plates of eggs and bacon and toast. They laugh with the waitress. Who looks just as old as the Formica countertop.

The smell of all the food hits me. The waitress watches me. Waits until I sit at a small two person booth as far away from them as I can to yell over what do you want. I think about all the things I want. Like my own plate of bacon and eggs. And another of pancakes. And a good life. Where I have money for things like that. And there's no rash under my eye.

'A coffee and a muffin,' is what I tell her though.

Sure thing, she replies. I watch her pour my coffee. Cut my muffin in half. She walks around the counter. Places it on the table in front of me. I look up at her. My sunglasses still on my face.

She asks if it's too bright for me. Points at my glasses. I laugh. Tell her no it's fine. Which I instantly recognize as a mistake. Because then she asks me why I don't take off my sunglasses. And insinuates I'm being rude.

If I was smart I'd tell her I'm blind. That I do this so she doesn't have to look at my dead eyes. That I'm being considerate. Which I am. Because I doubt anyone in here wants to see my scaly face while they eat their breakfast.

But I'm not smart. Or quick enough. Because I just blurt out that yeah, I have a fucking rash on my face. And I'm so embarrassed that I hang my head when I tell her. And I wish it was somewhere more exciting. Where this wouldn't even register with her as being strange.

Instead, she looks at me like I'm infectious. She backs away. Back behind the safety of the counter. Her voice turns to whispers when she's back standing with the men eating. I don't bother to look their way. But I know they're talking about me. Trying to guess what it looks like under the glasses.

But I don't care. Fuck her and them too. I eat the muffin. Drink the coffee. My spirits change. I forget about the rash. For a minute. Before it starts to itch again. And I notice my hand on my cheek.

Ignoring it stops being an option.

After my second coffee I count out a dollar and leave it on the table. Look at the clock. I have twenty minutes to get there. I walk out. The waitress eyes me as I do. I make an effort to stay as far away as possible. To ease the disgust on her face.

I take two steps out the door. Stop and light a home rolled cigarette. Made from the butts in the ashtray. It's strong. I wish I had another cup of coffee. I think about the meeting I have to go to. And how I can't remember what it's about.

Because I keep getting distracted. All I can feel is the spot just under my eye where it burns. I give up scratching. It hurts too much. And the amount of skin flaking off is getting distressing. Instead, I start pressing the side of my pointer finger against it.

It's the smallest relief. And my appreciation is great.

The day's too damn nice I tell myself. I should be in a park somewhere. Reading a book. Enjoying myself. Not going to sit in this stuffy office. Life should be about these nice days. Not preparing myself for a shitty job in a place I'll hate.

And as my feet keep moving in the direction of my appointment I can't wrap my mind around it. How people get up in the morning. Drag their asses out of bed to go to the same damn place everyday. It sounds maddening. Just thinking about it makes me want to start scratching myself. Pulling out tufts of hair.

I don't want to get a job. I just want to live.

Before I know it I'm standing out front of the unemployment office.

Just looking at the doors. Dreading going in. Listening to whoever is going to tell me the best practice for impressing an employer or some other god awful boring lecture.

I can't take much more of this. My whole life is just a stinking pile of shit. A tear rolls from my eye. Burns the rash. I look west. And think of the highway. And think of what it'd be like to just walk out there with nothing. Stick my thumb out and see where I end up.

But I don't have the guts for that. So I hang my head. Beaten. I open the heavy door and walk in. It's busy. It's always busy. Which doesn't instill me with faith. I walk over to the counter. Tell the receptionist that I'm here. She smiles and tells me that it'll be a little bit. And that I should wait.

I go over to the job bank computers. Scroll through all the jobs. I find all kinds of things I can do. Like paint or cut lawns or dig holes. But it's the same story all the time. 3 to 5 years experience. Or a driver's license. Or something else I don't have.

When I hear my name, I get up. I still have my sunglasses on. My employment counselor is standing at the desk. Waiting for me. Smiling. I want to be sick. I want to go home to bed.

I walk over and she says hi. We don't shake hands. We never do. She seems to want to keep her distance from me. How bad do I look? Do I smell? And as I'm wondering these things I hear her ask me to take of my sunglasses.

All I do is stare at her for a minute. Then tell her I can't. That I need to keep them on. She looks offended. And I can see that she's going to start exercising her authority. So I tell her what's wrong. That I'm embarrassed. That it isn't easy to look at it.

'Oh, I'm sure it's not as bad you think it is,' she tells me. And I sigh. Because I know in the face of this woman and her power I can't do a thing. She can just as easily tell my caseworker that I'm being uncooperative. That she thinks I'm undeserving of my claim.

And because it's that easy to get fucked I hang my head. And slowly take off my glasses. I sigh one last time. And look up at her. See her smile slide right in to a twisted scowl of loathing.

'Good god,' she says, 'I've never seen anything like that. What is it?'

I mumble that I don't know. That this is the first time I've ever seen it. That I don't have a clue what could be causing it. I keep my suspicions to myself though. That it has something to do with my lifestyle. That maybe I should wash my bed sheets.

I mistake the situation. Interpret her shock and horror for understanding. So I put my sunglasses back on. Feel better instantly. Calm. Like I can sit through whatever bullshit this lady is going to shovel on me.

But instead she tells me I can't wear them. I make a meek protest and she says that if it's that big of a deal we can cancel the meeting. But she reminds me that she'll have to call my caseworker.

I take the sunglasses off. Because it's the easiest thing to do. Welfare keeps doing this to me. Degrading me. Humiliating me. And I never get used to it.

I follow her back to her cubicle. And when she offers me a chair I take it. I'm exhausted. This day is beating the shit out of me. I wonder how much longer I'm going to be here.

'Now Stan, how's the job search coming along?' she asks me.

'It's not.'

'What do you mean?'

'I hand out resumes. Then nothing.'

'What do you mean nothing?'

'Well, no one calls me. Then I go back out and hand out more resumes.' I say.

'Why do you think no one calls you back?'

'Not sure. If I did then I'd probably have a job.'

'What kinds of jobs are you applying for?'

'Factories mainly. Some manual labour stuff. Anything that says no experience needed'

'Have you thought of something else?'

'Not really.'

'Well. I think you're gonna have to try some other places. Don't you have any friends that can get you a job? '

'No ones offered.'

'Have you asked?'

'No.'

'Why not?'

'If there was something, they'd tell me.'

'How do you know?'

'They told me.'

'Well, if you hear any one talking about jobs where they work, ask them.'

'Of course,' I say. This is the kind of shit she gets paid to tell me. That if I hear people talking about job positions I should ask them. Like I've never thought of that before.

'Well, I'm gonna sign you up for our job finding skill building seminar. I think you'll really benefit from it. It's next Wednesday. You can make it right?'

I tell her of course. That I can't wait. And that I'm sure it's really going to give me the leg up I'll need. She doesn't pick up on my sarcasm.

She types some things into her computer. Notes about my behavior I imagine. Then abruptly she stands up. Which catches me off guard. I stand up slowly. Then walk back out to the front desk. She follows me. When we get there I hold out my hand. Force her to have to touch me.

I wait for as long as it takes.

She tells me through clenched teeth to have a good day. After she lets go of my hand she takes a step back. Adopts her fake smile. Says that I should really check through the job bank while I'm here. That there's a lot of good stuff in there.

And I wonder if she's ever taken a look through it. Or has ever been standing where I am. With no experience. And no one willing to train me.

Instead of going over to the job bank, I walk outside. Put my sunglasses on. Light another of my homemade cigarettes. Decide what to do with my life. I figure since I'm down this way I'll head to the Salvation Army. It's a little late. But I'm sure I'll end up with something.

As I walk there I think about my meeting. Jesus, what a waste of time. All that I really did was get signed up for another seminar. And all the ones I've already been to have all been the same.

So I can't wait for next week.

At the door to the Salvation Army I stop. I take a second to hope for something good. Like maybe some strudel. Or cinnamon buns. I know they've been all picked over. Gotten by people smart enough to get here when the place opens.

The best I can hope for is a stale rye. And that's exactly what I get. I'll be lucky if it's still fresh enough for toast in the morning. I'm sure it'll be moldy by then. Rotten. But this is my life.

I swing it in my hand as I walk down the street.

22.

I get in from a walk. The red light on the phone is flashing. It's a message. Which are rarely for me. It's usually just my roommate's work. Trying to get him to come in early. But I've been spending a lot of my time alone. And hearing a voice might be nice.

Even if it doesn't even know I'm alive.

But I'm shocked when I start listening. Because for once it's for me. And even more surprising is someone's asking me to come in for an interview. I almost drop the phone. Miss half of it the first time through. Have to listen through another time.

The voice says he's calling from a gas station on the outskirts of town. One I dropped a resume off to just because I had one in my hand, and was coming home from a long day of walking along the highway. I saw the help wanted sign. Figured I had nothing to lose.

Now I'm sitting on the couch. Cold sweat running down the back of my neck. It's happening. This is it. I've got a job interview.

The place is on a pretty empty corner. The only people who use it are leaving town or going to work. Men and women in trucks and cars. With jobs in places where I get laughed at by the security guards.

I'll be serving the men I want to be.

I hang up and call the number the man left. When he answers I tell him my name. And that yes I am still looking for work. He asks if I can come in the next morning. I tell him of course I can. And that I'm really looking forward to it.

When I'm done I'm surprised I pulled off such a good lie. Because I'm not looking forward to this at all. I want to go lie on the bathroom floor. No lights on. Get a handle on things. But I don't have the energy. And I stay right where I am.

· · · · · · ·

The next morning I get up early. I know the bus doesn't go anywhere near the place. So like usual I'm going to walk. I take a shower. Get out and stand in front of the mirror. Wonder how I'm so fat for a guy who does so much walking.

I have to look good for the interview. My best even. At least that's what all those meeting at unemployment keep telling me. But I'm not sure how I'm going to pull that part off. I don't have much in the way of clothes. My closet is almost empty. And what I do have is dirty. Torn. Or stained.

I settle on a dark shirt. Not stained or torn but wrinkled. It's been lying in the bottom of the closet since we moved. I tuck it into my jeans. Convince myself that the wrinkles in it are hardly noticeable. Comb back my hair.

When I'm done I tell myself that this'll do. That it'll have to do. There's no other option.

I stand in the mirror awhile longer. Looking myself in the eyes. Trying to build up some confidence. To assure myself that tonight, when I walk through that door I'm going to be a man with a job.

A man with a purpose. As depressing as that sounds. Because I'm not sure why I think I'm better than this. That I'll be wasting myself at this place. That I am destined to do better things.

And the face that looks back at me. From the mirror. Doesn't look like the face of a man with a job. It hangs too low for a kid my age. I already look beat. And I don't think I look like someone who even wants a job.

Which I don't really. I like doing nothing. It's agreeable to my spirit. I don't do well when I'm required to be places. I barely made it to school. And I don't see how this is going to be any different.

I try to tell myself good things about the job. I'll be alone. I can read. But I have arguments. I can do those things at home I tell myself. And not have to walk across the city to do it.

I can lie to myself all I want. But I can't get rid of that face. And the lies it refuses to tell.

The interview is for 11. I go downstairs and check the time. Almost nine. If I hesitate much longer I'll never go. Or be horriblly late. Which is even worse than not showing up at all. I put on my shoes. Sigh. Go out into the world.

Which looks like shit today. This city rarely doesn't look that way to me. But when the sun's behind the clouds. Like today. It becomes unbearable. It feels smaller than it is. And I feel trapped. Like the air is closing in on my body.

The streets are already empty of the seven AM rush. There'll be another at three. And then again around 11. The city runs on rotating shifts. Those are the only times this place really moves. The rush of getting home. The last charge to make it in on time.

I stop in the first corner store I see. Grab a cup of coffee. A pack of smokes. There's no way I'm going to make this walk without a little something in my stomach. And the smokes. I'll never make it without them.

I start walking. Start chain smoking. Sip my coffee. Start thinking about the things I'll do if I get this job. I'll save my money. Get out of this shitty little town. Move somewhere where there's action. Opportunity for a young man like me.

When I figure I'm about halfway there, I stop. Sit down in some grass on the side of the road. The humidity is awful. I'm drenched in sweat. By the time I get to this interview I'm going to be soaking.

I start walking again. Only a lot slower. Keep my pace to just above a crawl. I don't know much. But I do know that men who smell like onions floating in vinegar usually don't get the job. It's not good for business.

At least no one has yelled at me from a car yet, I tell myself. Because sometimes it's too easy for me to give up. And if I can't see something good I might just turn around. And give up before I even give it a shot.

By the time I get there I'm ripe. I have half an hour before my interview. So I go around to the car wash bays in the back of the parking lot. I sneak into one. It's cooler in here. No sun. I lift my arm. Get a good whiff of the odor. Tell myself that you have to really get in there. Before it makes my eyes water.

I pick up the gun to the pressure washer. When I squeeze the trigger enough water comes out to get my hands wet. I rub the cold water into my face. Use it to slick back my sweaty hair.

It makes me feel a little better about myself. Like I can do this. Like I can get a job. Like I have some confidence.

I walk up to the plexiglass booth. Go inside. There's just enough room for a counter. Several bags of chips. A small cooler of soda. Cigarettes. The man working. And myself.

I tell him I'm here for the interview. We shake hands. He says that he wants to go outside. Stretch his legs. I wonder if it's because of my smell. Ah who cares. At least the smell of gasoline in the air will mask me.

'So, like I said on the phone. I'm hiring for the overnight shift, you okay with that?' he tells me when we get a little away from the both.

'Yeah man. It's just what I want. I like to sleep during the day.' I respond. When we get a safe distance from the pumps he pulls out a pack of smokes. And I realize that was his motivation all along. And not my horrible stink.

He takes a puff and tells me good. That's what he likes to hear. He needs a night owl. In between drags he gives me the run down. What the job entails. It's just sitting in the box. Behind the counter. People drive up. Pump their own gas. They come in and pay.

Easy peasy.

Then he starts asking me about myself. Like how come he didn't see me drive up. Or where I've parked my car. And I think about myself sneaking around the carwash. How I did a good job at not being seen.

I tell him I walked. And he asks me how close I live. I blurt it out. That I live downtown. He looks at me with dead eyes. His mouth hanging open a little bit. I've stumped him.

He takes a drag off his smoke. I want to light one of my own. But

I somehow feel it would be considered out of line. He asks me how long it took. Surprise in his voice and on his face.

'Maybe a little less than an hour and a half,' I tell him. And I can see him thinking. Which doesn't look good for me. He's bewildered when he asks if I'm prepared to walk three hours a day.

My only response is that I love gas.

I have to give him credit. Because he does his best to change the subject. Laughs and asks me if I still live at home. And I don't know why I do it. But I blurt out that I live with a friend. And that I'm on welfare.

Immediately I know I'm sunk. He does the math. A fucking lazy bum is going to walk three damn hours a day to pump gas. Those numbers don't add up. He starts picturing me not showing up with regularity.

That's when I learn something. Standing there with this man. Smelling the fumes of gasoline. A cool breeze coming off the field across the street. And it's if I'm willing to walk that much for a job, then I must be truly deranged.

And no one is going to understand my motives. Because I don't either. Like why in the hell I'd even walk here for an interview in the first place. I must have some kind of brain damage.

Or I really am that hopeless. I'm not even in my 20's. And I've already given up on any dreams I ever had.

'Well, you know you have to buy the uniform before you can start,' he tells me. This is how he's going to get rid of me. He knows. I'm a bum. I don't have any money. There's no chance I'll be able to come up with cash for that.

And even if I can. He's betting I'll spend it on something else. Which is pretty safe.

So I lie. Tell him that it's no problem. That if I need to, my old man will lend me the cash. But I'm not very convincing. And I don't think he has the faith that my father isn't a lousy deadbeat as well.

'It's just, you know. You gotta buy the winter coat as well. It's pretty expensive.'

I ask him how much. He tells me it's about 300$. He's trying to let me down easy. I'm not what he's looking for. I'm not what anyone's looking for. Why should I expect anything else. My own family didn't even want anything to do with me.

It's shouldn't be a surprise that welfare is the only one that'll have me.

After that he tells me thanks for coming. That he has a few more people to interview. And that he'll give me a call in a couple of days. And even I'm not dumb enough to think he'll actually do it.

He turns around. Walks back to his box. I stand there. I'm defeated. I want to cry. I want to run up behind him. Kick him in the back. Who the hell does he think he his. He pumps gas for a living. And here he is. Looking down on me. Like I'm shit on his living room floor.

Just tell me I don't have the job. Tell me that I'm no good. Or not what you're looking for. Because even though I know it's over, he intentionally gave me just a sliver of hope. Enough to make me sit at home. Staring at the phone. Willing it to ring.

Thinking I have a shot.

I don't have the energy to walk along the main road. To deal with the anxiety of the cars whipping by. I decide to cut through the residential section between me and home. I know it'll take me longer. But I'm happy about that.

Because my roommate is going to be home when I get there. And he's going to ask how it all went. We both thought this was the kind of job I'd get. So there's high hopes to crush when I walk through the door. And I'm not ready to live this afternoon over quite yet.

I walk slow on purpose. My head down. My feet dragging. Through winding streets I've never been down before. Lined with homes set back from the street. Boasting green lawns. I'm sweating like crazy. My feet hurt.

The thought of lying down sounds good. But this isn't the right place. It's too nice. You can't just go passing out on people's lawns, I tell myself. Next thing you know the cops'll be here. At least along the main road there's a ditch. Somewhere to keep hidden.

I smoke cigarettes to stay awake. I look at houses. Think about their air conditioning. Their pools. Their refrigerators and cupboards full of food. I think about what I have at home. And how sick I am of white rice and tall glasses of tap water.

More than once I walk by a place with a couple bikes on the lawn. And I start thinking about my feet. And how much they hurt. And how all I want is to sit down for a while. That I've had enough walking for the day.

No one's around Stan, just walk over calmly. Pick up a bike. Hop on. And ride away. This is your chance. I fight my morals for a minute. But when I see a red mountain bike I'll fit on I don't hesitate.

No one comes running out. No one points a finger. Or yells after me that they'll be calling the police shortly. Or calls me what I am. I ride away without a care. The sun's out. The afternoon breeze in my hair. Cooling the sweat.

I sing in my head.

. . . .

Instead of going home I go to a pawn shop. One that I don't go to very often. One where they don't know my face. I tell them I need a loan. That I'll come back for the bike. That I just need to pay the hydro bill.

The guy behind the counter looks me over. Then the bike. And I do the same to him. His dirty hair is thinning. His face looks shiny. And his black collared shirt is unbuttoned to the top of his enormous gut.

I guess he buys my story. Or thinks he'll make a pretty penny on the bike. He offers me $75. I take it. I wait as he writes out the pawn ticket. I'm just going to crumple the thing up and throw it in the gutter the second I get outside. But I guess there's no skipping the formalities.

Before going home I make a stop. Wait around out front of the liquor store. Find a kind soul who's willing to get me a bottle of whiskey. And by the time I get in the door I've had a couple of long pulls from it.

My roommate is on the couch when I walk in. He asks me how things went today. I tell him great. That the guy at the gas station loved me.

That he just had to interview a couple other morons but I was the man for the job.

'I should be getting a call any day now,' I tell him. He looks at the bottle of booze in my hand. 'Oh, and I found 20$ on the way home.' it makes me feel good to lie to him. To convince him I'm not a total failure. That my life does have a meaning.

He answers by telling me he has the night off. That he's going to go see a movie. Asks if I want to come. I shake my head no. He shrugs his shoulders. Tells me it's my loss.

After he leaves I open one of the big windows. Crawl out through it. Sit on the roof of the beauty salon downstairs. Lean against the brick wall. Open the bottle. Stare up into the night sky. Drinking. Wondering what the fuck I'm going to do with myself.

23.

A friend of ours hits the skids. My roommate and I have known him forever. Since the beach house days. Since before then. His older brother was something of a goof. A local loser of legendary status.

The reputation was inescapable. And it trickled down to our buddy Eric. He took a lot of shit for it. Got beat up and made fun of everywhere we went. But it never toughened him up. Like it's supposed to.

One day he shows up. I let him in. He says things are over. That his parents are getting a divorce. That the house they all lived in was up for sale. And that neither one of them could afford to keep him around.

Which didn't make any sense to me. Because Eric had a job. A friend's dad took pity on him. Paid him to help out at his landscaping company. Cart around the heaviest things. Dig the deepest holes. To me it sounded like a nightmare.

But still. I was envious.

I sat there thinking. As he told me about his folks. That maybe they just didn't want him any more. And divorce was the only answer. Because a few years back. He routinely stole from them. Took so much from his mother's purse that she thought she was going crazy.

Things after that were never the same.

He asks me if he can crash here. Just until he can sort things out. I couldn't care less. But I tell him we'll have to ask my roommate. That I'm not as sure how he'll take it. Eric nods his head agreeing. Knowing full well that he's unpredictable. That he might just feel like being an asshole for no reason.

I tell Eric we can ask him when he gets home. But that won't be until later. He offers to buy a bottle of whiskey. Some food. I don't turn him down. I haven't eaten yet today. And the idea of forgetting about my own problems for a while sounds nice.

By the time my roommate comes home we're both drunk. There's an empty pizza box upside down on the floor. Eric and I are sitting on the couch smoking. Yelling back and forth about music. And our parents. And where life is taking us.

I explain the situation to my roommate. Ask him what he thinks. He sits down in a chair. Opens his staff meal from work. Lights a cigarette. Looks back over at Eric and tell him he can stay. But he's going to have to start paying some rent. $300 a month. Directly to him and I.

Ah. The fucking genius. I never would've come up with that.

Eric agrees. Seems happy about the situation. That night Eric passes out on the couch. In the morning him and I go to his parents place. He picks up some things. Mainly clothes. Some blankets. A sleeping bag. Some hunting knives.

We don't have a spare room. So Eric has to get creative. He sets his things up under the stairs. Makes a pile. When he's done it looks more like a dogs bed than a humans. But he has as smile on his face.

The hundred and fifty bucks he gives me goes a long way. I start to live like some cocksure asshole with a factory job. I buy name brand cigarettes. Order extravagant dinners. Buy myself a new shirt.

For a while. I even walk with my head held up.

So for me. Things work out pretty good. Eric works days. Is gone by the time I get up. He always has some food. Something I can nibble on. I pick at his leftovers. Eat the edges of last night's meals while he's out there busting his ass all day.

After that I make sure to get out of the house. Try and avoid my roommate. I know he'll be gone by midafternoon. Then I can have the place to myself. Lay on the couch. Read. Listen to music. Enjoy the good life.

Eric usually gets home around six. As soon as he gets in the door he's looking for a drink. He has ideas. About what being a man is. And grabbing a beer before a shower is one of his main principles.

But he still has hang ups. Like he doesn't want to drink alone. He needs someone else along for the ride. So he pays my way. Even with his $150 still hot in my pocket. He comes home with bottles of good scotch. He likes to think he's doing his ancestors proud.

I pour myself large glasses. He tells me to drink more. So I don't slow down. Eric sits there and complains about his day. His boss. The clients. I get bored when he talks. My mind wanders. I only hear half of what he's saying. I only chime in when I think he needs to hear that I agree.

Eric pours himself another drink. Takes it to the bathroom. I hear the shower. I fix myself a glass. Lie down on the couch. Pick my book back up. And wait. Because I know when he gets out of there. He's going to have one thing on his mind. And I'll have to follow.

He comes down the stairs in his underwear. His black hair slicked back. He puts on a pair of pants. A clean, unwrinkled polo shirt done up to the top button. Some cologne. I smell like sweat. My pants are almost see through in the crotch. Beside him I look worse than normal.

But I don't really give a fuck. Because in a couple minutes. We'll be out that door. A shot of scotch warming our throats. Smokes in our hands and a lean to our walk. Laughing. Having the best time we can.

The bar we go to is an old shithole. There's never any girls there. Just the front room full of old men. Rotting factory workers who want nothing to do with us. Our youth. Or our loud voices.

So we stay in the back room. We sit in the corner. At a small round table. Eric buys a pitcher of watered down beer from the old crook behind the bar. We know he does it. And there's nothing we can do. Because the second we raise a stink he'll start looking for identification. Some proof of age.

Things we don't have.

So we take it. Because Eric likes the scenery. His old man works in a factory. His grandfather worked in a factory. It's all his family has known. And he wants to follow in their shadows. So even though he doesn't have the job. He can come sit here. And imagine what it's like to be one of the old men in the front room. Not talking. Watching a TV with the sound turned down.

Eric rambles on about it all. And I sit there. Drinking the beer he bought nodding along. Which is the only thing keeping me from telling him what I really think. That those old men just look like a long slow death to me. And life can't be all that good. If this is the place they come running to.

Our nights go on like this. The two of us in that musty back room. Eric buying jug after jug. We share a plate of pickled sausages and eggs. We get up and shoot pool. Talk about girls. And the lives we'll have when we finally get the job we've been told to shoot for.

The evenings always end the same. The bartender yelling over to us to hurry up. That 11 o'clock is fast approaching. The downside to drinking in an old man bar. They get sleepy. Stop drinking. But it works for Eric. His job. He needs to get up in the morning.

So we drink up. The bottoms of our glasses pointed to the ceiling. Then kick open the back door. Stumble the three blocks home. Smoking cigarettes. Eric singing old songs about labour. Unions. And striking.

I keep quiet. Wondering what the fuck is wrong with this kid. And why he wants to be a part of a union so bad. I don't see the allure. The charm. All I can figure is the poor kid is lonely. And wants to feel like he has a family. As perverse as that sounds to me.

The more and more I see of it I don't want it. The whole city stinks of it. And I start to feel like I need to escape. I feel like I need to know if there's more out there. Something better than the grim future Eric gets all worked up over.

Back home Eric pours another big glass of scotch. I take one for myself. I turn on the TV and before long Eric is passed out. Chin to his chest. When he starts to snore I turn up the volume.

My roommate comes home about an hour later. Slams the door behind him. I don't ask. But I get the impression he knows Eric will be sleeping. And likes to make him jump. That it gives him pleasure to shit on someone after a long night frying food for sports fans.

Eric pops up off the couch. His eyes still closed he crawls under the stairs. Pulls the blankets and sleeping bag up over his head. His boots and pants still on. Sticking out from under the mess. His half glass of whiskey still on the table.

Before my roommate sits down I pour Eric's drink into mine. I ask him how his day was. He complains about his boss. His coworkers. Everything. He rolls a joint while he does it. I know he'll smoke it with me. But his griping is the price I have to pay.

After that I go up to my room. Read for a while. Until the whiskey runs out. Then lie in bed with the lights off. Listening to the rumble of some video game from the living room. My roommate will be up until an hour before dawn.

I laugh a little before falling to sleep. Thinking of Eric down there. Under the stairs. And if it wasn't for the booze I'm sure he wouldn't get a minute of sleep.

The days go on like this for months. And every day I wake up I tell myself that it can't go on like this forever. We're having too much fun. And while it lasts it's nice. I can forget that I'm going nowhere. And there's no prospects.

One night I get stupid. Ask Eric if he can get me a job. He says he'd love to. But they just aren't looking for anyone. I nod my head. Say ok. But I don't believe him. I think that he doesn't want me to get the chance. That he wants to keep the work all to himself.

I pour another glass of his fine booze. Take a sip and tell myself he can go fuck himself. He can have his shitty job. What do I want it for anyways? Because right now, I've got all of Eric's perks. But I have nowhere to be in the morning.

But things don't last forever. The place Eric works at slows down. At first his hours get cut. Down to three days a week. He's in the apartment now when I wake up. I can't eat his food. I hide in my room on those days. Pretending to be asleep until the late afternoon.

His money starts running out. The bottles of booze become less frequent. The nights out are no longer nightly. We have to wait until Friday. Like all the other amateurs. The ones who don't have the strength. Or the youth. Or the cash to keep it going every night of the week.

Like we used to.

Now we just stay in. And without all the booze things get boring pretty quick. The only excitement is watching my roommate play video games. Praying that he'll smoke a joint with me. Anything to forget that I'm alive.

One night though,we get lucky. Some bum walks in the door. It happens so quick I just sit there. On the couch. Watching him get closer and closer. My roommate doesn't notice him. Too entranced in the game he's playing.

Eric is under the stairs. Polishing a pair of old black combat boots. And only looks up when he hears the door close. And by that time the drunk is almost beside him. The fear on Eric's face almost makes me laugh.

But I don't get a chance. Because the drunk trips over a bike lying in the middle of the floor. He lands chest first on Eric's tool belt. His short legs scraping over the bike. Which is the first look my roommate gets of him. And that's what I end up laughing at.

The drunk pops up like nothing. His eyes are rolled into the back of his head. Like a blind person. Or a great white about to bite down on a swimmer. He lets out a long drawn form of the English language. Something that sounds like 'Hey man, do you know where I can score a dime bag?'

My roommate tells him no. Sorry. Like this kind of thing happens all the time. He barely glances at him. Keeps playing his game. The drunk looks at him. Looks at me. Looks at Eric. Says he regrets bothering us. Bows like a gentleman. And like that he's back out the door. I never see him again. Or find out where he came from.

A week after that. Eric's boss cuts his hours back to none. He comes home with a pretty nice check. And he suggests we go down to the bar. Like we used to. I agree. But when we get there the old feeling is gone. And I no longer feel unbeatable.

We raise our glasses. Try to smile. Make a toast. We go home around nine.

He starts looking for another job. But it's tough. He wants all the same jobs that I do. The ones that aren't there. He tries to get a job with another place doing the same thing he had been doing. But he keeps getting told he doesn't have enough experience.

It goes on for a month. Until his money runs out. And we can't afford to support him. He asks me if I can float him a month. That he's sure he'll find something. And I almost laugh in his face. Because without his money. And kindness. I'm going right back to being a deadbeat.

I tell him that isn't going to happen. And he looks hurt. Like he really thought I'd be able to do something like that. Or that maybe I'd feel bad. And make an effort to buy back some of those drinks.

'Well,' he says, 'it looks like I'm going to have to go live with my mom.' and I don't blame him. The humility of it. Of having to give up like that. But she has a big place. On the other side of town in a social housing complex.

He tells me that he thinks his mom is starting to lose it. That even though his old man treated her like shit, she kept it together. He shakes his head. Says he's scared he's going to end up taking care of her.

I nod along. Tell him life's tough on people. But think to myself that his mom always seemed a little fucked to me. Her eyes were vacant. Cold and confused. Like she wasn't processing everything.

Eric sticks around for another week. It drives my roommate crazy. He keeps at Eric for money he doesn't have. I figure if he wants to starve under our stairs then good for him. But one day when I come home from a walk. All of his stuff is gone. And there's a key on the counter.

I take a look around. There's papers and pizza boxes everywhere. Two big garbage bags leaning against the television. Bottle caps and cigarette butts and empty pop bottles from one end of the room to the other. The place is beginning to look like a dump.

My reaction is to climb the stairs. Go into my room and shut the door behind me. Telling myself that things aren't going to be easy without all of Eric's booze. And I lie down in bed. Knowing I'll miss that the most.

24.

My roommate comes home excited one night. Tells me while we smoke a joint that he finally got his manager to give him the day shift. Because he's so happy I tell him that this is great news. But I'm too stoned or too slow to admit what it really means to me.

The way things work now is perfect. He sleeps all day. I see him for maybe an hour before he has to go to work. And then he's gone the rest of the night. Only returning late. When I'm about ready to go to sleep anyways.

It's like I have the place to myself. I feel good. I spend my nights alone. Reading on the couch. Ignoring the sound of the buzzer by the door. People downstairs wanting to come up. Spend their nights on my couch.

Ruining my solitude. My happiness.

And this is exactly what my roommate does. His need to be popular. Or loved. Answering the buzzer every time it rings. Inviting whoever the hell it is down there up.

Before I know it there's a party going on in the living room almost every night. I routinely find myself sitting on the end of the couch. Watching six or seven assholes running hash tokes into yellowed pop bottles off the ends of cigarettes.

I smoke their dope, but I can't stand them. They make me sick. I want them to meet with accidents. Car crashes. Violent home invasions. Or maybe a fire. I think of calling up my roommate's manager. Begging him. Pleading with the man to give my roommate all the night shifts. That he's ruining my life.

But I think better of it. There's no chance of it working. And then I'd have to explain myself. Of course his boss is going to tell him. That some crazed maniac claiming to be his roommate called up. Begging him to give him all the shittiest shifts he could.

Well, I could always tell him it was a joke.

Instead I do what I can to avoid the situation. Like take to walking the streets at night. Wandering up and down the deserted main street for hours on end. Until I get bored. Or tired. Or paranoid that the degenerate stoners my roommate has over are rifling through my things.

Most of the people who come over are just looking for a room to get stoned in. People who've heard that this is the place to sit around and watch TV in. But one of them is the little brother of our friend George Georgopolus. Another welfare bum tattooer.

The whole Georgopolus family is fat, sweaty and gross. George does all right. Because he can draw. Has a good attitude. Genuinely makes an effort. But his little brother Lou. Total opposite. As long as I've known him he's quick to anger. And defense.

But then again. Everyone calls him a slob. Or a fat fuck. So I can see his reasons.

So last winter he did something about it. He took to the Georgopolus' garage, which had always been George's art studio until he moved out with a girlfriend, and turned the space into home gym. No one saw him. He disappeared.

No one knew what happened. Sure, rumors floated around. But none were as strange, or as boring, as the truth. Because Lou was out there in that garage. Lifting weights. Shunning his mother's gravy heavy meals in favour of bars and shakes and brightly coloured drinks originating from a powder.

The fat fuck was getting skinny.

In the spring. People started to see him around again. No one could believe it. Lou was a new person. The first time I run into him in the parkette across the street from our place I don't recognize him. And when my roommate is done talking to him, I try to introduce myself.

And I feel like an idiot because he looks at me like I'm one. So I laugh at myself. And to cover I ask Lou where the rest of his ass went.

His reaction isn't much. A shy smile. The pride of his accomplishment in his eyes. The old Lou would've snapped. Been on the verge of tackling me down on the pavement. Beating me. And quite frankly, I'm lucky that by the look of things he's been practicing restraint.

Or he managed to sweat out being an asshole.

When he was fat he spent his nights somewhere else. Never at our place. He didn't like drugs or booze or good times. He was shy and angry. So he was at home. In his bedroom. Playing video games alone.

But now. His hungers are different. And he craves getting fucked up. Night after night I watch him. Doing his fucking best to outdo everyone in the room. If you smoked a gram he smoked five. Then drank a litre of vodka. And ate a handful of pills.

And for a few months he holds onto himself. Keeps the act under control. He laughs. Doubles over grabbing his sides. Has conversations. He shares himself. I learn more about him in a couple weeks than I have the years he's been around. Hanging out on the periphery.

And it's nice to see him like this. Happy. Because before last winter. I don't remember him ever cracking a smile.

He's got a nice one too. At least for as long as he keeps using it.

Because soon his new strength gets the better of him. He realizes he's stronger than most of the people that tormented him. And a lot that never did. He takes of advantage of it. His payback for all the years of shit that got shoveled his way.

And the nights of his laughter turn south. He starts to crack. To lose control. Flies off the handle. His tactics involve yelling and snarling an inch from your face. Like some wild animal is right there. About to sink it's teeth into your face.

It's terrifying. And some afternoons. When it's just my roommate and I sitting around. We start to remember fondly the shy overweight kid we used to make fun of.

His only other mood is somber depression. He smokes himself into a fog. Doesn't share with anyone in the room. Ignores all attempts at including himself in the conversation. And when it starts to turn into tomorrow he gets up and leaves. All without saying a thing.

I start to get sick of seeing him. And when he comes over. I wait until I'm good and stoned off other people's dope. Say I need some fresh air. That I'm too baked. I get called a pussy nightly. But it's worth it. I know no one will want to come with me. I know that I'll get some peace.

After a while Lou stops showing up so much. Disappears for a couple of weeks at a time. When he shows back up he looks scrawny. Has large black bags under his eyes. When I ask where he's been he doesn't look at me. And mumbles that he's been busy. Starts packing a bowl.

After that I write him off. Just another asshole here to take advantage.

One night it's just my roommate and I. We're having a coupe of drinks. I get loose with my words. Ask him how in the hell he manages to hang out with Lou. How he can stand the bullshit. Because in my eyes. The guy's not doing himself any favors.

He tells me he's been thinking the same things. That when he comes over he barely speaks to him either. He says that when he takes off for a couple weeks at a time. He's at an all night gym. Hanging with some meatheads. Lifting weights. Taking speed.

'That explains why he looks like a bag of shit,' I say.

We both laugh.

After that I don't see Lou for at least a month. And when I do it's across the street. In the parkette on the corner. Lots of people hang out over here. So it's s good place to bum a smoke. Get some air. See where the action is.

I go down there with my roommate. We sit on the bench. My room-mate talks to some other kids. People I only know as background characters in the places I go. He tells them stories. Tells them all kinds of shit. But I drown him out with my own thoughts. While I slowly smoke a cigarette and stare into the distance.

And that's when Lou walks up. The first thing I think is he looks damn awful. Like he's been crying. And I guess my roommate notices it too. Because he stops his tirade. Asks Lou what the fuck is going on.

He tells us a long story. One that involves him trying to buy some hash oil from a dealer known for being a piece of shit. That he handed over the money no problem. But when he got home. Rolled up a joint. He found out all he had was a couple ounces of tainted Vaseline.

Retail value less than $6.

Now Lou was out a lot more money than that. And he had no clue what he's going to do next. I can't help myself. And before I can stop. I'm asking him what the fuck he was thinking. That he should've seen it coming.

He stands there not moving. And I'm not sure if he heard a word I said. His face looks so fucking vacant. That I think he might be in shock. But then he pipes up. Starts asking for advice.

'Get those meathead speed freak buddies of yours,' I tell him, 'Go over to his place. Kick down the fucking door. Scare the shit out of them. What the hell else can ya do?'

But Lou isn't so sure. He's in way over his head. He's just a simple fat kid. He comes from a kind and loving family. One that's probably at home right now. Worrying themselves to death over him. He doesn't know the first thing about home invasions.

'Maybe if you knock on his door. Ask real polite. He'll just hand it all over.' I feel sorry for him.

'Really?' his eyes light up.

I shake my head.

The story circulates around. Rumors of the dealer bragging about his accomplishment. People start calling Lou a fool openly. He gets embarrassed. He stops coming around. He goes back into hiding. But we barely notice.

Until a few months later. A Friday night. Someone comes into some money. I know I'm told the reason why but I don't really care. Because they're over here. And the living room is full. We've got cases of beer. Bottles of whisky. And I'm just drunk enough to put up with it all.

So I have to say my spirits are pretty high.

When the phone rings I pick it up. Expecting someone who wants to come over. And when the voice reminds me it's George, the first thing I do is invite him over. Tell him about the booze. And the dozen or so girls that aren't normally among the regulars.

But he declines right off the bat. Asks me if I have seen his brother. I tell him that I haven't. That it's been weeks since he's been by. I ask why he's looking. And if he's called those weightlifter buddies of his.

He tells me no. But that it's a good lead. Asks for their number. Skips over why he's looking. I tell him we don't have it. That Lou was pretty tight-lipped about those guys. And the things they did together.

I apologize for not being more help. And he says it's no big deal. But if Lou does show up. I should tell him to give his brother a call. I try to convince him to come over and tell him himself in case he shows up. But he declines and tells me to have a good time.

So I hang the phone up. And start to do just that. I sit beside a girl I don't know. One who's thin and pretty and wearing the tightest jeans in the place. I ask her name. Take a puff from a joint that gets passed my way.

And before I know it. I forget all about George calling. And the tinge of fear in his voice.

· · · · · · ·

We don't get the whole story until Monday. When the phone calls start coming in. When the rumors start circulating. That Lou'd hit the skids. That after he got ripped off he felt like the whole world was out to get him. That no matter how hard he tried. He just couldn't win.

He spent all that time. Losing all that weight. But he felt like it didn't get him anywhere. That he still got pushed around. That he still couldn't get a girl to go out with him. He got more and more depressed.

He quit doing drugs. Things got worse. The Georgeopolus's got worried. They took him to see a doctor. And his opinion was that Lou's body was used to the drugs. And now that Lou cut them out he was going into some kind of psychosis.

So they gave him more drugs.

The night that George called us Lou had been particularly bad. He left in the middle of the day. Didn't come back. Didn't call to say he was all right. While George was calling around Lou was pretty close to home. Turned out he was only about a kilometer away. By the railroad tracks.

At two in morning a light came around the bend. Lou went into the middle of the tracks. Completely out of options. And laid down. We went to the funeral at the end of the week.

And that day. The one thing I could understand. Was how hopeless Lou felt. And I started to think he might be on to something.

25.

I'm down at the parkette. It's all concrete. Inlaid brick. There's two big long wooden benches. Some bushes in the corner to piss and do drugs behind. And a short walk along the back. The division between us and a dusty municipal parking lot.

Tonight I'm on the wall. Hunched over. Smoking a cigarette. Not involved in any of the conversations around me. But aware of them. Listening in a half-cocked sort of way.

And through the chatter I pick up on one. A kid I know. But only from around. He's a few feet away. Talking casually about the fast food joint he works in. How it's a god damned shit hole. But they're hiring.

For some reason. Through my better judgment. And total commitment to the factory life I have ahead of me. And my love for the life of miserable leisure I already lead. I get up. Interrupt their conversation. To ask if he can put a good word in for me.

I'm not all that quick. But the look on his face says he'd rather eat a shit sandwich. Not knowing what reaction to take, I stare at him. Not in his eyes, mind you. But through him. Through the city. Through time.

He has all the same fears as the guy at the gas station. That I'll show up late. Drag my ass through my shift. Be rude to the customers. Make an unimpressive burger. And leave a great big black mark next to his name in the process.

But he gives in. Says I should go in the next morning. Fill out an application. Then when he comes in for his afternoon shift he'll talk to the manager. Tell her that we're old friends.

I tell him thanks. Walk away. Sit down on the wall again. This time a little further down. I light another smoke. And think about what I've just done. Now I have to go there tomorrow. I have to fill out the application. Or I'll prove him right.

That I am a lazy bum. And I don't need that attached to me. Or else no one is ever going to help me.

But I'm not sure if I'm making the right decision. Is this what I want? Is this how I want to give up on my easy life. But I tell myself I've handed out hundreds of resumes now. No factories are calling. Gas stations reject me. And I can't even get a job as a janitor.

Which I thought would be a breeze.

I sit there. Oblivious to everyone around me. Telling myself that this is the only answer. That all I can do is give in. Get a job flipping burgers. Which for some reason I feel better than.

So I get up. Go home early. Spend the rest of the night in my room. Trying to convince myself that this is what I should do. And that I'm making the right decision. Because I feel like if I take this job. Then this will be the end of my life.

And in the morning I wake up early. Lie in bed and smoke a ciga- rette. Take a shower. Put on clean clothes. Comb my hair and brush my teeth. Tell myself that I look great. That I look like the kind of guy who can deep-fry potatoes with zeal. And who'll never ask any questions.

When I get there I ask a kid behind the counter for an application form. He looks annoyed when he ducks under the counter to grab one. A part of me hopes he'll offer up a free breakfast. Or at least an orange juice. But all I get is the paper I asked for. And a dirty look when he lets me borrow a pen.

I sit at a table in the dining area. Fill in all the boxes on the form. Every one of these at every place I go is always the same damn thing. Just a different company name at the top. I fill in my name. My age. My sex. My address. My job history.

I make sure all the lies I tell are the same as the ones on my resume.

Around me are people eating. And for the first time I notice the smell. And my stomach rumbles. I start to think yeah. This might not be so bad. At the very least I'll be able to eat better. All the free hamburgers I can handle.

So when I go hand over the pen. And my resume. And my application I'm feeling pretty good about the whole thing. That at least I won't feel these awful pains in my stomach anymore. The ones that wake me up in the middle of the night.

The ones caused by eating nothing but white rice.

I walk home feeling good. Like this is the end of having to go to unemployment meetings. And workfare. And dropping off my damn job search forms. I'll miss the meetings with my caseworker. And her beautiful skin. But I can't have everything.

In my head. When I pass other people walking I think, 'Fuck you. I'm going to have a job soon. I'm not a god damned bum anymore. I'm on my way.' And when I get home I tell myself this is the last pot of rice I'll be eating for awhile.

But the next day. When I pick up the phone. And the manager is asking for me. I'm frozen by fear. My attitude has changed. I've had time to think about it. That I like the pace of my life. And when I say sure, I'll come in for the interview, I can't believe it.

I watch my roommate. My friends. The poor saps. They might have more possessions. And brighter futures. But god damn, they work like animals. Come home sweating. Angry. Complaining that it's no fucking way to live a life.

And here I am. Walking right into it. Willingly.

But the next day, when the time comes, I'm ready. Dressed nicely. Which is tough. The shirt I'm wearing is too big. Is stained along the bottom. I tuck it in. Look in the mirror. I smile. Trying to hide my chipped teeth.

I shrug my shoulders. Because this is as good as it gets.

At the burger joint, I walk up the counter. A girl asks me what I'd like to eat. I tell her I'm here to see the manager. That I have an interview. She laughs. Tells me to go sit at a table in the corner. And wait.

I go over. Close my eyes. Take a deep breath. Dream the dream of burgers again. My stomach rumbles. I start to get bored. It feels like I've been sitting here forever. I'm beginning to get antsy. I think that maybe they've forgotten me. Or taken one look and decided it isn't going to work.

And just as I'm about to get up, to spare them having to tell me to leave, a hefty woman in a mildly better version of the dump's uniform comes over. Introduces herself. Sits down. Asks me why I want to work here.

I stall a second. My initial reaction is to tell her I'm running out of options. That I've handed out hundreds of resumes. And this is the only place that'll even consider me. But then I remember the meetings. All the tricks I was taught in that small conference room.

So I lie. Tell her I love cooking. Am thinking of becoming a chef. And I want a taste of what it's like to work in a kitchen. I lay it on thick. I'm pretty proud of myself. Because my on the spot lying is getting to be second nature.

I'm becoming a professional.

She smiles as I'm talking. And when I'm done she says that this is a great place to start. That I'm going to learn all the essentials of professional food preparation. And a lot of former employees have gone on to school for cooking. Made a life of it.

'Oh, great,' I reply.

She asks me what my availability is. I tell her that my schedule is pretty wide open. And she says that's perfect. That they need someone for the evening shift. From 7 pm until 3 am.

'That won't be a problem will it?' she asks. And when I say no she asks if I can start right away. If it would be too much to come back later today. I don't want that at all. I need a couple days to get used to the idea. But I know I can't refuse. Or there goes the job.

And I hear myself saying sure. I can come back today.

She tells me that I have to buy a uniform. That they take it from your first check. She looks me up and down. Assures me they have some pants and shirts in my size. That when I come back later the night manager will sort it all out.

I get up. Shake her hand. Tell her thanks. That I appreciate it. She smiles again. And then she tells me that one of the perks of the job is that when we're working we get a 25% discount. And then when we're not a 5% one.'

What the fuck. There goes my dreams. And I leave angry. Telling myself there has to be a way. That they can't keep their eyes on me all the time. That I'm sure I can still eat my fill of this garbage each day.

When I get outside I light a smoke. Think about what I've done. I've agreed to come back later today. And when I do the math in my head. I'm going to have just enough time to walk home and then back again.

I put my head down. Follow my feet in the direction of home. Start thinking about how this is going to change my life. That after a couple weeks of working here I'm going to have some big fat paycheck. Money in my pocket and the confidence that comes with it.

At home I run the kitchen sink until it's cold. Fill up a large glass. Sit down on the couch. And stupidly, before my first shift even starts, scared by the posters on the walls of the welfare office offering jail time for committing fraud, I pick up the phone and call my caseworker.

The first thing she does is congratulate me. Tells me that of all her clients, she always knew that I was going to do something with myself. That I have always had the power to make something of myself. I don't know how to respond. I'm embarrassed. No one's ever said they believed in me.

So I just say thanks. And before I hang up she tells me to call if I need any advice. She'll be happy to help. I nod my head even though she can't see me, hang up the phone and walk back across town for the 4th time today.

· · · · · · ·

I show up about 15 minutes early. I'm sweating and thirsty when I walk through the door. I don't know what to do. How to announce my presence. So I stand at the end of the line. Behind all the other fools in here. Jealous of everyone sipping on straws.

At the counter a dead eyed teenage boy asks how he can help me. I tell him I'm the new employee. He yells over his shoulder. Into the back of the restaurant. More of an announcement than I was looking for.

A hefty woman comes into sight. I don't think that she's the same one that hired me. Although I can't be certain. Because the hairnet and uniform make it hard to tell the difference between humans.

She looks at me with a scowl. Like I'm not supposed to be here. That she doesn't have the time to deal with me. The woman who told me to come in had been nice. Warm. But this one wasn't.

I get a grunt of a hello. She tells me to come on back. And motions to a door leading in behind the counter. When I open it I get a better view of the kitchen. I can see the guy who got me the job. He's standing at the grill. There's about 30 patties in front of him. He's sweating like a pig. He has a grease soaked apron.

His face is bright pink. He looks faint. He looks sick. He looks disgusting. I begin to question whether or not I've made an awful decision. That maybe I'd be better off sitting at home right now. Waiting for the first of the month to roll around.

He looks over at me, from the corner of his eye. But all I get in form of recognition is a barely perceptible nod. And then his eyes are back on the sizzling patties. I watch the sweat run down from his temples. Along his jaw. Until it drips off onto the grill.

And then the manager is imploring me to follow her. Past the grill and the deep fryers. Around a corner. She leads me deeper into the back of the place. Pointing out things like the freezer. The drive through window. And various machines I don't catch the names of.

The whole time we're avoiding other members of the staff. They run back and forth. Slipping on the wet greasy floor. They all look scared. Like what they're doing matters. Like one fuck up could mean something. Other than some over-cooked french fries.

The manager takes me into a small office. It's more like a closet with a desk in it. She tells me to sit down. That I have to sit here for a while watching training videos. So I know all the protocol. So she doesn't have to teach me.

There's a stack of videos on the desk. Before she leaves she tells me that I have to watch them in order. Starting with 1. Which I tell her makes sense. She gives me a dirty look. Her face goes red. And she asks if I'm getting smart with her.

'Um, no,' I reply. Feeling like I'm back in high school. Sitting in the principles office. Waiting to get shit on for some minor act of disrespect. Or individual freedom. She eyes me up and down. Her face a mask of disgust.

I don't have the heart to tell her I feel the same way. So instead. I give her the finger when her back is turned. Who does she think she is? Her problem is that she believes in the power of her slightly different uniform.

I have nothing else to do. So I pop in the 1st tape. The chain's founder is standing there. Smiling. Like someone's grandfather. I smile. Because I remember the news reports a couple years ago. When his heart blew up.

Yet here he is. Wearing a collared shirt embroidered with the restaurants name. Trying to make me give a shit about this place. These burgers. And his name. All from beyond the grave.

It's some accomplishment.

I sit in the office for an hour or two. The founder walks me through some important steps. Like the reason for a tucked-in shirt. And how to wash my hands. His teeth gleam as he happily tells me. I groan. Shift in my chair. Wonder if I can smoke back here.

On the fourth tape things get interesting. Actions shots of the founder looking over the shoulders of a happy employee. His calm serene voice calmly going over all the steps. The proper way to make a hamburger. There's a very specific style employed. It takes a sharp mind to get it right.

I start to panic. Lose any faith I have in myself. I can't remember the order in which all condiments must be applied. I feel sick. And wonder if anyone will know if I watch the tape over again.

But I don't get a chance. Because the manager is standing in the doorway. Telling me that the guy cooking burgers is going home. That I can fill in for him. I ask her if I can just watch that part over again. I want to make sure that things go smoothly. That I don't want to give the place a bad name.

'If you don't want to cook burgers. That's fine. Pack up your shit and leave,' she tells me. And I don't want to be cooking burgers. I want to be at home. Smoking a joint with my roommate. But I know I can't give up that quick.

So I shake my head and say no. She nods her head. Like she's won. And after she throws me a uniform she tells me to change and meet her by the grill. I think about shoving every burger in this place up her ass.

But my caseworker. She's so proud of me. So I just put on the pants. Which are too big at the waist. I need to use my belt. But strangely enough, the cuffs are so small I can barely pass my foot through.

The shirt feels damp when I put it on. A thin layer of grease covering it I convince myself. Better than the other theories I could think of. Like the shirt had already done a shift today. An idea backed up by a horrible odor seeping from it.

But I don't have a choice. When I get to the grill, I feel like a clown. The manager looks more annoyed than ever standing there. Asks me what took so long. Doesn't give me a chance to reply before telling me there have to be enough burgers on the grill at all times.

That I have to foresee the need.

'How d'you do that?' I ask. Certain I didn't see it in the training video. She rolls her eyes. Informs me that it will come to me. That I will get to know how to foresee the rushes. But I also have to make sure I don't waste any patties.

A thin line that I later find out doesn't matter. If I want to. I can cook them into black dust. They recycle those ones for the chili. And it's a good thing. Because for the rest of the night. Standing there sweating in front of that grill. I must burn a whole truckload of burgers to charcoal.

And no amount of cooking them in spicy tomato sauce will loosen them up. The manager gives me shit all night. And I get nervous. Start fucking up the order of the toppings. She chastises me more than once for spreading the mustard on before the mayonnaise.

I try to see her point. How people expect things a certain way. And I have a hard time not laughing in her face. Picturing some asshole out there in his car. Inspecting his burger. Flying into a rage about where the lettuce is.

The manager chews me out in front of the whole staff each chance she gets. And I remember the fear in the eyes of the employees when I came in. I understand it now. This woman's a pig. And I want to tell her. But I can't. I need the job.

And that's when I know what it feels like to be an adult. Someone without any power. I finish out the night with my head down. Doing my best to keep the old bitch from noticing me.

The dining room closes at eleven. And the manager goes home at midnight. It's like a thousand pounds of greasy flesh lifted from the back of everyone that works here. We all breathe easier when she's out the door.

The next manager doesn't come in for six hours. I fry 12 pieces of bacon. Slap four patties down on the grill. Make sure not to burn them. Toast just as many buns. Put whatever the fuck I want on them in whatever order. I lean against the ice cream machine. Eat all four.

A girl whose shift started later than mine comes over to me. Stands as close as she can. Tells me I shouldn't be stealing burgers on my first shift. That they know if you take them. Everything is checked off three times.

I look her up and down. And even in her ill fitting uniform I can tell she looks good with it off. I smile at her. Burger bits in my teeth. Tell her I've burned so damn many tonight they'll never know. And I'll be fine.

She smiles back at me. Tells me she doesn't want to see me get fired on my first night. That there aren't any cool people working here. She winks. Brushes her tits against me as she walks away.

And for a second I think I'm going to like working here.

When my shift is over I don't change clothes. There's no point. My skin reeks of fried cattle. I scrub my forearms in a sink in the back. I still have a sheen to me. Like a coating of Vaseline. If I put on my regular clothes they'll be ruined.

Instead I roll them up. Stuff them into a large paper takeout bag. I buy a large fry. A couple more burgers. A large cola. I take my time getting home. It's nice out. I'm glad the night's over.

I'm proud. I have a job. I'm a man.

28.

Even though I can't stand it. I get into the swing of things. I get out of bed in the late morning. Shower and put on my uniform. I haven't got paid yet. They say the first check takes a couple of weeks. So I don't eat before I leave.

I walk along the main street until I get there. My hands in my pockets. My head down. My stomach growling. And I'm not quite sure what's supposed to be better about being a working man. Because it seems like I have it a lot worse.

Because now I don't have any time. I can't take a long walk in the morning to clear my head. I can't spend days on the couch. The sun coming in the window. Reading book after book after book.

Now I have to be somewhere. Show up when they tell me I have to be there. Which is even worse than school. Because at least then I could skip. Come up with some half-assed excuse. And not have to worry.

I used to tell myself that work would be easy. That going wouldn't be this hard. That I'd see the money. I'd have motivation. But I was wrong. I realize something about myself. That I value time over dollars.

And the nights working behind the grill are already killing me. My back is sore all the time. I spent the last of my money at the pharmacy. A bottle of caffeine pills to keep me moving. And another of pain medication recommended by the pharmacist.

'It's the only one that still contains codeine,' he tells me. A smile on his face and an outstretched hand holding the bottle.

But he isn't running his mouth. Because they sure do work. And I'm able to start flipping burgers in a near sleep state. Semi-conscious of my surroundings. But more tuned in. And I start to feel the waves of people. The rushes.

Each night I burn fewer and fewer.

Which I thought would get me some praise. Some compliments. A pat on the back at least from the manager. But I'm way off. And every chance she gets she's wrist deep up my ass about something.

If she tells me to clean something I do it wrong. She tells me my uniform is a mess. That I need to look respectful. She's not wrong. The clothes are a damn mess. But I look at her like she's crazy. Wondering why. Because none of the slobs that come in here ever see me.

I spend my breaks past the drive through lane. Out behind the dumpster at a picnic table. Drinking cokes that are coming out of my check. Chain smoking cigarettes I owe to people. Wishing for an accident. Or a power outage. Anything that might give me a few hours peace.

It's not even the end of my first full week yet. And I hate it. I don't get it. I think about my father. And all the other people I've known who've been working their entire adult lives away. I can't believe it. That they go in day after day. And haven't managed to kill themselves.

Really, it's impressive.

On my walk home one night. I run into a brother of my stepmother. He tells me it's been so long since he's seen me. Asks me how I'm getting along in the world. I guess it's too dark for him to notice the uniform. The nametag.

So I fill him in. And he looks at me like I'm stupid. Like this is a job for a moron. Or some asshole teenager saving up for prom. He tells me to go out to one of the factories. Say that I need some work. Those jobs are for men.

'That's what my boy did. Now he's got himself a truck,' he lets me know while beaming with pride.

I tell him my story. All the long walks out to the factories. Months of it. All for nothing. I let him know that after all the work I never even got a call. That maybe I'm not what they're looking for.

He face contorts as I fill him in. He leaves shaking his head. Unable to believe that I can't get the job that seems to be so easy for everyone else to get. I begin to feel I'd have looked better if I just said that I was on welfare.

And I walk the rest of the way home confused. Because I thought that if I had a job I'd get less of those looks. Sure. I no longer get the abhorred look. The one reserved for snakes. Or shit on the bottom of your shoe.

But those were almost better. Because I understood them. Because collecting welfare I'm just fucking garbage. That's the run of it. But now. Here I am making a living. And it seems like everyone still disapproves.

It's impossible to please people, I tell myself. No matter what I'm doing I never get the approval of anyone. Not teachers. Not friends. Not parents. And I wonder if every move I've ever made has been a wrong one.

Which is easy to believe in. At least from where I'm standing.

· · · · · · · ·

I come into work. The manager is up my ass before I even get behind the counter. She tells me that I won't be behind the grill tonight. I'm relieved. I hate the pressure. And I've never fully gotten the hang of rolling with the wave of degenerates that eat here.

She tells me tonight's the night. That they need me to work the drive-through window. I tell her it's alright. I'll stay behind the grill.

Which she doesn't like. It's me being smart again. And she tells me I don't have a choice. Her ugly face scrunched up. Leaning towards me. Doing everything she can to intimidate me.

But by now I've come to realize something. She's just miserable with her life. Trying to rub her odor on me. And everyone else who works here.

So I'm not all that bothered.

She starts laying it out for me. How things run. That the voices coming through the headset are not the people currently at the window. I have to keep my cool. But I'm already panicking.

The last things she says to me, her words of encouragement, are that she'll be wearing a headset. Listening in. And if I get into any trouble she'll come to help.

And by the time a rush starts I'm sweating. Worse than I ever sweat standing in front of the grill. Another employee passes me food and drinks to put in bags. She looks at me with concern. Her light brown eyes crushing my spirits.

When she asks me if I'm all right I tell her no. And feel like crying.

I drop some fool's change between the building and his car. He gives me a dirty look when he opens his door to retrieve it. But I'm so backed up that I barely have time to shrug my shoulders at him.

When I knock over a soda. And it spills over the counter onto my lap, I give up. I can't take it. I've never been a religious person before. But I look towards the heavens. And out loud, so everyone can hear, I ask Jesus Christ to help me.

And in a way he does.

Because then the manager comes storming over. Her face so red her head looks like a balloon about to pop. Which I find comical. And I must smile a little. Relieved. Already knowing my time at the window is over.

She yells at me. Tells me to get out of here. Go in the back and wait for her. That she needs to talk to me. And even though I'm grateful to be rid of that awful nightmare, I don't like her tone. And on my way to the back I take my headset off. Throw it against a wall.

The sound of the cheap plastic shattering calms me down a little. But not much. And I'm still pretty angry when the manager comes back. So as she tells me I can't swear, I'm stunned. I think, When did I swear?

I tell her as much. And she says Jesus Christ is a swear. I laugh at her. The most spiritual moment I've ever had. Asking a savior for help in a time of need. It was biblical.

To her though, my explanation seems blasphemous. And she gets even angrier. She paces back and forth. Stomping like a horse. And maybe that's when she makes up her mind. Because the next thing she does is fire me.

And for some reason I'm surprised. I figured I was due for a stern talking to. A little pleading on my part. A faked apology. Then I could go back to the grill. Head hung in a mock shame.

So I ask her if she's serious. She looks shocked by my audacity. Tells me that it's not working out. That I just don't fit in. That they can't have me around anymore. Says I can come in and pick up my check on Friday.

'And don't forget to hand in your uniform. Or we'll have to charge you,' she threatens.

Which is about all I can take. And a translucent red film washes over my vision. I stand up. Point my finger about 5cms from her face and tell her she can shove this uniform up her ass.

And it's the first time I've ever seen her speechless.

I leave her standing there. I walk past her. Through the back kitchen. Towards the drive through window. And I realized I was probably yelling. And they heard everything I said.

No one's working. They're all just staring at me. And the girl at the drive through. With nice brown eyes. Looks like she's watching a monster kick down a wall and eat people.

But not for a second do I ever stop to think I might be overreacting. And the next thing I do is look at the guy who got me the job. The one who was so afraid of me dirtying his name. And instead of apologizing. Like a regular person. I tell him to fuck himself before kicking open the door.

Everyone in the dining room is looking now. I'm a path of destruction. And I'm incapable of stopping it. So I raise my middle finger towards them yelling 'I pissed in the Pepsi!'

I get outside. Take a deep breath of the grease-tinted air. And suddenly I feel better. Like I was never supposed to be there. I light a smoke. And slowly walk the long walk home. Never once concerned some offended diner might be on my tail.

And it's the closest I've felt to being invincible.

Until it starts to sink in. That I'm not sure what I'm going to do now. The check those bastards owe me isn't big enough to cover the rent I'm going to owe. And I'd like to eat.

My only option is welfare again. But I don't know if they're going to take me back. The rule is you have to wait 3 months of being destitute. Jobless. Or they just tell you to get lost. And I'm pretty sure I just fucked myself.

When I get home my roommate is sitting on the couch. He looks at the clock on the VCR. He looks at me. Asks what I'm doing home so early. And even before I tell him, he looks at me like he already knows the ending. And all I'm doing is filling in the details.

I go up to my room. I hide there for a few days. When I come out the first thing I do is call my old caseworker. I leave a message. Tell her a short version. Wait for her to call back.

When she does she sounds genuinely concerned. She asks what happened. I tell her a story that stops directly after I ask Jesus for help. I tell her the manager had it out for me. A real hater.

She tells me that it's terrible. I ask if there's anything she can do for me. And I'm told that it shouldn't be a problem. It hasn't been that long. My case hasn't been officially closed. And that she can get me a check for the first of the month.

And I fall in love with her all over again.

Before I hang up the phone she tells me that things are going to work out. That I'm not going to be stuck like this forever. There are bigger things out there for me.

After we hang up I can breathe easier. I'll be able to pay rent. I'll be able to eat. I pick up a check on Friday. It should get me though to the end of the month.

I sink back into the couch. And even though things are going all right I wish that it would swallow me. I wish that everything would just end.

29.

It's been the rumor for years. That the employees out at the Ford plant are getting old. That they'll all retire soon. And the factory will have to hire again. Young guys like me. Fresh out of school. No prospects.

But it seems like the whispers are louder these days. The men at the employment office with faded jeans are looking a little better. Livelier. Their faded faces now filled with hope.

Which makes them look more wretched to me. Because I feel like I can see the thoughts behind their eyes. Their dreams of striking it big. Good pay. Stability. The golden ticket.

I know first hand. I lived in the luxury the place afforded. My old man did all right by them. There was never a time when there wasn't food in the refrigerator.

Or gas in the car.

Or the boat.

Or the truck.

I sit at the job bank. Listening to them chat together. Corroborating evidence. A step brother or uncle or some other fuck lucky enough to already work there is always the source. A confirmation that the old men are leaving in droves.

So I begin to think this is my time. The stars are aligning. There's no chance of me failing. My old man's been working there his whole life. As long as the place has been open. He's worked in every department.

And I believe the job is my birthright.

A fact I'm proud of. Like I'm going to be continuing some grand tradition. A tradition of men with no education. Sweating their lives away. Happily collecting twice what I spend in a month each week.

I convince myself that I have the job already. And that these old fools sitting here are delusional. That they're heads are rotting with age.

Who the hell is going to want them. When there's young flesh like me. Ready to give up.

But to get a leg up I'm going to have to call my old man. We talk from time to time. But not often. And it's not for any reason. Other than we both share a dislike of the phone. And rarely have much to say.

I call when I'm sure my step mother isn't around. I don't want to hear her voice. I don't want to have to pretend to like her. I hope my old man is on night shift.

So I can catch him during the day.

He picks up. He doesn't sound happy to hear my voice. Or the opposite of that either. Just indifferent. It's his way. I ask how things are. He tells me it's all the same. That nothing changes. He asks me. And I haven't much to say either.

So I don't waste any time. I tell him about the buzz on the street. Down at the unemployment office. How Ford is hiring. And I don't say anything. But I wonder why he never called me. To let me know he has an application form for me. My foot in the door.

He tells me he's heard the same things. But he's not sure if he'll be any help. That he's not anything special out there. I tell him it doesn't matter. That it'll give me a chance. Compared to all the other deadbeats out there.

He says ok. That he'll grab an application when he goes in that night. But for some reason. I feel like he doesn't want to put in a good word for me. That he's concerned. Like the burger cook. Of me putting a smear across his name too.

And I can't guarantee that I won't.

He tells me he'll come by tomorrow. Before work. I can fill it out. He'll take it in with him. I tell him thanks. He hangs up. And this is it, I say to myself. The end of my poverty. I sit back in my bed. Light a cigarette. Put my feet up.

I begin to dream of all the things I'll buy. A great big truck. Eat steak every night. Have cold milk in the fridge. Pay my roommate to move out.

Then I'll finally be a big man.

. . . .

Every day after my old man takes the application in for me I expect to get a call. But I don't. I begin to think that it's just a rumor. That men with high hopes are spreading the vicious lie all over town.

I get angry. Depressed. Feel stupid for falling for it. The buzz around the local bums. I sit at home while my friends go out. Get drunk. Meet girls with pretty smiles. Soft skin. Jobs of their own. And money to spend.

So I start to get worried. That I'll never meet anyone. That I'm going to be alone. That I'll never have the life that I was told will be mine. I get depressed. I lose faith.

Months roll by. I haven't handed out a resume in ages. I don't see the point anymore. There always seems to be a better man for the job. One who's more qualified. Or whose clothes smell better.

And after the rumors of getting fired make the rounds I know I'm fucked. That no one will stick up for me now. Because I confirmed all their suspicions.

I'm a volatile loser.

My caseworker barely ever calls. Has stopped making appointments for me. She has fifty other people just like me. As long as I don't make any waves she leaves me alone. Deals with those that cause her the most grief.

She hasn't even sent me out for workfare since I've been fired. A fact that I'm not going to bring to their attention. One humiliation that I don't have to deal with.

One afternoon I go out. Walk around the city. Hit up the food bank. The Salvation Army. I score some good stuff. Margarine. Beans. Stale bread. I have everything to make the finest meal I've eaten in awhile.

So when I get home I'm in high spirits. Even though my roommate is sitting on the couch. And the place stinks of marijuana. He's got a smile on his face. He tells me that he's got the night off. That Max is on his way.

And that there's a message on the machine for me. I don't think anything of it. Imagine it's from my caseworker. Some meeting or seminar I'm going to have to attend. So I slide some bread in the toaster. Put the beans in a pot. Turn on the stove before I pick up the receiver.

I listen to the message. It's from Ford. They want me to go to a group aptitude test. Out at some hotel in the middle of nowhere. It's the priliminary test. To see if I have the brain power. The physical capabilites.

If I fit the mold of what they're looking for.

This is what I was born for. There's no chance for failure.

I can't believe it. I'd just about given up. Had become comfortable with the idea of my lifelong poverty. But here's my chance. To make a future for myself. To have all the things I'm supposed to have.

Like a mortgage and car payments and vacation photos from resorts in foreign countries.

I listen to the message three times. I can't get enough of it. I've suffered enough. And it's all coming together.

I hang up. Call my old man. This is it. I have something for him to be proud of. Finally. But when he answers the phone. And I let him know the good news. He just tells me not to get my hopes up.

Which crushes them more than anything. But I do my best to stay high. In my head I call him an old fool. He must know they recognize the family name. That he's been there 40 years. And how docile we must be.

So I tell him to have a good night. That I have things to do. Put the phone down. Look over at my roommate. Who looks back at me with the excitement I wanted in my fathers voice. He congratulates me. And I wonder why I don't give him enough credit.

When Max shows up he has a case of beer. We drink it. And I spend the rest of the night lying deep in the couch. Oblivious to everything around me. Completely content. Unafraid for the first time in a long time.

. . . .

The day of the interview I'm too excited to sleep. I get out of bed with the sun. Walk west along the main street of the city. Look at the way the light hits the old beat up buildings. And I don't remember the city ever looking so pretty.

The interview is in a hotel convention centre. Way out on the highway. I have no idea how long it's going to take to hitchhike. So I figure what the fuck. I might as well start now.

When I get to the edge of the city I turn around. Walk backwards. My thumb in the air. It's not long before I get picked up. A woman from Quebec. Looking to practice her English.

Too bad for her though. Because I'm damn nervous. And in no mood to speak. So her attempts to get a conversation going are pretty much hopeless. I look out the window. And answer her questions with as few words as possible.

She lets me out in the parking lot of the place. I thank her for her time. Tell her that her English sounds good to me. She smiles. And I notice how pretty she is. And wish I'd noticed when I got in the car.

I light a smoke. Walk across the parking lot. There's a line of men coming out the front doors. At least 75 of them. People like me. Ones who couldn't sleep. One's who figured what the fuck.

When I get close I ask one of them, and I was right. People been here since five AM I'm told. I shrug my shoulders. Find a grassy spot in the shade. Smoke cigarettes and wait.

After an hour or so the line's three times as long. But at least it starts moving. I wait a little longer. We all got the same call. It's not like I'm going to miss the chance. Why stand when you can sit.

When the end of the line snakes into the building I get up. Walk over. Look through the main door. To me. It seems like there's hundreds of men. And they all look as excited as I feel sure. That this is it.

And it reminds me of the days at the unemployment office. The same desperation is in the air. Except here there's men and women from all over. This is the kind of job you drive two hours for. This is the kind of job you move your family for.

I look at them all. So hopeful. Thinking of the many ways this day is going to change their lives. And I laugh at them. Every single one of them. These poor fools. Don't they know that they don't stand a chance against me?

And most of them are so old. In their thirties. Their forties even. I snort indignantly. I'm a baby. Full of strength. Ready to just put my head down. Do whatever they fucking tell me.

More or less give up.

Everyone is walking up to a long table. Like the ones in the school cafeteria. It has a table cloth draped over it. The car company's logo printed huge across it. Two pretty girls sit on the other side.

I announce myself when I walk up. Like some kind of rural dignitary. Neither one of them look at me. But in unison they tell me to go into the conference room. Find an empty seat. And fill it.

The exchange leaves me feeling queasy. Like maybe I've made an awful mistake again. Because if I do well here. Then it's the end of the line. A job for life. No other reason to ever try again.

But I stop thinking about that. Inside the massive conference room. Just beside the door. Is a table full of pastries. Doughnuts. Giant percolators of coffee. Christ. It's like something from a movie. I stack a paper plate high. Grab a coffee.

I find a seat. Sit down. In front of me is a stack of papers. A blue pen. A pencil. I put my coffee and plate beside them. Look at the guy beside me. Wink. Pull my chair in.

'You think ya got enough there, buddy?' the guy beside me says while jerking his thumb towards my plate.

'Yeah, I don't know. I didn't see any bigger plates. I 'll have to fill my bag before I go.'

He rolls his eyes. Looks around for someone to make fun of me with. As far as I'm concerned he can go fuck himself. He clearly came from a home with food in it. Didn't have to hitchhike here on an empty stomach.

So what does he know about anything? I figure nothing. And start my breakfast.

About fifteen minutes later a man walks to the front of the room. Stands behind a podium. Explains the test. The time frame in which it must be completed. If we're caught cheating, it's all over.

He tells us to start. The sound of all those booklets opening. Pens being picked up. Several cleared throats. This is it. All these lives on the line. And I'm certain of my ability to pass. To leave the assholes beside me in the dirt.

The test is pretty easy. Basic math. Reading and writing comprehension. Reasoning. The kind of thing the school board throws up every few years. An effort to categorize you. Get a handle on where your life is going.

Which doesn't make me feel good about my decision. That I showed up. I should be back in bed. Because the whole thing does remind me of school. And I remember the words my father said to me a few years back. When explaining his work. That life doesn't change much from high school.

And I don't know if I have the guts to carry that out.

I take about an hour to finish it. But I haven't seen anyone else get up yet. I don't want to be the first. It doesn't look good. Like I've not understood and given up. So I wait. Let some other fools finish. And when a healthy amount has passed their test to the man behind the podium I do the same.

But before I leave I grab another coffee. Two more doughnuts. Then walk out into the sun of the early afternoon. I walk by a few men. I listen to their conversation. They brag about how easy it was.

And I wonder if that's how I'd sound. If I joined them. And started to say the things in my head out loud. Would I be just as big of a prick? Would I sound like some cocky piece of shit?

I walk across the parking lot to the gas station. I buy a pack of smokes. Find some shade on the side of the highway. Tell myself I can't remember a nicer day. And that I feel like celebrating.

When I finish my doughnut and coffee and butt out my smoke I get up. Walk out to the highway. And start my efforts of getting home again. By the time I get picked up I'm beat. Covered in dust from the shoulder of the road.

And when I get home. I don't feel much like celebrating anymore.

31

A couple of months roll by. I tell myself things. Like it's a long process. There were so many people there. Hundreds easy. And I've heard that there were other days like it. Two groups a day.

Now that's a lot of fat to trim.

I get by on these lies. They make it a little easier to sleep. Because if I didn't have them, I'd have to give in. To the anxiety. And the voice in my ear that keeps reminding me of the truth. That I'm no good. And destined to fail.

But then it happens. A phone call. An official sounding voice on the other end. Asking me if I can come in for an interview. And when I say yes I squeak. Like a 14 year old. You damn fool, I tell myself. They're probably taking note of this.

The voice tells me I need to come out to the factory. They want me to come talk to someone from human resources. I tell her yeah. No problem. I'll be there. Before she hangs up she tells me to have a nice day.

And before I put the receiver down I'm already having a hard time breathing. I don't know if this even happened. It seems like a dream. I have to go out to the factory. Shit.

I remember driving by it with my old man. When I was a kid. And I wanted to go in there so bad. To see where he spent all his time. To see what it looked like inside that huge steal box. And now I have an invite.

The dreams just don't stop coming true.

For the next couple weeks, before the interview, I run my mouth. Tell people I have it in the bag. That there's no way I'm not going to get offered a job. That before they know it I'm going to be driving around in some nice car. Living in the suburbs. Tasting the high life.

Everyone smiles. Tells me they're proud of me. That I deserve a break.

That this is my chance. And I agree with everything they say. I do deserve this. I feel like some great king's son. Ready to take the throne. My future laid out in front of me. Like a plush purple rug.

I've never been more happy with myself. And it shows. I walk around like I've got a big bank account. Smoke name brand cigarettes. Drink imported beer. Because I don't have it figured out yet. That I should be humble. And keep my mouth shut.

On the day of the interview it threatens to rain. But I don't give it a second thought. Or even notice. And I walk out to the edge of town in a blur. Thinking of the good life that's waiting for me. Just a few hours to go. Just a few kms down highway two.

And it doesn't take long. A good sign I say. Before a sedan made by the factory I'm on my way to pulls over. Tires crunching the gravel. I hustle. Run to the passenger side door. When I get in an older man is driving. Looking at me with a smile.

We drive off. He asks me what I'm up to. I tell him about the interview. How it's just for show. That my old man's been there since the day it opened. I start to outright lie. Tell him my old man knows all the right people.

That there's no chance of failure.

He's happy for me. His smile getting even bigger. He tells me how things are getting tough out there. That we're lucky the car plant is still here. And how young men just don't have the same kinds of jobs they had when he was my age.

'Used to be you just walked right from the high school to the factory. And life was in the bag,' he tells me. And he sounds just like my father. My uncles. And everyone else who's been working since the 70's.

He offers me a smoke. I have a pack in my pocket. But I take his anyways. I light it. And wonder if these welfare habits will stay with me. Always trying to stretch what I have. Always thinking about survival.

We pull into the parking lot. I stare at the building. No windows. Just large boxes made of sheet metal. Painted the same blue grey as the sky today. I open the door. Step out. The old man wishes me luck. And I can feel a light rain starting to fall.

I find it refreshing.

Before he leaves I ask the time. I have enough time to smoke another cigarette. And after the old man pulls off I do just that. I stand under the overhang in front of the door. And I start to feel the fear. I start to second guess my chances.

And by the time I open the door I'm sweating. I'm shivering. I think about turning back running across the huge parking lot. Out to the highway. And trying to find my way home.

But I can't. I have to do this. So I walk the long corridor. Looking for the office. And trying to keep my heart from beating so fast. My head sways a bit. I know I need to sit down. But I tell myself, Soon. I'll find where I'm going any minute.

I haven't seen a soul since I opened the door. And just as I'm about to give up. A man comes from around a corner. I ask where the hell I'm going. And he tells me it's just ahead.

I sigh. Relieved. When I walk in the office I tell a permed woman sitting behind a counter my name. And why I'm here. She looks over a list. Tells me that I can take a seat. It'll only be a few minutes.

I take her up on her offer. I sit down on the long wooden bench along the wall. I'm reminded of high school. There's not much of a difference. The counter. The woman behind it. I might as well be waiting for the principal. Coming up with lies.

And my heart doesn't stop beating any slower. And my head still sways. The fear is getting the better of me. I'm certain that I'm going to blow it. I'm looking at these bland walls. But all I see is my future sitting dead in the water.

It's up to me to flush.

I don't know how long I'm sitting here but it feels like forever. And I get caught up in my thoughts. Like how I can't hack it at a burger joint. How I get passed over for self-service gas attendant positions. And how guys on welfare don't get loans to go to school.

So by the time a man in a nice tie comes over, smelling strongly of cologne, and introduces himself to me I'm not very confident. And it shows in my weak handshake. And his lack of respect for me shows on his face when he pulls away.

He asks me to follow him. So I do. This close to him. His back right in front of me. I notice how big he is. How he eclipses me. And I start to feel like a little boy. Trailing behind some huge monster. I shrink into myself.

In the office he opens the door to there's already another man sitting there. He doesn't get up when we come in. Nor when I'm introduced. I ready myself. Stretch out my hand. Do my best. And still pull back a sore hand.

At least I'm consistent.

I'm told the other man is just going to sit in. Watch. They ask me if I mind. I figure it's going to be hard to say that I do. So I nod. Tell them that I don't mind one bit. I try to act casual. Put my arm over the back of the chair. Then realize it's not very professional.

The man I followed in sits down. Tells me I did very well on the aptitude test. I say thanks. I get the impression I'm to be silent. He asks me a couple standard questions. Why I want to work there. What interests me about the job.

And I tell him all the stuff I've been told to say. Like I want to settle down. Buy a house and get married and have kids. This is what they love, I tell myself. It's just as good as saying I don't want to do anything with myself ever again. And that I live to work.

I like what I said. Feel like maybe things are going to go my way. But that's when they jump on me. Fire off question after question. Both of them. I don't have the time to answer one before the other is yelling in my ear.

Now I get it. Just sitting in my ass. They're here to destroy me. But even though I clue in to what's going on, it's too damned late to stop. Sweat is running down my face. They ask if I'm good under stress. I tell them I am. A terrible lie. I'm not fooling anyone.

I start to panic. And then it's all over.

Tears start building up. And by the time they tell me they've seen enough I'm full on crying. The two men look away in disgust. I get up and leave. Half hyperventilating. When I walk past the receptionist I try and hide my head.

Completely embarrassed.

Outside it's raining. But I don't think I'd notice if it wasn't for my smoke going out. I don't even try to hitch home. There's no way I can sit in some strangers car. Hiding my eyes. Coming up with lies.

So I walk. On the shoulder of the road. In the gravel and dirt turning to mud. I barely hear the scream of diesel engines going passed. I'm having a hard time concentrating. I wander in the direction of home in a daze. One thought on repeat.

I've just cemented my life as a deadbeat.

By the time I get back to the city the rain has stopped. A small miracle. But I'm soaked through my clothes. Its mid-afternoon. I have nothing to do for the rest of my life. And I don't feel like keeping up the joke any longer.

I sit in a park. Ones I know I won't see anyone in. Down the hill from the railroad tracks. The one Lou went and lay down on. And I admire his guts. Or his pain. Or his sadness.

Because it's more than I have. And I know I'm going to go home. My roommate's sitting there on the couch. Expecting to hear some good news. But I'm going to have to tell him I left crying. Like a baby.

I stay where I am until after dark. Then I walk slowly home. I can't bring myself to go in. So I climb up the fire escape. The lights are on in my place. I peek in. Hidden by the glare.

My roommate and Max are sitting there. It looks like they're having a good time. But I know I don't have that in me. And they're not going to let me go up to my room to hide. So I give up. Lie down on the roof. Watch the sky.

I fall asleep. And when I wake up it's the middle of the night. There's no sound. Just the hum of the electricity running through the wires. I get up. Look behind me. My apartment is dark. I go around front. Open the door. Walk up the stairs to my room. I don't bother with the light. I smoke cigarettes lying in bed. Telling myself that this is it. That this is my life. That I'm not meant for anything else.

That I've proved everyone right. I'm a loser.

31.

It's hard for me to face people. After all that gloating. Tooting my own horn all over the place. And of course everyone asks me how things went. When do I start they say.

And I don't even bother to lie. Because I don't have the energy. I just say that I fucked up the best thing that ever landed in my lap. That I was broken. And I left the place in tears.

These people. The ones who ask. I thought we were friends. But they rarely hold back their laughter. Tell me how much of a pussy I am. And there's nothing I can do. Because I have to admit. It looks pretty bad.

But I figure it serves me right. And this is the punishment I get. The last little kick. The sharp jab to my stomach. I thought I had it all. But instead I've sentenced myself to a life of handed out hot dogs. Old worn through clothes. Loneliness. And days spent with nothing to do.

Because what am I going to do? I've burned it all down. If the place my old man has worked for 40 years won't give me a chance what hope do I have. Is some stranger going to reach out? Take a chance?

I don't see it happening.

And now I get asked what I'm going to do. What's my plan? I don't have a clue. So I can't say a thing. And I notice this makes people happy. They need me on the bottom. And to keep slipping.

I make them all feel better about themselves. I see it on their faces. It's nice to have a failure around I guess.

So I start to avoid everyone. Never leave the house. The only person I ever see is my roommate. When he comes home at night. With his pocket of money. And his free staff meal. Burgers or steaks. Thick fries. All the things I've forgotten the taste of.

And like all the other times. I sit here. Pretending not to watch him from the corner of my eye. Hoping. That just once he won't want it. That he'll ask me to finish it for him.

But like always it never happens. I hate him for knowing how to live. When he's done he always smokes a joint. And he always passes it my way. I'm thankful for every puff. It distracts me from my thoughts.

Not well enough though. Because I can't shake the feeling that my entire life is a mess. And that I'm starting to crumble. That I need to change something. Because I'm beginning to hate the sun and the sky and everything in-between.

I start having a hard time making the rent. I spend my money on cheap booze instead. Each month I give the landlord a little less. So I fall farther and farther behind. I give him just enough to keep him from getting angry. I make up lies. Say I'll be back soon with the rest.

And even I don't believe me. So I wonder why he doesn't kick me out. But it's because he's a fool. And wants to believe in me. So I learn just how little you need to give a man to keep him off your back.

A lesson I figure will come in handy.

Some days the landlord gets up his courage. Comes around and bangs on the door. I ignore it. Hide in my room not making a sound. Praying that he doesn't decide to use his keys. And come right in.

So most of the time I keep to the streets. Which are beginning to bore me. Few people are out during the day. Just the same bums I see at the unemployment office.

People I've grown to hate. I don't have any real reasons. I don't even know any of them by name. But I'm envious of them. Their age and wisdom. They've been at this a lot longer than me. Seem to have it all figured out.

Maybe after a few more years Stan, I tell myself, you'll get the hang of this. And be able to manage your depression. And I start to see myself in all these bums.

Just older. Dirtier. Lonelier. Sadder. More accustomed.

And when I walk the street I know I'm in a bad place. Because I can't get a job. And I don't even want one. I see the money my friends come home with. How much easier their lives are. But I don't want it. I don't want anything.

I just want to lie in grass all day. Stare up at the sky. But those aren't options. And I don't have any ideas. But I know the end of the road is coming up fast.

So I spend my days wandering around. Trying to avoid my roommate. And everyone else in the world. I do a good job. I only end up talking to the women who give out hot dogs. And the people behind the counter at the Salvation Army.

It's good for me though. It clears my head. I start to see what the city is now. After all the bridges have been burned. It's a trap. A cage closed behind me. I feel doomed. I find it harder and harder to breathe.

So I blame this city. I tell myself that it's the reason I'm suffocating. Because I came here looking for something. Some excitement. But it's not here. And I'm stagnating like everyone else. I need more from my life.

I start thinking about packing up. Filling a backpack with the few things I have left. Take off while my roommate is at work. No word of goodbye. No note. Get to the edge of town.

Stick out my thumb. See where I can go.

But I have to wait till the end of the month. Get one last check from welfare. Cash it. Then take off. A small stake. I'll have to be crafty. But I think I can make it last. If I skip on the rent I should be able to last a few months.

I start to fantasize. About some romantic life hitching around. Not a single care. I can see Toronto. The east coast. Maybe even cross over into America. And I start to believe that my failure was the best thing to happen to me.

Because if I got that job. I'd be fucking stuck here. All that money and comfortability. I couldn't just walk away from it. So the job was the trigger. The one that closed the trap.

So I convince myself I made off with the cheese.

I'll just start over somewhere else. Find another city with fast food joints. Landscaping companies. Factories. Where no one knows me. I'm just a guy roaming the country looking for work.

I try to find some reason to stay. Because a part of me is scared. That pulling up is a big move. I don't know anyone anywhere. But I can't find a reason.

I fucked up the only job I think I can get. The guarantee. The one that was going to keep me going. Compared to that no matter what I do won't be as good. I'll be wondering what if.

My family and I don't really speak. We never really had much in common. Or I was too busy pushing them away. I want to blame them for it. But they all seem to get along.

And I'm sure by now my old man has heard how the interview went. That his boy left the place crying. A fact I'm sure no one is going to let him live down. So I'm probably a disgrace. Not welcome back into the fold.

I'd stay for a girl. Or a bunch of friends. But neither of those are in supply. I have my roommate. But I'm really just half the rent to him. Or else he might throw me some scraps from time to time.

So I think of places I can go. All the older brothers of friends have gone west. Off to Vancouver. They rarely come back. There has to be something to it. I tell myself that it will do.

At night I lie in bed. Dream of the rocky mountains. Good weather. No more snow. It's enough to make me feel good. I tell myself that I've found a reason to keep on breathing.

It's just two more weeks until the end of the month. But I want to go now. I try and think of some way to get the cash. I remember long ago when my parents told me there was money saved for me to go to college.

I figure it's worth the try. Maybe they'll feel bad. Give it to me just to get rid of me. So I call. My old man answers. We don't talk about the interview. I don't have the balls to bring it up.

After all the small talk I ask about the money. He tells me I'll have to talk to my step mother. He puts down the phone before I can tell him not to bother.

She picks up the phone. Asks me how much I need. I ask about the college fund. She laughs. Tells me that they spent it years ago. Asks me if I want my old man to come by on his way to work the next day. That he can give me $50. Before hanging up I tell her not to bother. Neither of us say good bye.

So I wait. The end of the month is only a couple of weeks away. I just have to keep my mouth shut. Cash that check. Get the fuck out of here. They are the slowest two weeks of my life. But they pass.

When I get the check I go straight to the bank. Take the whole thing as cash. Six hundred dollars. I don't know how long I can make it last. I'm scared. But I don't have any other idea.

I go to the grocery store. Buy bread. Peanut butter. A few cans of tuna fish. I don't know what else to bring.

At home I pack a backpack. A couple books. Some extra shirts. Socks. Lots of underwear. I put the bag at the end of my bed. Shut the door of my room. Wait.

My roommate gets up around three in the afternoon. Comes downstairs. I'm on the couch. Reading. I thought he was never going to get up. That I'd have to wait another day.

I want him to see me before I leave. I don't know why. I think it'll give me more time before he gets suspicious. He goes over to the kitchen. Takes a can of spaghetti from the cupboard. Roots around in the cutlery drawer. Lifts some dishes in the sink.

I don't bother to tell him he won't find what he's looking for.

'Have you seen the can opener?'

'Nah man,' I say even though it's under my clothes. In the bottom of my backpack.

He gives up. Sits in his chair. Watches television. For fifteen minutes I pretend I'm reading. Waiting for him to get up. To go. When he does he leaves the television on. So I decide that I will as well.

He goes back upstairs. I hear the shower run. It's getting to be too much. But I know I have to wait. To let him leave first. And after about half an hour he comes down. Reeking of cheap cologne. Before he leaves he tells me to have a good night.

After the door shuts I get up. I go up to my room. Wait ten minutes. Just to make sure he doesn't come back in. Sometimes he forgets his work keys.

When I'm sure. I put on my shoes. Close the door behind me. The TV still on.

It takes about forty-five minutes to get to the highway. I still have a couple hours of light. It's cool. Fresh. The backpack's weight feels good on my shoulders.

I think of everything waiting out there for me. The whole world. And I don't know what's going to happen. But it can't be any worse than what I was doing.

So when I get to the edge of the city I turn around. One last look at what I was supposed to be. One last taste of my defeat. I walk backwards. Thumb out as my farewell.